And a Long, Slow Rain

Howard Gengarelly

ISBN: 0985054700
ISBN 13: 9780985054700

Growth Rings Press
Gainesville, FL

For Margo

Prologue

So, Mr. Pete Krekow, you finally did it, you pulled the plug on your dear old oscillating fan. It's been pushing dead air since 1963, over two decades of rattles and squeaks. After all those years, you cut the cord. Now, no more nights of watching that wire-mesh cage twist and turn on each slow return. No more nights of stale, hot air. Finis.

Yeah, check that out, a trim little window unit, an air conditioner. With the flip of a switch, she'll take the edge off the night. You'll hear a sweet hum, feel chilled air blow across you as you read, contented in your old, fat chair.

Of course, for the first time your windows will be closed, and that sweet hum will tend to drown out the sounds you know so well: traffic on Dixie Highway, sirens, stray cats, boat horns from the waterway, and lately the growls and howls from the newlyweds across the street. Sounds you love.

So you sit, unwilling to turn it on quite yet, and wonder how long it will be before you regret not being able to open the windows, let the outside world back in, stick your head out and talk to Willie Dee, the gardener, who talks mostly to his flowers, rarely to people, but he'll talk to you.

It's funny how life can go for years, decades with little change. Then, before you have a chance to ask what's next, your whole world is turned upside down.

It began a few weeks back when the newsroom scanner spit something out about police activity near the Intracoastal. You're a reporter, what you found was a beautiful woman dumped on a bed of rock and rubble at the edge of a seawall decorated with floating garbage and sick fish. And the woman had a secret, a twelve-year-old mystery that would draw you in as no story had done before. But it's supposed to be over. The story is filed. Yet you seem unwilling to let go. It's the last move in the story. It's your move.

Go ahead, take one last look back at the lonely, golden-haired princess whose death changed your life. Then do it — hit the switch.

Chapter 1

"Please, my angel." He stood next to the silver ice bucket and slowly turned the cold, green bottle. "Once more."

She lay with her arms reaching back, loosely holding the underside of a large cushion. Her long, elegant legs stretched into a pile of colorful, wrinkled pillows at the end of the bed.

The light from a tapered, white candle fashioned a bouncing shadow on the wall of the cabin. Its light imaged her slight, firm stomach, as it seesawed in breath with the swell of her small breasts. Perfumed wax sweetened the scent of passion.

A framed photograph of an attractive woman in smart, conservative swimwear and a girl of about twelve years, lounging near a large pool in the yard of a very large mansion, stood nearby on a small table. They smiled for the camera.

Ivy looked at the picture, which was subdued in the shadows, and wondered what the woman in the picture had to do to keep her place by the pool. Did she have to choke back cries from pain he inflicted with such pleasure. Or was that just for his whores.

The sound of ice making a grinding noise attracted her attention. He lifted the bottle from the bucket at the foot of the bed where he stood, watching in the half-darkness.

Watching as the pool of perspiration grew at the rim of the knotted place in the middle of her abdomen. Watching and waiting for the fluttering flame, the only light in the cabin, to dance with light and shadow on her splendid, naked body.

Water rushed down the bottle, splashing into crushed ice, leaving a thin trail across the sheet as he brought it to the table where the candle stood, flame swaying, near the top of the bed.

She watched the reflection of the flame as it danced in his blue eyes, flashing off tiny red threads that streaked the whites.

"You're a rather expensive child," he said, filled two wine glasses, and handed one to her. Then, with the bottom of the chilled, wet bottle, traced a route from her chin, down her slender body, climbing and circling in broad sweeps around and over areas of unblemished real estate.

"You hurt me, you know," she whispered. Her nerve ends both recoiled from and enjoyed the freezing, wet glass. She touched his pale face with the tips of her fingers, gently.

"Your cry was but a whisper." He bent over her and kissed her nose, then her chin, finally her mouth.

He closed his eyes as she brushed his light, blonde brows and skied slowly down a surgically perfect nose and stopped, resting on a fleshy, lower lip.

"And, I think you like it, the pain." He stood over her and drinking the last of the wine directly from the bottle, took her empty glass and set it on the table.

She blew out the candle, throwing the room into darkness.

She turned, away from him, and opened the curtain over the small porthole next to the bed, and knelt with her chin on the edge of the window.

It was raining.

The storm swept the Intracoastal with rain and thunder without rocking the large yacht, whose mass insulated them.

"A penny for your thoughts, Ivy." He caressed the back of her neck.

"Oh, it's just, I don't know. History, ancient history, I guess," she said. "A better day. A day without rain."

"Stop this," he said, pouting. "Ivy, you make me feel as though I don't take good care of you."

"Oh, I'm sorry, really." She turned and held his face in her hands, gently kissing him. "I'm sorry," she whispered.

He turned her back to the small porthole, and, kneeling behind her, rested his chin on her shoulder. "Tell me about the day without rain," he said.

"Once, when I was little," she said. She felt him touch her.

"Once upon a time, there was a little girl named Ivy." His breath was sour.

"Yes," she tried to ignore his touch. "Once upon a time, there was a little girl named Ivy. One day her mama took her to a street fair, over there, on Flagler Drive.

"They were alone for the only time she could remember. No brothers, cousins. No sisters, aunts, uncles. They held hands and laughed and danced as artists, and musicians, and street actors filled her day with things she had never seen before."

The sound of the rain pounding on the cabin muted her story. She wondered if he was listening. She wondered what her mama was doing just then. At home, surely, cooking. The eternal mess of noisy kids, probably playing shoeless in the muddy yard. Filthy. Happy.

"And she wore her best dress, the only one that hadn't needed mending by the time it was passed to her by an older sister or niece. Mama had bought it at an Easter fair, at church, and it was as close to new as anything she had ever owned.

"At the end of the day they sat alone on the seawall and looked across the water, looking at the yachts floating where we are now, and wondered what people did on such large boats." Her eyes closed, feeling for a sigh that had been used years before.

"Such a charming story. So, quaint." He turned her head with the tips of his fingers and pressed a long-stemmed pipe gently against her lips. "Here, smoke this, Ivy. I blended it just for you. It's traced with the dust of an angel." He lit the contents of the bowl. She inhaled slowly, deeply.

"This too." He held a small mound of powder in the palm of his hand. "And if you're a good little girl, I have something even better, a very special treat just for you."

She reached over, held his hand and pulled it toward her. Bending forward, she inhaled in short, sharp breaths. When she pulled back, slowly, she saw, in a narrow band of light from the porthole, that he was holding a small framed photograph. It was the picture of a thin, blonde-haired, young woman, standing with an older man in front of a large, stone-carved fountain.

"Pretty, isn't she?"

"Yes, very."

The woman was dressed in a full-length, black formal evening gown, and wore elbow-length black gloves. There was a gold necklace with a small medallion around her neck. The man also was dressed formal, black tie and tails. He stood sideways, looked off the frame, uninterested in the camera, rather more intrigued by a school of street urchins grabbing at his outstretched hand.

The woman, however, did not watch the man play his private game with the ragged children, rather, she watched the camera, as if distrusting the lens, cautious, with neither smile nor frown.

"Have you seen her before, Ivy?"

"Maybe." She felt the drugs working, felt herself drawn into a peaceful, inner silky-spun cocoon, from which she did not want to unwrap. "Once, with Mr. Thady, I think."

"You don't know who she is then?"

"No." Ivy slowly shook her head.

"She is my sister," he said. "My beloved little sister."

He held the picture closer to Ivy. She focused on the long blonde hair and the thin face. "She is pretty."

"Yes," he said, and placed the picture at the foot of the bed. "How much you look like her."

"Do you think so?"

"Yes, very much."

"Is that her husband?"

"No, just one of many admirers." He reached into an opened, gold-padlocked, polished mahogany sea chest next to the bed, and took out a small, ebony box, from which he removed a gold chain and medallion.

She felt the cold of the gold chain as he put it around her neck. "For me?"

"How much you remind me of her," he said. "For now, you will be my little sister." He drew back and looked at her. His fingertips brushed her face.

"Don't hurt me," she said. "Please."

He held her close, rocked her gently. "My angel." He felt her warmth against his body, patted her softly. "Would I hurt my own sister?" He guided her down, onto the bed.

She rolled over and stretched so that her feet were over the end, and wrapped her arms around the pillow. She held it very tight.

"A white gown, Ivy, a very expensive white gown, that will be my special present to you, my little angel."

She wouldn't cry, she thought, she was a lady, a lady with a new Sunday dress.

Chapter 2

A late afternoon thunderstorm brought cool showers and a soothing breeze that for a few welcomed moments relieved the city from the oppressive summer heat.

In its wake, asphalt streets steamed, buildings cooled, and darkness completed its westward sweep across the Atlantic Coast.

The rippled surface of the Intracoastal waterway mirrored the change as the soft glow of bridge and street lights gradually replaced the setting sun.

In the water, next to the seawall, a slender body lay, unbreathing, among the rocks, clothed in a delicate, white gown, and darkness.

Chapter 3

The alarm on my old windup cut short the agony of a nightmare that hurt so bad it made my teeth ache. This one had been around for a few days. It had a way of returning every time I got a call from the lady who had given me six of the best years of my life, a starring role in the creation of our daughter, then ran off with another guy, leaving me with a light bill, phone bill, a full pot of my favorite coffee, and a dozen years of child support.

It had been about fourteen years since I finished that pot of coffee when, Kay, the former Mrs. Pete Krekow, had ruined a record two years of unbroken silence with not only a phone call, but one of those directives that said it had to be done face-to-face. Alone together. Same time, same station.

Formula: nightmare.

She said it was about our twenty-year-old daughter, Robin, which was no surprise. The only time she called was when it was about our girl. The calls had usually been about money: she needed more. Never the other way around.

But with that in the past, hearing she had a problem to discuss was the last thing I expected. This was particularly true because Robin had grown into a lovely, young lady who, I inferred from our phone conversations, spent all her time at her studies at the junior college. She did not sound like she had time for trouble.

"I don't know how bad or how far advanced this thing is," Kay said. "I want it nipped in the bud. You have to do it. She won't listen to me. So, for once, you have got to take the reins, Cowboy, and act like a father."

Given the direction of our generally one-sided dialogue, which was typical, and despite the cowboy references, which were something new, I passed on any "back in the saddle again" witticisms and told her she could count on my help. In what, and how far involved, I had yet to learn because she said the substance of her concern was not for the phone.

She said she would explain in detail when we got together. No, it was not urgent. Yes, it was important. Very important. Then she made a comment, the old dig, about my showing up on time.

A difficult side of a reporter's job is that news, particularly the good stuff, rarely breaks at convenient times. That had always been a sore point. However, I thought we had argued out on that subject years before. She, it seemed, did not. Thinking back, it was difficult to figure which was worse for our marriage: my need to be always wrong, or hers to be right.

We agreed to meet the following Monday night at the same hotel cocktail lounge we had used over the years when the phone didn't get it done. It was dark. It was quiet. It was about thirty minutes midway between homesteads.

I lived in an apartment a short drive south of downtown West Palm Beach, three blocks west of the Intracoastal, and a stone's throw from Dixie Highway, where the offices of the News & Journal, where I worked, were located.

In fact, I was still curled up, snug as a bug in the same rug my new bride and I had made our first home over two decades earlier. I had never left studio apartment number 33, top floor of the Rainbow Apartments. Thought about it many times. Just figured the old fan would not look right any place else. That was the first thing we bought when we moved in. The oscillating fan.

Her spread was on the other side of town. It was at the north end of the county, where Robin, a few horses, some exotic farm animals, and the ambulance chaser she married a month after our divorce, were housed.

They had met while he, Grant Rutos, was working in the public defender's office. She was on the other side of the law, driving a green-and-white, and arresting criminals as quickly as he got them released. I remember listening to her snorting with some good old Republican indignation over the failure of the system, failure of the church, failure of the family, and so on.

With so much failure in her life, I guess the failure of our marriage must have seemed a natural sort of progression.

I figured she won her "failure of the system" argument because within a few months of their marriage he, Grant, left the public defender business, and began a law practice that was anchored by radio ads that rivaled the bad taste and annoyance of folks selling cars, tires, and insurance. She was still on the same police force, only now she was a detective.

We agreed to meet Monday night when she got off work, which would be after eleven. I would have preferred an earlier meeting. Monday was my day off. Still, I figured I could run weekday chores and still have time to read and relax later in the day. If I wanted to take an afternoon nap, which I sometimes enjoyed on my day off, I could set the clock to allow plenty of time to get ready for the meeting, avoid trouble by getting to the lounge early.

With that agreement, I was left to cool my heels for a few days, and wonder what kind of trouble my daughter had gotten into, and whether I could help her.

I knew that when it came to being the kind of father who was at the starting gate when he was needed, my track record was a sorry list of no-shows. Over the years, I had tried, in my own way, to let Robin know how much I loved her. Cards, phone calls, an occasional movie or Sunday at the park. I just could not be a father on a court-appointed timetable. I could not begin a new, half-a-life with her. The weekend visitations that began each

Saturday morning with smiles and laughter would end Sunday evenings in tears and agony. It did not seem humane.

The family thing slipped away. I had, over the years, dated some very nice women. Lovely women. However, I was somehow never able to make a commitment to settle down, to start a new family. Some people begin again. Most, maybe. They start over: new kids, new dogs, new friends. They balance the past with the present in households filled with children coming and going on a rotating basis -- summer here, weekends there.

Yes, the holidays, those damned holidays. Decorating a Christmas tree, then sitting alone watching bulbs blink. Waiting for my baby to show up, knowing soon after she arrived she would have to leave, presents in tow. Then back to watching lights blink in a dark, empty room.

I decided finally that no lights burned brighter than half the lights. I did what I thought right, I headed for the hills. Alone. And I stayed that way until about the time that alarm went off and interrupted my nightmare.

Or so I thought at the time.

So Monday rolled around, the alarm went off, and I cut a path to the shower, where I turned it on hard. I felt the cold water beat on my head, concluded there is little better than being hammered with cold water, in the summer, in West Palm Beach.

I got out feeling cool and ready to tackle any problem. I dried off, brushed my teeth, threw on some fresh, unpressed clothes. I had a glass of orange juice and checked the time. I figured it was early enough for me to go downstairs for a quick visit with two of my best friends, the owners of the Rainbow Apartments, an old biker couple who had finally retired from the road.

Frankie and his wife, Cricket, had bought the complex about a year earlier, when the previous owner, an insurance company in Miami, tired of bleeding what had been a rather nice complex before they had bought it a few years earlier.

The first thing they did was root out trouble, something at which they were particularly adept. They had lived on the hard edge of the road, traveled more tough miles than most third world armies. And fought more battles. Cleaning house was no problem.

They remodeled the place, stem to stern. First class. Then they retired to apartment number one on the first floor where they could oversee everything. I kept in their good graces by never asking where they got the money to develop such a prime piece of real estate.

I was halfway out the door when the phone rang. I hurried back inside, worried something had gone wrong, gave a healthy yank on the phone cord which, as always, was a tangled mess of tight curls, "Kay?"

The curt voice of Bill Latham replaced my anxiety with anger. And relief.

"Look out your back window and tell me if you see any police activity down by the water," he said. "The scanner just spit something I couldn't read. Something about the waterway 'south of the bridge.' I couldn't tell which bridge."

I walked over to one of the two windows that faced the water. Although I lived three blocks away, my apartment had a partial view of Flagler Drive and the Intracoastal. I didn't see anything unusual. The street, at least as much of the drive as I could see, a short block, was quiet.

"Looks peaceful enough," I said.

"Never mind. Get down there and look around." Latham, my city editor, had, over the past few years, developed into a particular pain in my side.

"No can do," I said. "I've got an important meeting. I was just out the door."

"Pete, two minutes, there and back."

"Where's Cooper?" I asked.

"Up to his ears in scrap metal out on the Turnpike," he said. "Two minutes."

"Yeah, " I said, thought of Kay, and her shot about being on time. "I'll call right back."

I decided to walk the few blocks. There was no parking on Flagler, so I figured it would be easier, quicker. In the limited time it took to hit the street, I was damp with sweat. A welcomed, light breeze from the ocean helped, cut through the stagnant air and turned the beads of moisture into facets of coolness. I stole a few seconds, just long enough to stand, close my eyes, and listen to the sounds of the city, with its urban snore of tightly wound engines, sirens, and screeching tires. It was beautiful.

Up the Intracoastal, I could hear the powerful blast of a boat's horn as it traveled north along the path of the waterway. I followed the sound, walking quickly toward the water. As I walked, I thought of Robin. I wondered if she might possibly need my help. If so, could I help her?

I looked down at my ever-growing form, knowing that the days of 195 pounds, the thirty-two inch waist, were history. And it hurt to look in the mirror of the past and remember the years when it all seemed so secure. When I was at the top of my form.

Those were the years when, just out of the Army, I walked lightly, and punched the typewriter fiercely. Those were the years I was the top reporter on staff. I got the best stories. I was the man other writers came to for answers. Pete Krekow, that was the byline people looked for, and read first.

I was the man who hammered out hard-hitting copy that was read and respected by friend and foe. Those were the years when bad cops and dirty politicians watched me sideways.

And then the divorce. Things were never the same after that. I lost my fight. Gave it away, I guess. Gave it up for the loneliness. Gave it up because that was the easy way. Write the ham and eggs stories by day. Live on a reputation. Let me tell you, it ain't hard to kill a bunch of years.

Anyway, I was about a block from Flagler when I saw the first flashing lights, blue and red, bouncing off a street sign. I could smell the water as I crossed Flagler, and headed to the seawall where two city patrol cars were parked on the sandy, grassed area next to the wall.

I went to the edge, walked quickly to the place, about two blocks south, where three officers stood looking into the water. "Got a Sad Sally down, Pete."

Chapter 3

By the time the oldest officer, a man named Higgins, spoke to me, I was close enough to see the body in the water, at the edge of the wall.

"She's a beaut, this one." Higgins shook his head. "What a waste."

The other two officers, both women, remained silent. They were tough.

It was a young woman clothed only in a delicate, white evening or perhaps nightgown. The wet cloth clung closely to the contours of her shapely body.

"Yeah." I answered. Indeed, she had been a very attractive lady. A beautiful, dead lady.

Chapter 4

The owners of the stately, Spanish-style house across the street were not pleased to be disturbed, but seeing my press card rallied to the occasion, and had their housekeeper show me to the phone in the kitchen. And stay to make sure I didn't dial Hawaii, or walk off with any silverware.

I called Latham, told him what I had found, and said I would be in with a story shortly. Then I checked the number of the lounge in the phone book, called, and left a "may be a little late" message for Kay with someone named Crystal.

I walked back to the seawall. Higgins was in his car doing paperwork, and the women in blue were leaning against their car, talking quietly.

"Any idea who she is?" I asked Higgins.

He just shook his head, went on writing.

I walked over and sat on the seawall, near the Pretty Lady in White. She seemed vulnerable, lying there so quiet, childlike in her innocence. She rested with arms raised as though waiting for me to lift her from her cradle and share her last dance. Her shoulders and neck were partially covered by waves of long, blonde hair. Escaped strands followed the rolling tide and played around her cheek and mouth, the lips parted slightly.

I felt a chill as I sat there, watching her lifeless dance, and thinking that my own daughter was about the same age as this young woman. The same age, and every bit as beautiful. They were, in appearance, very much alike. A sense of urgency began to wind a path through me.

Three days had passed since our phone conversation. "No," Kay had told me, it was not "urgent," just very important. I took some small comfort in that. But, I knew I needed to write this story, then get moving up the highway. The chill was not going away. A fear one associates with the unknown was growing in me.

Finally the crime boys with their cameras and brushes swept me away. "Sorry, Pete, got to ask you to move."

One of the detectives, a lieutenant named Flowers, said he had seen her before on an undercover assignment. "If I could forget her, which I couldn't, I'd never forget that little sparrow." He pointed at her hip, at the tattooed bird caged by her gown.

He said she was a dancer at a strip joint out on Military Trail. "I remember she did this slow routine she called a Sparrow Dance. It was like nothing I ever saw before or since.

"Poor Butterfly music. Seemed like she died as her clothes came slowly off. You see that, you never forget her. Only time I ever heard the joint quiet."

"She was that good?" Higgins asked.

"She brought a tear to my eye," he said. "I saw a drunk cowboy cry like a baby, and didn't anybody say a thing."

"Where did she work?" I asked.

"Last place in the world you'd expect for someone who could dance like that," he said. "Speed Stick T's."

Higgins groaned. "Bucket of trouble."

"I remember doing a background check on her. I expected something, and came away with nothing. She didn't figure into the investigation, so I kind of forgot about her, until now."

Flowers and I had done a lot of work together over the years. He knew me well enough to bench the them-against-us attitude that many of the younger officers and detectives had when dealing with reporters. I was glad to have him on the crime scene.

18

Chapter 4

I nodded, told him I knew the place. It was the kind of sweat factory that incubated news stories. Over time, I had been in and out of there enough that I was on a first name basis with the head bartender, one of the bouncers, and the slime at the bottom of the barrel, the owner, though for him our relationship was on a last name basis, because nobody, at least nobody I knew, called Mr. Thady by his first name.

I didn't, however, remember knowing any of the dancers. The action, the kind that makes headlines, is more often away from the glistening flesh. The bouncers see to that. They don't waste time with rowdy customers, who are quickly thrown out, often with both feet in the air. And that's where most of the bloody trouble finds a place to happen, or continue, in the parking lot.

We turned at the sound of the guys in coveralls lifting Ivy's body out of the water and onto the wall. Higgins stood near her as they climbed over the wall, and quickly placed her on a stretcher on the grass, and covered her.

"I was at the edge of the water with her a few minutes ago," Flowers said. "Nobody should end up down there."

I asked him if he saw anything that would indicate the cause of death.

He shook his head, frowned. "I wonder what went wrong in her life tonight?"

"If I had to make a guess," I said. "I'd say things started going wrong a long time ago."

"Yeah," Flowers said. "But there's wrong, and then again, there's real wrong. Know what I mean?"

I told him I did. Flowers was a diner special kind of guy: meatloaf, mashed potatoes and gravy. His wife dressed him in expensive suits because that's the way she wanted her suburban neighbors to see him. She put uptown ties on him, but they never were tied correctly.

He was a big kid in an uptown suit, and a great cop. It didn't surprise me that he would care about the death of a young dancer. He wasn't a cop who had become hard-edged: he was neither disgusted with, nor corrupted by, the system. He still felt deeply about his job, about doing it well. He felt for victims. I liked him plenty.

"I even remember her name, Ivy Mitchell," he said, scribbled in a notebook. "Young lady, you made quite an impression."

I asked him if he remembered anything else about her.

He said he thought maybe her folks were from one of the old, dirt road communities out west. "If I remember, she grew up out there, but I don't think she still lived there. Seems like she had an address somewhere over in the Flamingo and Parker area. It was sometime back, but somewhere in that neighborhood."

"She really was beautiful," Higgins said. "It's a shame to see her washed up here, like this."

I asked Higgins if he had seen any indication of the cause of death.

"No," he said. "Which, these days, usually seems to end up having something to do with drugs."

"Strange place for a young woman in a nightgown to choose to do drugs," Flowers said.

"I guess," Higgins agreed. "Strange place for anyone, other than a fisherman, to be hanging out."

"Dirty as that water is," I said, "I'd find it a strange place even for a fisherman."

"People fish canals, hook cars, beds, sofas, even bodies. They'll fish anywhere," Flowers said. "But this didn't have anything to do with cane poles."

"I wonder what it did have to do with?" I said, and looked around the manicured-lawn neighborhood. "Cane poles and death, neither fits this place."

As I gave a quick look around the area, I noticed a white sedan pull around the corner of my street. The car drove toward us, slowed as it passed, and the driver, a young woman, gave me a friendly nod and a nice smile. I returned her gestures, and tried to hide my surprise that, in the shadows of the evening, her long blond hair and attractive thin face made her look very much like Ivy.

"Did you see her?" I asked the officers, but they had their backs to the road, and did not.

They turned as the car made a turn onto one of the side streets. "Who?" Flowers said.

"Nothing," I said. "Thought I was seeing things, that's all."

"You feel all right, Pete?" Higgins asked.

"Sure," I said. "I've got a meeting with the former Mrs. Krekow after I write this story. That's probably what's got me on edge."

"How's the lady Sheriff doing?" Higgins asked.

I told him I hadn't seen her in a couple of years. "Tonight is for something about Robin."

Both Flowers and Higgins said they hoped everything was fine.

I said, "Sure," and finished writing notes in my reporter's notebook, whose pages I had been filling with things Flowers and Higgins had said, along with odds and ends I picked up, mostly local color, which on a story like this was mostly shades of darkness. "Mitchell, Ivy."

"I remember she seemed like a cute kid," Flowers said. "Pretty way about her. Not tough like a lot of them. Soft. Childlike."

"Robin?" I asked.

"No, Pete, Ivy." Flowers patted me on the shoulder. "My friend, you need to get along now."

"Yeah," I agreed.

Between Higgins and Flowers I had a good start on what I needed to file a brief. The cause of death would be established by the coroner's office. I was leaning against a tall palm, finishing my notes, when Flowers walked over, reminded me that her family had not yet been notified.

"Next I have to find, and notify her family," Flowers said. "You know she's still an unidentified white female, right?"

"Yeah," I answered.

"I hate this part of the job."

I watched him walk to his unmarked car, then I headed to the newsroom, thinking I was glad I did not have his job right about then.

I stopped off to get my car on the way, drove to the News & Journal building. It was nearly ten when I pulled into the parking lot. The sun had set on us back there. For Ivy, it would be the last time.

Chapter 5

I passed the guard at the front door, didn't feel like waiting for the elevator, so I walked quickly up the side stairway. The news cycle had wound down for the day, leaving the newsroom reduced to about a dozen desk people. Some were still pushing copy, a few were doing the head, jump, wrap thing on early-edition page proofs.

For the most part the room was decorated with rows of clean-topped desks, empty seats and blank-screened computers. It left the place looking more like an insurance or stock brokerage office than a newsroom.

Gone were the Teletype machines that cranked out reams of paper, reporting news, weather, sports. Gone were the IBM electric typewriters that filled the room with clatter. All replaced with plastic, soft-ware silence.

Bill Latham and a cityside copy editor were working the wreck story Cooper had filed from the Turnpike. The police scanner ran red lights on the desk next to them.

"Get anything?" Latham asked me.

"Not much," I said. "I'll put something together and send it over."

Latham was a typically arrogant young college-of-journal-ism type who had impressed some people at the top with his sound-bite-style editing, and back-stabbed his way into a management position.

"Don't hurry, we're making over for a society party that turned into a brawl. Take your time, send a short, and if it sings, who knows, maybe I'll find a piano player for it."

"Sure," I said. "A society brawl?"

"Palm Beach benefit turned into a shouting match. Then someone hit a socialite on her jeweled head with a Faberge egg or something like that," Latham laughed. "Tall's writing an epic on this one."

"Yeah, thanks," I said. "An egg on the head. Sounds painful."

I looked across the room and saw Don Tall, the society writer, working himself into a frenzy over the fractured Faberge egg story. He was a young guy who kept pictures of himself on his desk. Just himself.

We had locked horns a few years back over a story he wrote that played loose with the truth. He called it new journalism; I called it crap. His editor called it creative nonfiction and sent me back to cityside. Told me to mind my own business. So be it.

I could feel a headache coming on. I grabbed some aspirin out of my desk drawer and walked back to the water fountain. Swallowing pills with only a small squirt of water shooting in the air is a cute trick I never learned, so I simultaneously choked on the bitter tablets and dribbled water down my chin, onto the front of my shirt. I was wiping my face when I turned to see Tall's grinning puss.

"You hear about the big brawl?" He was wired, anxious to talk to somebody, anybody. Even me.

If I had been inclined to bury the hatchet, break an arrow, chew the fat, or any such thing with this fool, I still had a story to file, and a date to keep with Kay. I was worried about my kid, and in no mood for this turnip.

"I'd like to chitchat," I said, "but I'm not dressed for the occasion."

Tall shrugged "And I thought you never washed your shirts." He walked away.

"Jerk."

I went back to my desk, did a library search for Mitchell, Ivy, got a message that the system was taking a time out. I thought of Ivy, a lifeless dancer, dressed in white. Man, there had been so many beautiful victims in the past twenty years. And so many young ones. Age and beauty hadn't protected them, not in my world.

Politicians stealing from people who voted for them, pastors soliciting favors from little girls who trusted them, that was my world. Pimps, whores, drug dealers, car thieves, street people, lawyers, bail bondsmen. Car wrecks, suicides, murders. I had spent over two decades writing about all the things that went wrong in the city.

I was beginning to tire of the way the lives of people were abbreviated in stories I had written, then were buried on pages dominated by ads that promised sustained pleasure, youth, beauty, whatever. It was an insult to reason.

I went back to the library and went through the clip file drawers. I wasn't sure how much I would find because the library staff was in the process of transferring all clips into the computer. The hard copy was scheduled to be packed away or destroyed. I wasn't sure which, and I guess it didn't really matter. The short of the issue was that more and more the computer was replacing footwork for reporters. Quick, easy access.

Investigative reporting with your feet on the desk and a keyboard in your lap seemed to be the future of the game. From what friends around the business had told me, we were the last of the papers to make the conversion. Still, until they did away with file drawers, I liked rooting around in them. They smelled of old paper, old stories. And old reporters.

I found Ivy, and not in just one, but two files, cross-listed, Mitchell, Ivy (see also) Mitchell, Mary Jane.

The Mary Jane Mitchell folder was very old, the name on the edge of the file handwritten in ink. The librarian had not taken the time to type a label, which seemed an indication of the lack of importance someone placed in the file.

There were three clips, all old, yellowed. The first story was a two-paragraph brief about fourth-grader Mary Jane Mitchell, winner of the Lower Division county spelling bee, called affectionately, the story pointed out, the "Bee-Have."

The second was, again, a two-paragraph brief of, now fifth-grader, Mary Jane Mitchell, winner of both Lower and Middle divisions in the same spelling championship. With the second clip was a photo of a smiling Mary Jane Mitchell, wearing, according to the cutline, "her favorite ruffled Easter dress," holding two small trophies, and smiling proudly.

The third clip was a longer story about sixth-grader, Mary Jane Mitchell, whose award-winning essay had earned her a place with two other students, one from Dade and the other from Monroe county, as one of three outstanding South Florida middle school students. The students were awarded a college-trust scholarship by an association of state banks and a group of South Florida contractors who, the story said, agreed these students "were the pride of South Florida middle schools." The photo that ran with the story was of three young girls holding large plaques. Ivy was in the middle, smiling, and wearing what seemed to be, without the ruffles, the same Easter dress.

The Ivy Mitchell file was recent, the label typed. Inside, the clips were still stiff, the paper white, the ink dark, and the photos as clear as newsprint allows. There was nothing regarding criminal activity; in fact, all the clips were photo story items, about local social, benefit functions. I read the stories, none of which mentioned Ivy, however, she was the bright spot, no matter where she was standing, foreground, background, anywhere, in the photographs. And the photographers had been diligent about getting her name for the cutlines. When Ivy was in a photo, it went from society ho-hum to excitement. I noticed she seemed always to be on the arm of a different, but always very expensively-dressed man.

I wondered what she was doing with these guys. I amused myself wondering what they told their wives about the woman they had been photographed with the night before. Anyway, looking at her pictures, I figured she must have been worth the risk. Good God she was beautiful.

Then I began thinking about the kid in the old dress, the student, scholar-turned society escort, stripper, whatever. I remembered Flowers had said, "There's wrong, and then again, there's real wrong." I had thought at the time I knew what he meant. Holding both folders in the library that night, I wondered. Sometimes, it seemed just "gone wrong" could be bad enough. Bad enough to change your life, bad enough to get you dead.

Flowers had been right about the addresses. I got the family homestead from one of the Mary Jane Mitchell stories. The other was torn from a reporter's notebook, probably by a photographer, and clipped to one of the society photos. The first was out west, and the other over on Flamingo, near Parker. I knew both areas. The later was not far from the paper. A couple of miles, maybe less. I wrote them down. That was all I got from the clips.

I left the library with a notebook that had more blank pages than a reporter might hope for, and wrote the best story I could with what little I had, or could use, and sent it to the city desk, then I dialed the lounge. I asked for Crystal. Somebody put me on hold.

I checked my watch, it swung eleven just as Crystal brought the phone back to life. "Mr. Krekow?"

She said the place was nearly empty. "Just a few regulars and a pair of salesmen from somewhere in the Panhandle making my life miserable. Hope they tip as well as they play grab-ass."

"No lady sheriff looking angry?"

"No way," she said. "But before the night is out, one of these jerks from the Redneck Riviera is gonna need one to protect him from me."

I asked her to tell Kay I was on my way. She said, "Will do."

I stopped by the desk and told Latham I would check family and friends first thing in the morning.

"Right." He reached for a dictionary and began fanning pages. "I've got a head looking for a story."

"Yeah, sure."

Chapter 6

*I*t was nearly eleven-thirty when I walked into the lounge. Crystal, who turned out to be a knockout, nearly matched my stride as we crossed the room. She had soft features, brown eyes that seemed to sparkle, the reflection of streaks of grey in her shoulder-length, brown hair. She looked too young for grey, but didn't hide it. I liked that.

She took me to a table in a dark corner at the back. Kay was seated, dressed in an attractive suit, looking more like a model than a cop.

"Sorry about being a little late," I said. I sat in a comfortable chair across a glass-topped table from Kay, who sat with her back to the wall. Crystal wiped my side of the table with a damp cloth.

"A young woman was found dead, floating in the Intracoastal, not far from my place," I said. "Cooper was late shift, but he was covering a car pile-up, so I had to cover the story."

"Drowned?" Kay asked.

"I don't think so," I said. "Probably a drug overdose."

"And?"

"And, all she had on was a nightgown," I said. "One of the detectives knew her, said she was a dancer, over at Speed Stick T's."

"Get you a drink?" Crystal asked me.

"Just a beer, thanks. Draft is fine."

Crystal looked at the empty in front of Kay. "How about another?"

Kay nodded. "Light on the vermouth."

Crystal walked away. I loved her walk.

Kay played with her empty. "Anyway, it's a guy."

"What's that?" I asked.

"The problem." Kay looked suddenly annoyed. "The reason you're here."

"Sorry," I said. Somehow I hadn't thought about my girl with a guy, at least not in a way that could lead to a problem. I knew she had boyfriends, but that was kid stuff. "Why don't you tell me about him?"

I waited, watched the tips of her fingers move lightly around the edge of the glass in slow circles. "You know Robin has been taking acting classes two nights a week down on the Lake Worth campus?"

I said I did. I thought that was great.

"You would," she said.

"Let's not argue, Kay," I felt that old flutter in my gut. "She met him in her acting class?"

"You could say that," Kay said, went back to playing with the edge of her glass, this time not quite so gently. "It's her teacher."

"Her teacher?"

"Yes."

"How old is he?" I asked.

"Not too old, if that's what you're asking," she said. "I thought colleges had rules against things like this."

"I don't know," I said.

"Our daughter is mixed up with an acting teacher." Kay made a facial expression that left no doubt about her opinion of acting teachers. "He comes from California." Same facial expression.

So much for California.

"Have you met him?"

"Not yet," Kay said. "Robin wanted to bring him home for dinner. I guess I blew it. Or Grant did. We said no way, the wrong way."

Crystal brought the drinks. We sat for a moment in silence, leaving them untouched. Leaving each of us to our own thoughts about this meeting.

Did these few times alone together get more or less painful as the years passed, I wondered? I noticed small indications of aging in Kay. A few grey hairs, small creases around her eyes, hands weathered from years in the blistering South Florida sun. The blushing bride was a woman now. She still looked great. But I thought she looked troubled as well.

I thought about Robin and her teacher, and couldn't stop wondering whether I should be relieved or frightened. It seemed like a modest problem with a simple solution. I really didn't understand why Kay had gone to this much trouble just to talk to me alone. This was something we could easily have discussed over the phone. Something, I felt, was missing. The trouble was not yet on the table.

She took a picture out of her handbag, handed it to me.

"She left a picture of him in her room. I made a couple of copies."

I looked at the picture of a rather nice looking, neatly dressed man who might have been as young as his late twenties, or as old as his mid-thirties, no older. I thought he had a nice smile. He didn't look dangerous, and I wasn't sure if it really was any of my business.

I felt badly about looking at a picture that had been lifted from my daughter's room, and by a cop no less. "You know his name?"

"Of course," she answered.

I noticed she was slurring her words a little. That was not typical.

"Here he's Sheldon Lennox, though his real name is Bobby Randahl." Kay took out a notebook and flipped through a few pages. "Lennox could just be a stage name. I'll find out. I have some friends in LA who are downloading what they have on him, which isn't much yet."

"Do you know how long this has been going on?"

"It's still pretty new," she said. "I would guess it has been in the making for a couple of months, not more."

"And Robin says?"

"She's in love," Kay said. "What does she know? Apparently he has been telling her she's a great actress, etc., etc., she'll be a star, etc., etc., ., she should move to California and study with him." She made a fist, a reflex action. "Now you have to tell her, she will not."

She seemed to have something more to say, I waited, sipped my beer.

"Pete, he could ruin her life."

"I'll do my best," I said.

"Good." Kay was wound pretty tight. "This can't slide. You need to get with them, her and him, but particularly him. You're a man. Tell him to lay off your daughter."

I said I would get in touch with Robin this week. I wanted to ask Kay if this was really the way to handle something like this, but decided against the argument that was sure to follow.

"She is not moving to California," she said. "That is final. I'm counting on you to get that message through to her."

"Maybe I could ask them to dinner."

"Look, I am not asking you to make a new friend." Crimson, again.

I wondered how much she had had to drink. She had been here, maybe an hour. Probably less. I had never known her to drink much.

"Just sit down with her. She listens to you." Kay looked around the room, probably looking for Crystal, who thankfully had disappeared. "Tell her to take her cute little fanny home, and park it. Engine O-F-F."

I wondered if her "cute little fanny" might be part of the problem. I had heard of mother-daughter rivalries. But it did not make a lot of sense. Kay looked great, but who knows. Who ever knows.

"I'll get together with her this week," I said. "I promise."

"Thanks." She got up, put her bag over her shoulder. "This has been a long day."

"Yeah." We gave a light hug, I held her a second. "Kay, I'm glad we did this. It's been a long time."

"Me too," she said.

"No problem," I said. "Still, I'm concerned. I mean, I'm glad we got together, but we could have done this over the phone, right?"

She sort of shrugged, nodded.

I thought she looked like she wanted to say something. "Is there anything else?" I asked. "Something else you want to talk about?"

She rested lightly against me, her head against my chest, a brush of hair against my cheek. "Maybe I just wanted to see you." She pulled back, though not away, said with a nice smile, "I miss you sometimes, I guess."

"Is everything all right?"

"She grew up overnight." I felt her grip tighten on my arms. "One day she was a kid, next thing I know, she's a woman."

"Yeah." I thought I saw tears in her eyes, so I didn't push it.

"Thanks," she said, gave me another hug, a soft kiss on the cheek, turned, and walked away.

While I watched Kay leave, a bit unsteadily I thought, Crystal came by with the bill. "I'm glad to bring your change," she said. "But, long as you're up and about, I'd appreciate it if you'd save me a round-trip ticket."

"Always glad to fly one-way with a lady," I said, and followed her to the bar. She walked behind the counter and rang my bill up on the register. I paid, said "Thanks," and slid a generous tip across the counter.

"How about a cup of Irish coffee?" Crystal asked. "Before you run off, I'd appreciate a quick word about the young woman you told your friend about. I'm concerned it might be someone I know."

"You mean the young woman we found dead in the Intracoastal?"

"Yes, a small group of dancers from the place you mentioned, it's not far from here you know, come here rather often. I've come to know a few of them."

"Speed Stick T's?"

"That's right. Most just 'yes ma'am' me, but a few have taken time to swap names, a few words. 'How's the kids?' That sort of thing," she said. "You're a reporter, right?"

I told her I was.

"Well, they come here when they want to have a quiet drink, a sandwich, away from the lights and whatever else they don't want to deal with for awhile," she said. "Sometimes they come with a friend, if you know what I mean, though I don't stick my nose where it doesn't belong."

I sat on the stool next to the register. "You think you might know the woman who was found dead tonight?"

"I hope not."

"My name's Pete Krekow." I reached my hand across the counter. "I write for the News & Journal." We shook hands. Hers were soft.

"Nice to meet you, Pete."

I watched her work behind the counter. She moved beautifully, swirled whipped cream on two cups of Irish coffee and placed them on the counter between us.

I picked my cup up, and gently tapped mine against hers. "To new friends."

"New friends," she said.

I took a sip, it was very good. "Good coffee," I said. It was, I thought, as good as the Irish coffee I had had at Shannon airport, though perhaps not as good as the cup at the crowded tavern across the street from Fisherman's Wharf in San Francisco. That was the best I'd ever had. Then again, I've never been as cold as I was that night.

"You Irish?" I asked.

"Farenzella?"

"Italian?"

"Bingo." She tapped my cup again.

"Anyway, you make great Irish coffee."

"Years of practice, Pete."

"Does the name Ivy Mitchell ring any bells?" I asked her.

"We're just on a first name basis here, but Ivy was one of the names I was afraid you might mention," she said. "A very attractive woman with long, blonde hair, a lovely smile?"

I nodded. "That could be the same woman."

"I'm rather good at placing names and faces together," she said. "It goes with the territory. Do you have a picture of her?"

"I'm sorry I don't," I told her.

Crystal shook her head. "I hope I'm wrong," she said. "The lady I'm thinking of is about as nice as they come."

"Then I hope you're wrong," I said. "The description you just gave me could fit a lot of people. How about if I stop back by here with a photograph?"

She said "Sure" to me, and "Good evening" to a customer she cashed out.

"I'm curious, Crystal," I said. "What are they like, the dancers who come in here?"

"Quiet mostly."

"Quiet?"

"I think, like I said, they come here to get away from things," she said. "The women are mostly soft-spoken, polite. If they are with a friend, they stay mostly to themselves."

"Could you tell me a little more about the men?" I asked. "Are they generally the same men or different?"

"Pete, if I started talking about things like that, I'd be looking for a new job before the week was out," she said. "I'd like to help, but I have to draw a line at putting my job in jeopardy."

"Your help could be very important."

"I'd rather not."

"Okay, I understand," I said. "But how about if I just bring some clips by, some photos of Ivy at society parties with different men. Could you just tell me if you ever saw the men before, with her?"

"Could I just blink 'yes' or 'no.'" She laughed.

"Or wiggle your nose."

"You win. But don't bring them here. Call first. We'll get together."

"You work most nights?" I asked.

"I swing shifts some. Please, it would be best if you called first." She wrote her name on a napkin.

I thanked her, put the paper in my pocket.

"You doing a story on the lady sheriff?"

I shook my head, smiled. "We have a grown daughter. She brings us together every once in a while."

"Yeah, I could write that story," she said. "Only my guy hightailed it back to Oregon, where he was from, never heard from him again."

"You have children?" I asked.

"Two boys. Harry, the oldest is six, Joseph, he's five," she said. "We're real happy together. I have a sixty-foot double-wide, in a nice trailer park. The boys do well at school. I'm a lucky woman."

"Sounds like you are," I agreed. "Want to talk about what happened?"

She shrugged, "Not much to say." She said she had married a minor league baseball player who had a few good seasons, but not good enough to put him in the majors. "When he finally quit the team, he went back the way he came, alone. Even left his spikes behind."

"Still," she said, "we had some good years. I know folks who have never looked for the end of the rainbow. We did. I'm thankful for that."

With the end of her story, we tapped cups together. "And, I'm thankful for you, Crystal Farenzella," I told her.

"Give me a call, Pete," she said. "But not too early. After I get the boys off to school, I ususally grab a few extra winks before I have to think about heading back here."

I told her not to worry. "I'll be spending the morning talking to Ivy's family and friends. Just hope you don't forget how to make Irish coffee," I said.

"Not a chance." She had a great goodbye smile.

Chapter 7

A dirty, near-naked five-year-old, dragging a broken two-wheeled tricycle down the middle of the dusty limerock road, pointed the Mitchell house out to me. He was crying. I asked what was wrong, but I didn't understand the answer. Assuming it was an answer.

"Gerald. Ya'll git your butt here. Now." I couldn't see the woman who called the kid, but Gerald screamed something else I didn't understand, began washing his face with tears and snot, and took off running with the bike dragging behind.

I pulled in front of the house Gerald's dirty finger had indicated. The mailbox looked like it had never been new, and the family name had never been painted on it. I hoped this was the right place because this was the kind of dirt-poor, redneck neighborhood where city folk were neither trusted nor encouraged to wander. This was a place where action carried more weight than words, and disputes were more likely to be settled in the front yard than in a courtroom. Slick words did not settle here. Neither did strangers.

If the wood-framed house had ever been painted, that paint was well past the final stages of peeling off. Landscaping consisted of sandspurs, broken toys, a rusting swing set, assorted automobile parts and two out-of-action automobiles.

A dozen small, dirty children played in, on, and around the wrecks while a young woman beat a dusty rag rug against a skinny palm tree.

I walked across the littered yard toward the front door but was cut off by the young woman. I told her I was a reporter from the News & Journal. "I need to speak to Mrs. Iris Mitchell," I said. "It's important. Please."

"You lookin' at troubled times, mister."

I told her I was sorry, though looking at her I figured troubled times were not a unique feature of her landscape.

"May I ask your name?"

"Gloria." She frowned as she watched me take out my notebook. "Townsend."

I spelled her name aloud as I wrote it down. She nodded when I finished writing.

"You live here, Gloria?"

She shook her head and pointed to a rusting travel trailer that was parked in the back of the house across the street. It obviously had not traveled in years. There was more plywood in the windows than glass, and its sides were streaked with layers of aluminum paint and tar that had dripped off the flat roof.

"We're in mourning." She didn't look sad. It was more like a tired hostility. And she seemed too young to look quite so old.

She might have been attractive if the strain of having too many children when she was too young hadn't stretched her body unforgivingly, and the fruits of love in her marriage hadn't included a bruised eye that was nearly healed, and a split lip that was raw and swollen with blood.

"This is the Mitchell residence, isn't it?" I asked.

"These sure enough are Mitchell places. You got that right. Here and over there, and over there, too." She pointed at two other houses as well. She was proud of the homesteads. One was where her trailer was parked.

"I would be thankful if you would tell Mrs. Mitchell I would like to talk to her."

Gloria gnawed on a thumbnail.

"Please.

"Mama," she called to the house.

I noticed that a few women were just inside the front door, listening. None looked old enough to be the mother of a grown woman.

"Who is it, Gloria?" The question came from inside the house. I did not see who had answered. The voice was soft though. Not educated, but not the shank drawl I had been hearing since I first turned onto these limerock roads.

Then she came through the door, and stood on the block steps. And it could have been Ivy, except her hair was grey, tied back in a tight bun, and her body was slightly stooped with age. Her eyes looked tired, sad. She must have been beautiful, a long time ago. She had to be Ivy's mother.

"Mrs. Mitchell?"

"Yes." She came down the steps and walked toward us.

"I'm sorry to bother you." I told her I was a reporter. That I needed to ask a few questions about Ivy. "I know these are troubled times for you and your family."

I looked to Gloria for help in making this interview a little easier. Her lip was bleeding. She licked it with her tongue and spit the blood on the ground. No way.

"I would appreciate just a few questions. About Ivy, please. I would like to write something nice about your daughter. I need your help."

She stood next to Gloria, who moved over, close to her mother. They stood silent for a long moment.

"Nice place you have here." I jotted a few notes in my notebook. "Gloria said your family lives close by."

As they watched me in stone silence, I noticed a frown begin to form on her face. Gloria, who watched us both, noticed as well, and mirrored the deepening expression.

"Having family close must be a comfort," I said. Still, they stood silent.

"Please, Mrs. Mitchell, just a few questions."

She shook her head. "I thought it might be you when I first saw you from the steps. Then I thought, 'No, it can't be. After all these years, not him. Not again.'"

"I don't understand," I said.

"You people smell suffering, don't you?"

"No Ma'am. Sorry, but, I know this is a bad time for you, but I think you've got me confused with someone else."

"I'll talk to this man alone, Gloria." She patted Gloria affectionately on the shoulder. "Go on inside, hear?"

"I really hate to have to bother you. It's my job," I said.

Gloria nodded, reluctant, then turned and measured me with the kind of glare she probably learned from her husband. It was not pretty. She then went in the house and joined the half dozen women who waited and watched just inside the torn-screen front door. The yard kids stopped playing and looked at the stranger with distrust.

"I'm really sorry about your daughter, Mrs. Mitchell."

"Sorry?" She moved close to me. Close enough so I could see the deep blue eyes with coal black centers. "You don't give a damn about my sorrow."

I moved back one step, away. But she pursued me, stepping forward. I took another step back. I must have looked something like Gerald, the last time I saw him. Only I didn't have a broken tricycle.

"I don't understand." My throat was rough, dry. I noticed the gaggle of women stepping out of the house, huddled together, moving slowly like a storm cloud. Heading my way.

Her voice was a whisper, but her eyes were hard. "You don't remember, do you?"

I told her I didn't.

"It's twelve years ago when you wrote a story about my girl. After she was, after her stepfather had taken her." Her deep blue eyes watered. She took a long breath.

"You said if we allowed you into her nightmare, you would see that justice was done." She lowered her head and walked around me, towards my car.

I followed, looking back just briefly. The whole family was outside now, watching. Even the smallest toddler stood anxiously, in silence.

She stopped and picked up a piece of broken glass on the ground. "Mary Jane Mitchell. Her friends called her Ivy. You couldn't use her name, so you called her 'the golden-haired princess of our sweetest dreams. The blue-eyed daughter of our darkest nightmares.'"

Her finger nervously brushed the sharp edge of the glass. "Mary Jane was the child of every mother's prayer. She was the best student in her class. Her teachers loved her. She went to church on Sundays.

"She was the prettiest child. The one who was on her way out of this place, Mr. Krekow." The edge of her thumb started to bleed slightly as the glass cut her, but she did not seem to notice.

"You sat with us, Mary Jane and me, in that hospital room. You held her hand, and told her that if she would share the pain of a child who just had the inside of her body bruised and torn by someone she trusted, you promised action would be initiated.

"I remember that word, 'initiated,' it seemed so rich, so unlike any word a poor country woman would use. She trusted you. She held your hand and trusted you."

We were standing beside my car. She looked back at her family, her expression frozen in grief and rage.

And I remembered. And she saw I finally remembered.

If Ivy's name had been used in the story, a clip would have been automatically cut and placed in the library files. In any event, though her name was withheld because she was a child, someone in the library should have checked and filed a copy of the story properly. I had missed the most important connection I had to her.

"He was so cruel. He tortured her body. He stole her innocence, her youth. He destroyed her trust, forever." She stood, frozen with hate, with memory. "I guess the police figured with her background, she'd be having babies in a year or so anyway, so who cares. Why chase some drunkard stepfather, when the next'll be the same. Poor country women don't know no better.

"Something died in her that night, you know. In a way, she died when she was only a child."

I didn't say anything, I just turned the handle on my car door and started to open it. I thought I was going to be sick.

"You came here to help, Mr. Krekow. You want to help my Mary Jane? My dead baby." She finally cried. "You want to help? Do what you said you'd do. Initiate something."

She pushed against the car door, blocking me from opening it enough to get in. "Go get him, like you said you'd do. He's up there in Cedar Key, where he's from, where he ran back to after he hurt my girl. Go up there, and tell him what he's responsible for. Punish him the way I've been. The way she was."

"Mrs. Mitchell, I'm sorry if you think somehow I failed you," I said. "I'll see if there is something I can do. But it's been so many years now."

Her rage was my terror. I tried to open the door, but she hit me with her left hand on my right ear. I reached up to block more blows as she used the piece of glass in her right hand to tear my arms.

One of the grown women came between us, and tried to calm her. "Mama, please stop now," she said, and held her mother in her arms as the others crowded around.

Gloria came close, "Years hell," she shouted. "He come back twice this year. Jumped up out of nowhere, slobbering at the place where she worked. Looking at her like that."

"You did this," the daughter who held her mother shouted.

I forced the door open, got in and locked it. Iris broke free and pounded on the window and kicked the door, and stones and cans began pounding from the other side, from the yard. I saw a spray of spit and blood leave Gloria's mouth as she threw a rock against the window of my car.

I drove quickly away.

Chapter 8

The first thing I did when I got back to my apartment was to open the windows and let fresh air rush around the room. I turned on the old fan and listened to the sweet clatter of the venetian blinds as they danced in the warm breeze.

Then I went to the bathroom. My short-sleeved bare arms were cut and bleeding, my face was scratched, my right ear a nasty shade of red. I washed my face and arms, carefully. I wiped on alcohol and picked out a small shard of glass. When I finished, I noticed it wasn't half as bad as it had looked at first.

I took a cool shower, changed into a clean, long-sleeved shirt and two-day pants that were folded a day earlier and thrown on top of the dresser. I tossed the bloody shirt in the garbage, and the pants into a corner of the closet.

Then, the call to Robin. I sat by the phone, after a few minutes of dial-gazing, I picked up the receiver, listened for a tone, dialed. Robin helped me out of the decision-making process with an answering machine message. She was not home. She was, "sorry to miss this call, but if you will please leave your name and number, I'll be delighted to call you back. Thanks."

I told her I was sorry I hadn't seen her for a few weeks, and would like to get together, soon. "Maybe I could catch up with you on a school day, in Lake Worth. We could meet at the cafeteria. Or go out. Whatever you want. Will call again soon. Miss you. Love, Dad."

I walked to the office. On the way I remembered I had forgotten to close the windows. Hamlet time: to go back, or not to go back. Only a few white clouds floated under a background of blue sky that disappeared into a clear, circular horizon. No way it was going to rain.

It was about eleven when I walked into the newsroom. The place was busy with day-shift bustle. I was glad to see Johnny Reilly, an old reporter-turned-copy-editor, working the lead seat. Reilly was already a seasoned reporter when I began working at the paper. We worked police together for about five years, then he did a long stint on the county commission beat. He had been retired to the desk for about five years. We had remained friends.

As usual, he had a cigarette behind one ear. I knew he would rather be smoking it, but administration had recently put the kibosh on smoking in the workplace. Pretty soon he would make a break for the door and head down to the front parking lot, where he would join the seemingly ever-present group of folks who stood around outside, looking lost in a world that no longer tolerated their needs.

I never particularly liked cigarette smoke, but felt we could treat people better than to make them stand around, dodging cars, just so they could blow a wisp of smoke here or there. It seemed to miss the point of ways to deal with addiction.

"Hey, Johnny."

"Missed you this morning." He played with the hinged lid of a Zippo. "Latham left a note about you doing something on the Mitchell thing. I expected to hear from you sooner."

I told him I'd had some trouble with the interview.

"I can see that. Nice shade of red. What's the other guy look like?"

"The other guy was an old woman."

He laughed. "I hope you got a good story out of it."

"I wish."

"Don't sweat it, just write up what you got. Take a quick lunch. Then I need you to spend the rest of the day on a rest home protest up in Riviera Beach."

While we were talking, our new managing editor, a woman who had recently been brought in from a company newspaper in Virginia, where she had earned a reputation for trouble, came over and stood behind Reilly. Her name was Barbara Dreggs. She wore a corporate frown.

Her goal, as described in an office newsletter, was to "work with editors and reporters in an effort to improve the copy flow, and streamline the assignment process. To facilitate greater productivity without threatening quality."

Or, as those of us in the pit interpreted it: increase work load, cut staff, consolidate departments, cut positions, do wah, do wah. What it boiled down to quite simply was -- increase profits.

So far, she had encouraged one reporter to quit, and put two on probation. All three were relatively new people. All three positions were left unfilled. Meanwhile, the Old Guard waited, watching which way the tide would flow.

We had been introduced as part of a first-day, getting to know the troops. The whole thing was kind of a white-collar boot camp, with a lot of hand-shaking and back-patting, some tennis and football talk, and plenty of ass-kissing. I guess they wanted her to appear like a competitor.

She was a big, raw-boned woman who made the ivory tower dorks who were leading her around like a prize filly look like children. They made her look butch.

We had not talked since then. Actually we had not talked then, just shaken hands, limp-smiled and nodded. So it seemed natural to assume she was waiting to talk to Johnny. I saw relief in his eyes when it turned out she wanted to see me in her office. "Right away."

I shook my head at Reilly and shrugged. He matched my shrug and headed out for a smoke. I followed her to her office.

She was already seated behind a large, cluttered desk by the time I got to the doorway. On the wall in back of the desk was a large graph that tracked daily circulation. The line moved up steadily. She wadded a piece of scrap paper and shot it across the room. She bagged a pretty good two-point trash can shot.

"Very nice." I stood in the doorway.

She motioned for me to sit in the only chair on the visitor's side of her desk. As I sat, I noticed front and inside pages of the newspaper spread over the desktop. The pages hemorrhaged red grease pencil. Heavy circles orbited headlines many times, and short words, mostly slang, were adorned with exclamation points and question marks. I hoped the exclamation points meant trouble for Latham, not me.

"Thanks," I said.

She picked up a rolled copy of the newspaper and pointed one end my way. "They tell me you've been writing stories like this one for over twenty years. That right?"

"Which one?"

"The body they picked out of the Intracoastal."

"Yeah."

"You must get bored, doing the same thing all the time."

"Not really."

"Feel like a change?"

"Nope."

"Bill Latham tells me he thinks you need a new beat."

"What's he got in mind, parking ticket circuit?"

"Actually, he said writing for the television page, with some fills on the Sunday TV booklet."

I leaned over to her desk, picked up and wadded a blank sheet of paper, and drove a hook shot hard into the can.

"Good arm."

"Thanks," I said. A disturbed fly buzzed in the can. "Anyway, I don't own a television. How about he writes for television, assuming he can write, and you give me the Palm Beach vice scene."

"Funny," she said. She didn't smile, looked more like she had swallowed the fly. "You have any idea what a team player is?"

"Learned a bit about that in the Army."

"You Army?"

"Yeah."

"My father was Marine Corps. Career."

"Tough guys."

"You bet. I didn't like the service brat thing." Her usually spiritless eyes showed some feeling. "But I loved my dad. You like the service?"

"I guess. I sat in a tank on the Czech border for a couple of years. Drank a lot of beer. Made some very good friends. The food was wonderful. So were the people, the Germans, they were great."

"You serve anywhere else?"

"A year driving around Fort Hood, in Texas."

"I know where it is. I lived there when I was a kid."

"In Texas?"

"Texas, Germany, you name it." The spiritless eyes returned. "How'd you get into this business?"

"After the service, in college, it fell that way. I hated math and science. I loved to read and write. Journalism seemed like a great choice. No addition, no subtraction. Plenty of words. Words that I thought reflected life."

"Florida your home?"

"No, my family has been around the eastern end of Long Island so long they know which relatives stole the land from which Indians. It was a point of honor when I was a kid. Now, I suppose we claim Native American blood, and say we only wanted to share the land, but another family, probably of another religion, or national origin, did the dirty work."

She reached into a desk drawer and took out a pack of chewing gum. "Like a stick?"

"Thanks." I hadn't chewed gum in a long time. As I removed the paper and foil wrapping an old, familiar fruity aroma came my way. "Speaking of childhood."

"Yes?"

"The smell of gum conjures up some images."

"Like what?"

I rolled the thin strip into a bedroll shape and felt the smooth, powdered surface. "The smell of burning leaves in the fall, of suntan lotion in the summer, basketball games in the winter."

"Fish in the cafeteria on Fridays," she added.

"Yeah." I put the sweet memory in my mouth and slowly chewed through the layers. "Trips to the dentist."

"Ugh. You're a hard man to kick around memories with."

"Not really, it's just I'm getting a little nervous about being here," I said. "Over the years I've found the only time I've been invited to this office, either I've done something spectacular, or somebody is about to chew me out for something I did wrong." I paused.

"I can't think of anything I screwed up. I haven't earned any awards lately, so, I guess I'm trying to ask, other than the fact Latham doesn't like me, and that's nothing new, why I'm here?"

"It's to discuss your future."

"I didn't know it needed discussing."

"Your editor thinks it does. He thinks you are burned out. He wants you off city side, and buried somewhere between real estate and used cars."

"Cemetery plots?"

"Maybe." She showed a slight smile.

"What do you think?"

"That was precisely what I was trying to find out. You would have been well advised to run with the childhood memory thing a bit longer."

"Too late now."

"He says your attitude is getting in the way of your work."

"I never think on the job."

"You are about to fall off the edge."

"It was a rough morning."

"Aren't they all?"

"No, they are not. You're holding the paper, but you haven't read the whole story yet. She was a young woman who began her life in poverty. No pride-of-the-land crap either. I'm talking the real thing: rags, lice, ignorance, hunger, rage. She survived all that just long enough to do some dirty business to make a few dirt-balls some pocket money, then her life ended washed up on a bed of rock and rubble at the edge of a seawall." I watched the frown lines deepen at the corners of her eyes. Her mouth got tight, turned down hard.

"And as a child, when she was about to trade the rusted swing set in on some middle school textbooks, she was raped by her stepfather. Her life was never the same again. That's the story I've lived for the last eighteen hours. No, I'm not bored by it. It makes me angry as hell. It makes me sick." I wedged my teeth into the gum, trying to slow the anger that was building in me. I took a deep breath, as I let it out slowly I leaned forward in my chair, talked slower.

I could tell by the way she held her pencil, the way it was bending under the pressure from her thumb, that if I didn't back off quickly, she was going to send splinters of wood, lead and orange-yellow paint across the room. "Now she's dead, and he's over on the Gulf Coast, probably still in the child-molesting business, and Lady, that stinks no matter how much perfume you spray on it."

"My name is Barbara, not 'Lady.'" She put the pencil behind her ear before it shattered, and did some tight-fisted knuckle cracking.

I nodded, watched as she did a good job of winding down, calmed a bit before finishing her thought. The idea ran through my head that she had come close to giving me the sack. I had one foot out the door, and that was startling. The other guys' story had nearly been mine.

She brushed her mouth with the back of her hand, a nervous reaction, like a fighter wiping away the taste of sweat, blood. "It's nice to hear you still bring passion to your reporting, Pete. But get to the point. Tell me why I should not have you check in for duty at the entertainment desk."

I took another deep breath and let it out slowly. The flash image of hitting the streets, unemployment lines, interviews, moving to god-knows-where, planted the notion that if I wanted to stay a reporter at this paper, and I did, I would have to get along with this woman.

Yet, I wasn't so frightened that I would end my career working on the entertainment side of the newsroom. No sir. I had to find a way to make her understand, believe I was a very good reporter, who was of more value on the hard news beat than anywhere else. And, Iris Mitchell had been right. I had let them down. Let Ivy down, and though it was too late to save her life, I could clean the slate for both her sake and mine. I needed this story because I had let myself down.

"Barbara, the point is, I've just spent the morning with a mother who has waited years for justice. Now her daughter is dead, and she does not believe that anyone cares. And from where I'm sitting right now, I think she's right. We are the gate-keepers, and we are about to bury the Ivy Mitchell story in a file cabinet along with a pile of other yellowing clips on her life, so that I can grab a quick lunch, then drive up to Riviera Beach, where I will cover some kind of rest home protest that will probably be the lead story on the evening news tonight, and be old news in our newspaper tomorrow."

She stood while I was talking, and began pacing behind her desk.

"Pete, this is not a news meeting. You are not here to sell this story. You are here to let me know if you still have what it takes to cut it on city side."

"Let you know if I can cut it? I've been cutting it over twenty years. Pretty Boy out there was still playing with finger paints when I was winning writing awards."

"At ease, soldier."

She did some shoulder-rolling and dipping while she talked. I thought she was about to do some shadowboxing when she abruptly flopped back down in her large swivel chair. "You don't like editors do you, Pete?"

I didn't answer.

"How about officers?"

I remained silent.

"He never could get along with officers either, my dad. In a way, just now, you reminded me of him. You look a lot like him: tall, dark eyes, black hair. He could have been any rank he wanted, major, colonel, even general. Except, he never could polish brass. Even when it would have been clearly in his best interest to do so." She tapped the fingers of her right hand on the desk in no particular rhythm, just absently counting, irregular.

"But, my friend, he was solid in build and spirit. He treasured his men, loved to fight, drink beer with them. Talk loud, laugh louder. You like to kick down doors, Pete?"

I smiled and shook my head. "But I love the sound of laughter."

"Yeah. Once, when I was little, we lived in Oklahoma for a short time. Somehow I locked myself in a storm shelter under the house. The doors sloped off on the side of the building. I don't remember why, I could not push them open. It was terribly dark. I was frightened. When he heard me cry, he tore the wood doors off their hinges. The wood doors snapped, like kindling."

We sat quiet.

Just about the time Barbara seemed ready to get back to business, Latham stuck his head in the door. He said he was sorry for the interruption, and asked her a quick question about something or other. It was only pretense. He was overjoyed, figured I was getting trashed. He gave her an ingratiating smile, the kind I figured her father never would have given a superior. Then he aimed a sour-ball sneer my way, and started to close the door.

"Hey, Latham," I said.

He stuck his head back inside the room. "What?"

"What branch of the service were you in?"

Barbara leaned back in her chair, and closed her eyes.

"The Kick-Ass Corps." He laughed, and left, closing the door rather gently.

"Tough guy."

"Pete, help me. Tell me that you understand that the day of the rogue reporter who does business in back alleys is an anachronism." She had not moved. Her head still rested back, her eyes still closed.

"You believe that?"

"Pete, I'm really trying hard to help you." She sat forward and put her elbows on the table, and rested her chin in her hands.

"Okay, okay. I get the message. I'll walk the straight-and-narrow, I'll even be nice to that twit. But you know, and I know you know, I am not a rogue reporter looking for a bone to gnaw. I'm just a writer who is tired of watching the glitz get the front page, while the real stories lie around and nobody seems to want to run with them."

She reached for her phone and made a call. She turned away, and talked quietly. I could not hear what she was saying. It was a ten minute call, maybe longer. It sure seemed longer. When she was done, she turned back to me.

"Tell me more about the stepfather."

I told her what I knew. I did not mention the altercation with Mrs. Mitchell.

"Does the story tell how he got away without prosecution?"

"No, we never got that far."

"Why not?"

"It was a series about child abuse. Ivy was one of four other children. We never did a follow on that angle."

"Why?"

"Time. Finish one, on to the next. That's what I have been saying since we started talking."

"Did the dead girl's mother talk to you about the stepfather this morning?"

"Yeah. She believes the police, society, let him walk without a fight because they think poor country girls have a different standard of behavior, of expectations," I said. "You know what I mean?"

"I think so," she said. "Do you agree?"

"I think there's truth to what she says. If it had happened in another part of town, it might have been handled much differently," I said. "Still, there are other reasons that might explain letting him walk away."

"Like?"

"Maybe the case workers didn't think sending the father to prison, which, for a variety of reasons might have been difficult to do, was worth dragging a child into the court system. Ivy was already badly wounded. Why take a chance on ruining a kid emotionally who already has been put through something no human deserves.

"We know Ivy was an excellent student. Perhaps they thought it might be best for her to try and put it behind her. She had a large family support unit," I said. "Justice sometimes has an awful price."

"Good points," she agreed. "And, you're sure the mother is a reliable source?"

"Very." I instinctively touched my sore ear. "Yeah, I believe her."

"Pete, I agree. The Ivy Mitchell story has the potential to show how the long-term effects of child abuse can end in a sad death. I want you to find all the missing little pieces that led to her ending up on the rocks," she said, leaned forward. "If you are right, and this is a story of betrayal, failure, and neglect. I'm going to give you a chance to write this story, and to prove yourself at the same time. You have two weeks to put a package together. Meanwhile, you are off the desk. You work for me."

"Career change?"

"Maybe."

"Sure, what the hell." I should have felt defensive, but didn't. I was a reporter who said he wasn't looking for a bone to gnaw, and yet there it was, in a dish with everything but Fido written on it. And it looked pretty good.

"Fair enough," I said. "But, seriously, two weeks is not much time for a story that spans more than a decade."

"Two weeks."

She made another quick call, then left me alone in the office for a few minutes. When she returned she did not sit, instead she extended her hand. I stood and shook it. She had a good handshake.

I left her office, went to the library, where I copied a few photos of Ivy, put them in my pocket, and left the newsroom.

As I walked out the front door, and passed into that fine Florida sunshine, I felt good. I knew I was on thin ice, but I also knew I was a good reporter. A very good reporter. I hadn't felt this good about my job for years.

Chapter 9

As I walked across the Rainbow parking lot, my stomach shared a deep rumble with my soul, reminded me I had a package each of my favorite deli ham and swiss cheese in the refrigerator. I checked my watch. It was nearly noon.

I was on my way in the back door when I decided instead to take a chance on catching Trevor Black at his favorite lunch stop. I got in my car and headed to downtown West Palm Beach. If I was lucky, my old friend, the medical examiner, would still be at lunch in the same restaurant, at the same table he had sat at every lunchtime for as long as I had known him.

Black and I shared a friendship that went back a long way. We both had started work in West Palm at about the same time: he as the new medical examiner, me as a reporter.

My best story that first year, had been about a procedural complaint filed against him that could have cut short what was to become a solid career.

At the time I was assigned the story, for some reason, and I don't remember exactly why, the investigation had bogged down. It looked like the police inquiry might drag on long enough to ruin his ability to function in his position.

After pounding the pavement for three days solid, I was finally fortunate enough to have the overtime legwork pay off with the kind of information that gave me the story that cleared him, and sent a jealous assistant, who had been passed over for promotion, packing.

We had been friends ever since. He had, over time, been my best, most reliable source for critical death-related information.

I pulled into a parallel parking space in front of the little restaurant, The Elbow Room, put change in the meter and went inside.

Westy Brook, a guitarist with a flair for mixing jazz and classical, was playing when I walked in. He saw me, smiled, and plucked out a rhythm that mimiced my footsteps as I walked across the hardwood floor to where Trevor was just getting up to leave.

"Sorry, Pete," Trevor said. "Got to get going."

"Mind if I walk you to your car?" I asked.

"Don't mind at all." We stopped at the cash register, where Trevor paid. I waved goodbye to Westy, and walked outside.

"I'm working the Ivy Mitchell story," I said. We headed toward his car which was about halfway up the block.

"I haven't had a chance to do more than draw blood, and take some swabs for the lab," he said. "I got some heavy pressure to do two of the folks who were involved in a very nasty mess out on the Turnpike last night."

"Did you notice anything unusual when you were taking swabs?" I asked.

"Perhaps," he said, "but I'm not ready to discuss it."

We stood by his car. I leaned against the parking meter. He stood at the edge of the curb, rubbed the sole of his shoe against the concrete, trying to get something off that had stuck there.

"I'm very interested," I said.

"Sorry," he said, "got to get going." He opened the door to his car. "You all right? You look pale."

I nodded, told him it was important.

"I'll be doing her first thing tomorrow," he said. "Come by and see me later in the morning."

"I planned on going to Cedar Key tomorrow," I said. "I don't know what time I'll be back, probably late."

"Well, I'll be around."

"I suppose I could drive over tonight," I said, talking mostly to myself.

"Why don't you go back inside and get yourself something to eat," he said. "Get your mind off this woman a minute or two."

He got in his car, started the engine. The window rolled down. "You sure you are all right?" he asked again.

"I'm fine," I said. "Really, I am."

I walked back to my car, got in, smiled. After years of sliding, all of a sudden I felt like I was back in the reporting business. Driving to my apartment I thought, life sure had some strange ironies.

The venetian blinds greeted me with a festive flap. The windows were open; the floors were dry. Things were going my way. Even the fan seemed to hum a sweet tune as I settled into my dear old fat chair, and shared my good mood with a ham and swiss on rye.

I called Robin again, no answer, same sweet recording. I left another short message.

I could hear the gentle voice of Willie Dee, the gardener, as he talked to his leafy friends in the yard. He spoke to them like a parent, offering praise, encouragement.

I raised the blinds and leaned out the window far enough to see him working below me. He was talking cheerily, and raking leaves and cuttings into a large compost pile directly under my window.

"Hello down there. Is it Mr. William Dee, gardener par excellence I hear talking to all the little Dees this fine afternoon?"

"It is, indeed, sir, the family Dee," he said with pride. "But, my children, what a pleasant humor Mr. Pete Krekow has about him this day."

"And how sir, may I ask, does your family bloom?"

"We, sir, are blooming quite nicely, thank you."

"So, Mr. William Dee, shall I tell the bishop that his soil-bound flock is blooming quite nicely, sir?"

"Religiously, sir."

Willie Dee had been a resident of the streets when the new owners first moved into apartment number one. Frankie had found him burrowed in an overgrown mess of vegetation on a corner of the property. He was about to evict him when he noticed the plants in the thicket where Willie had made his sleeping place for the past few months looked healthier than others in the area. He asked Willie if he was a gardener.

"No," Willie assured him, he was not. "However, sir, because I live closely among them, I feel the way a man feels about his own. Duty-bound to share a bit of water and some small words of encouragement with his flock, if you will, sir."

He and Willie had spent the rest of that evening sitting on a curb, drinking bottles of cold beer and chewing on Cricket's delicious fried chicken.

Willie Dee had started life with a proud old New England name. "One, sir, with a quantity of syllable, and character of letter, that bespoke an unbroken lineage of five generations of silver-spoonery.

"It was, however, in those halls of ivy, where this master William VI was absorbed with papers on medieval religion and romance, that he met and fell in love with the damsel whose blue eyes would teach him of love, and, if you will, distress. Not, unfortunately, hers.

"He exchanged, then, my dear sir, the love of a woman and, alas, his family, for the love of a bottle of porter. Stout. Or otherwise, when the occasion arose." Willie held a half-finished bottle of beer to a street light and gently rocked it, like a pendulum, side to side. He then drank the sudsy remains in one swallow.

"Well, I ain't sure about bespokes," Frankie told him. "But I know a good man when I drink with one. So how's about you grab onto a bunch of them flowers that needs someone to tend them? You do that, and I'll keep you in enough beer to keep your whistle wet. And maybe I'll find a tent for over your head. But no falling down drunk or sleeping in the yard. And no asking the folks that live here for spare change. Do that and I'll break your arms. How about it?"

Willie agreed, and by the end of the beer and chicken, he had a home, a job, and a new family. He spent a final night in his little thicket, far in time and place from those halls of ivy, but sheltered still by his beloved foliage. Next day he and Cricket cleaned out an old laundry room that had not been used in years. With the help of a plumber and an electrician, both of whom lived with their families in the Rainbow apartments, they created a studio apartment where Willie could be close to those things he loved most: his new gardening tools, his small refrigerator filled with beer, a cupboard filled with canned vegetables, and outside, his most prized possession, his garden.

From that day forward, Willie ceased speaking directly to people. He spoke only, one might say, in the third person, through his plants, his children. He was, in turn, provided for and protected. The tenants treasured him, and the results of his work, which were glorious.

"And may we ask what bringeth forth these expressions of zeal, sir?" Willie asked me.

"Gardener, I travel this day to far off lands. I go in quest of a lost soul."

"A lost soul, is it then? Gracious, mercy. Cover your ears, my darlings, lest tales of infidels and demons trouble your sleep."

I was just beginning to enjoy the knight-in-shining-armour thing when I heard the phone ring.

"Alas, my friend, a signal sounds, I must 'farewell.'"

"And we bid you a fond 'fare-thee-well, brave knight.'"

I answered the phone. "Merlin's Emporium. Swords sharpened, armor polished. Used battering rams and shields. Merlin speaking."

"Hello, Dad? Sounds like you've been talking to Willie Dee. How'iseth he?"

"Sweetheart, Dee is dandy. How about my favorite girl?"

"Super. Glad I caught you."

"So, can we get together soon?"

"Sure. I can't make it this afternoon, but how about tonight? I've got someone you just have to meet. He's a new friend. A really great teacher."

The cuts and bruises from my encounter, the image of Ivy, dead on the rocks, knowing her stepfather had been back to watch her dance, and my deal with Barbara Dreggs, all combined to make me believe my trip to Cedar Key was a priority. If her stepfather had anything to do with her death, I wanted to find out as quickly as possible, before he had a chance to knit a cover for his actions.

I thought of Kay, who had let our meeting slide a few days so we could meet in person, and hoped I was making the right decision. "I can't do it tonight, Sweetheart."

"Ugh. We never seem to be able to get this together lately."

"I'm sorry, but I have to drive over to Cedar Key tonight. If things go right, I'll be back tomorrow, but I can't promise. How about Thursday?"

"Thursday is great. Just great. I have a class at eight, so we can have dinner in the cafeteria, then you can sit and watch this kid do a monologue that she has been working on for a week."

"Where do I buy a ticket?"

"Oh, this is wonderful."

"Cafeteria at 6:30. My treat. Bring your new friend."

"Absolutely. Gotta run, Dad. Thursday."

"Thursday." The line went dead. "Love you, Baby."

I looked out the window. Willie was gone. Time to get back to work.

Next stop, Cedar Key. The first thing I needed was the name of the stepfather, which -- and I did not remember why -- had been held out of the story. That might have been part of the reason he split without a problem. Anyway, I knew his name would be in my case notebook that I kept with all my other story clips and notebooks in a file cabinet in a corner near the front door. After an hour of searching through stacks of old files, I found a clip of the story with notes stapled to it. I read through the notes and found his name. Robert "Robbie" Provot.

I called Cedar Key information, got his number, dialed. A woman answered. I asked for Mr. Provot. "Which Mr. Provot?" the woman asked.

I said I didn't know, but I had a '65 Ford pickup for sale and heard some guy named Provot, from over in Cedar Key, might be interested.

"Well, could be either Jasper or Robbie. They're twins, you know. I'm their mother." Great, you must be very proud of them. "Oh, yes. They are the sweetest boys." Yeah, sure.

"So, I'll be in town tomorrow. I'd like to see them."

Simple. They ran a ham and egg joint on 24, J&R's, just this side of the pier. "Best damn sausage gravy you ever heaped over a biscuit." I'll bet.

"What'd you say your name was?"

"Merlin."

"Merlin?"

"Frank."

"Now listen up, Frank. You don't come to Cedar Key without fillin' yer tank at J&R's. Hear?"

"Yes ma'am."

"There's a good boy."

"I'm coming over from Jacksonville. Spending the night in Lake City on some business, but I should be in your neck of the woods first thing in the morning. If I get there early, will the boys be there for me?"

"Frank, they have that grill sizzling two hours before the old rooster remembers he's supposed to get me up."

"Thank you kindly. I can smell that sausage cooking from here."

"Well, stop that smelling, and get on over and get yourself something to eat."

"Yes ma'am."

"There's a good boy."

I hung up the phone, closed the blinds, set the alarm for seven-thirty, and snuggled under the sheets. I planned on leaving at about eight. I figured it was about a seven-hour drive, probably more. Allowing for finding the place in the middle of the night, I would get there at about four. I wanted to get there first thing in the morning. First, I needed some sleep.

Chapter 10

The phone started ringing at about the same time the alarm on the clock rattled to life. I gave the pin on top of the alarm clock a hit, lifted the receiver. It was Kay. She said she had just talked to Robin, and was pleased we were getting together Thursday evening. However, she thought we should have one more session alone together before I met "him."

"Kay, there's no way," I said. "I'm going out of town tonight, and I'm not sure if I'll be back tomorrow afternoon or evening. I may even be as late as Thursday morning."

"That's a bit unusual, isn't it?" It seemed like she wanted to chat, which itself was unusual. "Running away with the waitress?"

"Nothing that exciting." I said. "Listen, Kay, would love to talk, but I have to get going."

"She was pretty, I thought."

"Who?"

"The waitress."

"Sure," I said. "Kay, I have to go."

"I get the message," she said. "Call when you get back."

"You got it," I said, and hung up.

I dressed, threw a change of clothes in a duffle bag, and headed to my car. I tossed my bag on the back seat, started the engine, drove out of the parking lot, and headed west.

The road that crossed the state was rural Florida. It was dotted with farms and a few small towns along the path. I thought about Ivy and her family, about Ivy's mother and what she had said, what she wanted.

I finally reached the Gulf Coast. I turned right, headed north with still over two hundred miles to drive.

I wondered about the man who left so much misery behind him. Over the years I had done enough stories on criminals to know there are no guilty men in prison. State and county facilities are filled with innocent people. The courts and judges are wrong, the police are bad, this or that forced them into a life of crime. It's never their fault.

I thought back on stories I had written; stories about wives who felt the beatings they got were their own fault because they had not had dinner ready on time, or not cleaned quickly enough, or didn't encourage their husbands with praise. Or the rapists who believed women drove them to it because of the clothing they wore, the way they walked, smiled. Sometimes God made them steal and kill; sometimes it was for love. "Robbie Provot, what's your story going to be?" I wondered.

Chapter 11

I made decent time, grabbed a quick bite at an all-night burger joint. I finally reached 24, the last leg of the trip, hung a left and headed toward downtown Cedar Key.

I drove a dozen miles, and finally found the diner on the corner of a street of run-down warehouses and closed fishmarkets. I slowed as I passed. The place had big front windows and was well-lighted inside. It was a small joint with seating for about forty at old Formica-topped tables, and a counter across the back of the room with about a dozen wood stools.

The only customers I spotted through the windows were two guys dressed like construction or warehouse workers who were seated at one end of the counter. Behind the counter was a big, hairy, ugly guy who had on a camouflage hat and a black and white cowboy shirt.

"Wonder if that's my boy?" I said to myself. I was hoping for something smaller.

A few blocks down the road I turned and drove back. I pulled into a parking space in front and cut the engine.

Inside, a country singer whined on a jukebox that had been hit too many times. Now all the lights and tubes and bubbles that must have once made it a classy machine were blown out, kicked out, or had fallen out.

I walked over to the counter and sat at one end, away from the construction workers.

"Be right with you," the big guy behind the counter said. He was joking with the construction boys. I heard him call the one nearest me, Sammy. They were mostly listening and sometimes laughing while they ate from plates piled high with food.

He moved down my way, placed a menu on the counter. "Find what you want, name's Jasper," he said, began to walk away, then changed his mind. "Say, you ain't here about selling a pick-up are you? Mama said someone called yesterday about a Ford truck. Wasn't sure if it was a '55 or a '65 truck he was wanting to sell."

"Quite a difference," I said.

"Say that again. About like the difference between Mama's fresh hush puppies and road kill." He laughed.

Jasper and I were bonding nicely, so I didn't ask which of the aforementioned foods he would prefer, though his appearance might have suggested a preference for a roadside dinner of tire-tracked armadillo.

Still, if he was ugly, he did not seem mean. In a way, there was something likable about him. The lines around his eyes showed humor. It crossed my mind that it wasn't right to judge one brother by the actions of the other.

And neither was it right to judge by the head of long, stringy hair or a grey-streaked beard that hung down his barrel chest to his huge belly that jiggled when he laughed. He could just as easily have been a jolly red-neck, a soup kitchen Santa Claus, or a former governor of Florida.

"We specialize in biscuits and gravy," he said. "Make'em just like Mama, and her mama before her."

"Sounds good," I said. "I'll have sausage gravy and biscuits, and two chops, burned."

"You got it," Jasper said. "Eggs and potatoes?"

I nodded.

"Coffee?"

"Sure thing."

He finished filling out the order, then disappeared into the kitchen in back.

On the jukebox a long-winded singer lamented the fact that his daddy spent his life on an assembly line, his mama took in wash for rich folk, and his wife had just left town with his best friend. I figured his dog must be hiding, knowing he was next in line for a heap of trouble.

Jasper came back out, poured a cup of coffee and set it on the counter along with a frosted chrome tin of cold milk.

"You here for the fishing?"

"Afraid not," I said. "I'm here on business."

"Come a long way?"

"Palm Beach County."

"That's a heck of a drive," he said.

"The name is Pete Krekow. I'm a reporter for the News & Journal."

"You here in Cedar Key for a story?"

"Actually, all of what I need for my story is here, in this diner."

"This diner? You all heard of J&R's all the way down in Palm Beach County?" He smiled, showed his amazement. "Listen to me now, I can get Mama here quicker than two shakes of a gator tail."

"I'm afraid that's not the story, though I can see it's a mighty nice place, and I look forward to breakfast." I could see the disappointment in his face. "I'm doing a story on a family that lives down in West Palm Beach. I understand your brother, Robbie knows them. I'm hoping he can help me with some information I need on a few of the family members."

Jasper showed caution, extreme caution. Our friendship had turned a corner, screeched to a stop, parked.

"Still," I said quickly behind his pause. "I might be better off just writing about your mother's biscuits and gravy."

Jasper didn't smile. "My brother, Robbie, he don't like talking much."

"Just a few questions."

"Yeah, well now you notice the kitchen wall don't have that little hole in it like most places, where the counter person in front can talk to the kitchen person in back? And the customers can shout jokes through?"

I told him I had noticed the kitchen was closed off from the rest of the place.

"Well, that's cause Robbie don't take to people. That's why I'm out here with the customers. But he sure can cook, mister. My brother can make two biscuits dance at the country fair."

"If you would tell him I'm doing a story on the Mitchell family."

"Mitchell?" Jasper frowned. "His wife send you?"

"No, but the family is on the worst side of troubled times," I told him. "I was hoping your brother could help me understand some things I need to know about the family, so I can help them tie up some loose ends in their lives." I sipped my coffee.

"Well, he weren't down there for but less than a year, closer to eight months, before they busted up." Jasper clearly did not want to ask his brother to come out and talk to me. "And that was years ago."

"Please, just tell him I'd like to talk to him."

Jasper nodded. "When I pick up your plate, I'll say something. I can't promise nothing."

"That's fair enough," I said.

He went down to the other end of the counter with the coffee pot, refilled the empty cups, then put the pot back on the heater and went back into the kitchen.

The song ended about the time I heard somebody roar something, not so much a word, just a sound, then a pot or pan banged once, hard on a counter. Jasper came back with my plate.

Robbie came out, but stayed in the doorway. He wore a white tee shirt stretched tight against enormous arms and across his muscular chest, with 'Raging Robbie' in red letters across the front, spelled him out as the baby I was looking for. And he was one hell of a baby.

They were the only twins I have ever seen with so little in common. Other than their general bone and face structure, they seemed to come from different families. Robbie was bald and so close shaven that his cheeks were pink with scraping. His body was tight, steel. His mouth was turned down, hard; his eyes held no joy. He stood flat-footed, stooped with his chin forward, defiant.

"You the one come looking for trouble?"

I told him I was not looking for trouble, just information.

"I got nothing to say about nothing. Much less Mitchells." He spit in a garbage can nearby.

"I think if you would talk to me about the time you spent there, you would say some good came of it."

"No good comes of messing in another man's business."

At the other end of the counter, Sammy piped in with two cents coined to make himself look good to Robbie. I didn't catch what he said, all my attention was on Robbie. He was certainly a big, bad package of trouble.

If Sammy had planned on opening a comedy club, Robbie slammed the door on that idea. He looked over at the boys and told Sammy, "Shut your goddamned mouth or I'll throw you both through the plate glass window."

It was obvious why Jasper ran the counter. Sammy went back to picking crumbs on his plate, though I didn't think he looked smart enough to know to keep his mouth shut very long.

"Eat and get gone," Robbie told me, and went back into the kitchen.

"Don't seem like my brother wants to talk today." Jasper set the plate down in front of me.

My chops looked nicely burned, but I noticed the biscuits were missing. "Jasper, seems like my biscuits are still in back."

"Sorry, I'll get 'em."

"Jasper?"

"Don't ask."

"Tell him Ivy is dead."

Jasper looked pained. I wondered if he knew her and was sorry, or if he was frightened at the prospect of bothering his brother again. "Be right back."

This time Jasper and Robbie came to the counter together. Jasper put my biscuits in front of me. Robbie stood over me. "You ain't getting till you rile me something terrible, is you?"

"No," I said. I put my fork on my plate, picked it up along with my coffee cup, and stood. "I'll take this over to a table in the corner where we can talk alone."

I walked over to a table near the jukebox. I heard Robbie tell Jasper to "put this on his tab." I didn't look back to see what 'this' was, or if he had followed me. I simply sat and began eating. Robbie came over and sat across from me. I noticed he had a bottle of beer.

"Well, you come all the way to talk," he said. "So, talk." He wiped the top of the opened bottle with the end of his shirt.

I knew that unless I could wind Provot down, the interview would go nowhere. All the travel time would be for nothing more than to watch him stomp off, back to his kitchen. He wouldn't come back out a third time.

I took a bite of biscuit and gravy, tried to express my satisfaction by sounding a series of rhythmic grunts that I meant to show enthusiasm. "You're brother is right," I said. "You sure could make biscuits dance a two-step." I smiled my appreciation.

He took a sip of beer, nodded. "What'chu want here?"

"I'm a bit surprised you don't seem at all interested in knowing anything about Ivy's death. When or how or where it happened."

"I don't get paid to ask questions, that's your job," he said. "I don't mess in business that ain't mine."

"So you're not surprised to hear she is dead?" I said.

He shook his head. "I don't know nothing," he said. He looked troubled. "I'll say, I'm sorry enough to hear the girl is dead. She was the best of a bad bunch." He didn't look sorry, but, then again, he didn't seem like a person who knew how to express sorrow. "How long's it been?"

"Since she died?"

He nodded, took a long drink from the beer bottle.

"Monday night." I ate small bites of biscuit, watched his eyes.

He drank more beer, then set a flaming wood match, that he sparked with a fingernail, to an unfiltered cigarette. "What'd she die of anyway?"

"I'm not sure," I said. "I'm still waiting for the coroner's report."

"Don't sound like you know much of nothing."

"She was found at night, in the Intracoastal, dead," I said. "She was only wearing a nightgown."

"That's it? Nothing else?"

"That's it."

"Hope that ain't what brung you here," he said. "It is, you wasted your time."

"You were her step-father, that's what brought me here."

"I ain't been that for so long I almost forgot," he said. "Anyway, you come a long way to tell me that. What else you got tucked in your pocket?"

"Have you been to Palm Beach County recently?" I asked.

"Got no reason to go there," he said. He finished his beer and set the bottle hard on the table. "Kids today. Don't pay a bit of attention to their betters. Take drugs, hang out all hours of the night. Got no respect. And her, in that family, I could've told you she'd end up like that."

"Where did you meet Iris Mitchell?"

"I was on a construction project in a place called Padarkee or Pudeekee, something like that, when me and a bunch of the boys went on into West Palm Beach, mixed hands at a bucket of blood, cleaned out a freak show someplace in the middle of nowhere, ended up in the hospital with a busted skull." He laughed, showed me the top of his head, where a few pink scars crisscrossed white skin.

"Iris was mopping floors in the place, some Catholic hospital, Saint somebody." He tried to laugh, but was not a man to laugh easily. It seemed more like a cough, a sick, strained sound. "She was quick enough to bed when she found I had a steady job."

"How long were you married?"

"About long enough to get divorced."

"You have any children with her?"

"Ain't you talked to her?" A storm formed in his voice, his eyes lowered to mine. He crushed out the cigarette hard in an ashtray.

"I saw her the morning after Ivy was found dead," I said. "She wasn't in much of a talking mood."

"Yeah? I never could get her to shut up." He frowned, licked his teeth. "Without a slap to get her attention."

"It must have been a hard family to be a stepfather in."

"You ain't shitting." He held up his empty and shouted back to his brother. "Jasper, another on Mr. Big Shot here."

"How many kids were there?"

"Counting home'uns, cousins, all the little crappers that didn't know who the hell their parents were, must have been a dozen or more in that little place at any time, day or night."

Jasper brought the bottle of beer.

"That what caused you to leave so suddenly?"

"Who said I left sudden?"

"Ivy's mother."

"She's a damn liar." He pounded the table. "I knew Ivy would end up like she did because she was too much like her mama. What else kinda bullshit she tell you?"

I looked at Robbie, at the veins pulsing in his bald head, at the way his nostrils flared, at his eyes, his gaze, that turned into something more wild than human, at the muscles in his arms and chest that were beginning to move in quick, irregular jerks.

I hadn't been in a brawl since Army days, when I was stationed in Texas. A few buddies on the boxing team and I were doing the backroads tavern circuit one weekend when I ended up mixing with a country boy who looked a lot like Robbie.

That was a long time ago. The fight had been between two young guys who couldn't hold their beer. There was no fancy footwork like we practiced in the gym, just some pushing and shoving, a punch or two. I don't think either of us got hurt, a bruise or two, some scratches.

Still, there's a way things feel when something is about to happen. Something bad. Most times, if you're sober, you find a way to blunt the hard edge. I knew I should back off, but for some reason hesitated.

Barbara wanted a story, but I wasn't Clark Kent's alter ego. I was a reporter, and driving all the way to Cedar Key just to fight with Robbie Provot was beyond reason.

Still, a good reporter asks good questions. Sometimes the answers are what you expected, sometimes not. Either way, you toss a pit bull a bone and hope he gnaws on it, not you.

"She said you hurt Ivy badly enough to land her in the hospital," I said. "Then ran away before the police could get to you."

"She's crazy," he said. "I don't know nothing about nothing, except that kid was always an uppity little snot."

"Ivy?"

"Thought she was too good for folks." His mouth was wet with beer and spit. He wiped it with the back of his sleeve. "If the law wanted me, they knew where I was. I never hid in my life."

"You want to tell me about what happened?"

"All the women was stuck on me. Know what I mean," he said. "I was the only man in that sorry bunch of white trash."

"Ivy?"

"All of 'em," he said. "I was the only man they ever knew who didn't think food stamps was the only thing you put in your wallet for spending." He lit another cigarette.

"I don't see what that has to do with you leaving."

He drew deeply on his cigarette, blew the smoke towards the ceiling. "Iris was one good looking woman, you know," he said.

I told him I thought she still was.

"Yeah?" He seemed about to say something, then changed his mind, took a drag off his cigarette. "Kids need a swat on the flanks now and then. Especially that bunch of little shits."

"That's what happened with Ivy?" I asked. "You spanked her?"

"Maybe. I don't remember. If I did, she needed what she got. They was all, like you said, always hysterical about something," he said. "Maybe that's what they should be called instead of Mitchells, Hystericals." He laughed. "Anyway, if that's all you came for, that's all you got."

"Robbie, I've come a long way to find out all I can about Ivy Mitchell."

"I told you what I know," he said. "Now, finish your breakfast and get on along with you."

"I know you've been back at least twice in the last year," I said. "And I know you saw Ivy both times, so how about telling me about it."

"I told you I ain't got reason to be there, especially with her."

"You went to the place where she worked."

"What if I did?"

"Maybe you went back to apologize for the spanking."

"Mister, if you're pulling my string." As Robbie talked, he pointed the hand that held his cigarette at me. As the hand made choppy, up and down motions, the smoke drifted in small bands off the tips of his fingers. "You pull my string, and you gone be sorry. You hear?"

I nodded.

"I said she was the best of the worst. Understand? I don't remember nothing more than saying 'been nice' and hightailing it out of there." He took a short puff off his cigarette. The smoke drifted out his mouth, got sucked up his nose. He coughed when he tried to speak again.

"You all right?" I asked him.

He nodded and wiped his mouth with a paper napkin. "Thinking of them chokes me up."

"Robbie, tell me what you know about Ivy's death."

"Her death? How the hell would I know about something I don't know nothing about?" He wiped sweat from his forehead. "You ain't too bright, is you?"

"Robbie, I know, and the police, if they don't already know, will know very soon about your trips to see Ivy," I said.

"I'm free, white, and twenty-one. I go where I want. I see who I want. And by the time I finish this here beer, I advise you better get." He finished the beer in one long tilt, then banged it on the counter. "And, what the hell the police got to do with anything?"

From across the room I heard Jasper call to his brother, ask if he wanted another beer. Robbie shook his head, and started to

74

get up, but I reached across the table and placed my right hand on his shoulder. He knocked it off, but sat back down.

"Stranger, you playing a dead man's hand you ever do that again." Robbie still held a stub of cigarette, he drew on it hard, the tip glowed red, his eyes shut, squinted tight.

"Robbie, we both know you didn't just spank Ivy, and say 'be nice' when you left Westgate," I said.

Robbie started to get up again, then changed his mind. "You talking like a man with a paper asshole, Mister Newspaper Man." He held a balled fist up to his face and began gnawing a knuckle.

"I figure, after all those years, you began to wonder about Ivy." I felt the perspiration roll down my underarms, off my forehead. "So you went back, sat around and watched her dance. She was very pretty. A woman now."

He unclenched his fist and pointed a finger my way. I did not understand what he said, the sound that came out of his mouth did not seem human. Saliva was forming in pools at the corners of his mouth and spilling onto his chin.

"That's what the police are going to think," I said. "I'm surprised they haven't been here yet."

He didn't say anything. His eyes showed caution.

"You went back, watched her take off her clothes." I stopped talking because he looked like he was going to jump at me over the table.

"And, I told you, I don't know nothing about nothing." He was half-standing, his fists balled.

"That would be easier to believe if you would tell me the truth about the last time you saw her."

"Boy," he shouted. "You don't know when you about to retire to the chicken coop, do you?"

I slid my chair back, shook my head. "Robbie, I didn't come here for trouble. I just want you to tell me if you were in West Palm in the last few days, and if you were, did you see Ivy?"

"And I'm telling you this for the last time." He was stooped over the table, his large hands held the edge of the table. "I don't know nothing about nothing, except her making a spectacle of herself in front of those yackos. Revealing herself like a slut, with no bit of shame." He trembled as he talked.

"When was the last time you saw her dance, Robbie?"

"I don't have to tell you nothing."

"You went back this weekend didn't you? Saw her dancing." I said. "I guess you figured she needed another spanking?"

I heard a voice across the room. "Yo yo, big Robo," Sammy hollered. "Knock that city boy on his ass."

I had been right, Sammy wasn't smart enough to keep his mouth shut. I stepped back as the table erupted, exploded in a blast of Formica, food, plates and silverware, bottles and splinters of wood. The first punch drove me back like I'd been hit by a train.

"I ain't been there lately," he said, and tore off his apron, threw it behind him. "But, city boy, you about to go home minus some teeth to chew with."

I got up fast, jumped out of his way and he crashed into the table and chairs next to the window. He was up, and back on me so quickly that I was still standing flat-footed in front of the jukebox. When the two of us hit it, it exploded.

I tried to push Robbie away from me but he hung on and we rolled on the floor a few turns, then he hit me real hard in the face. We did some more rolling and dancing, he did some more punching, then he pushed me against the counter and was slapping me with an open hand on the same ear that had been hit earlier. It made a high-pitched kind of scream.

I covered many of the blows by reflex, with my arms, like the Army days. Only I was blocking, not counter-punching. And not blocking enough. If I didn't do something quickly, I was going to be the victim in the next day's newspaper.

Then I saw her. Through the red mist that clouded my eyes, I saw the body on the rocks. I saw the child, beaten, torn, in the hospital room. I saw myself there with her, and I didn't like what I saw.

The first shot was free, easy, because he was wearing himself out on me. It was only because he was a street fighter that he hadn't taken me out yet. Or, maybe he just didn't want to.

Anyway, I'd seen guys in the ring take the kind of hit on the side of the head or jaw that turns the whole head like a whip. Sweat and mucous and blood follow the motion in a wide arc, and the body ain't usually far behind.

My first punch was an inside right uppercut from tight up against my body to the bottom of his jaw. I heard some teeth fracture. It startled him, knocking him back enough for me to push him with my left arm to that place you see fighters measure with their left arm extended. Yeah, that place.

Robbie got careless and gave me that distance, and failed to get his head back. I took it as an opportunity to clean up the mess. He crumbled and his head hit the floor with a crash. Blood from his mouth and the side of his head made a small but growing red, liquid pool on the floor.

I reached in my back pocket and took a business card out of my wallet, stuck the card between two fingers of Robbie's left hand.

Jasper was next to his brother by then, with a towel, wiping blood from his face. He looked up at me. "I think you've done my brother wrong."

"When your brother left West Palm Beach years ago, he left a lot of pain behind."

Jasper shook his head. "I know he felt bad for something, but that's why he went back this year. He told me he had to make peace. That was about six months ago, the last time he went down there. I believe him."

"I'm glad to hear that, Jasper," I told him. "Why didn't he say that to me?"

"My brother is a good man," Jasper said.

"Your brother don't help with that chip on his shoulder."

Jasper stood up. "I think you better leave now." He looked pained, betrayed.

On the way out I wondered if I had done the right thing. In my car I got my overnight bag from the back seat, changed to a clean shirt. Then I buckled myself in, dropped the stick to drive, and I was on my way home.

As I drove, looked in the rearview mirror at the diner, saw the bare yard, the newspaper clips of Ivy in her Easter dress, with her trophies. Saw Iris Mitchell's finger bleed from broken glass as she said, "the blue-eyed daughter of our darkest nightmares."

I gently rubbed my face. It burned. I believed Iris, Robbie Provot did assault Ivy Mitchell when she was just a child. He ruined her life, and despite what Jasper said about him making peace, he didn't show a bit of remorse. The guilt faded quickly as I drove away.

Chapter 12

The highway burned bright as I made the cross-state run home, drove through a series of small farm towns, finally into West Palm Beach. It was almost one o'clock when I made Dixie Highway. I figured Trevor Black would be finishing lunch, so I headed downtown.

I drove up to the restaurant just in time, noticed the rear lights blink on Trevor's car as he slipped into reverse. I honked, pulled in next to him. I walked quickly over to the passenger door, heard a click of the locks, opened it, got in.

"That's pretty fancy timing, Pete," Trevor said. "What happened to you?" He played with the air-conditioning. The car was still hot.

"You should see the other guy," I said, yawned. "Sorry, I just got back from a cross-state drive. Glad I caught you."

"Well, I haven't finished writing my report, so I'm not going to go into detail, and this definitely is between you and me," he said, played with the air vents. "She died of a drug overdose."

I was not surprised, said, "Unfortunately that's not a unique cause of death."

"Yeah, well there was also trauma that I would not associate with consentual," he said, seemed troubled, "intimacy."

"This is taking some nasty turns." I watched a tiny sparrow worry a large crust of bread that had fallen on the ground beside a sidewalk dining table.

"Pete, you would think, after all these years, I wouldn't be upset by the death of a young lady."

"I hear you," I said. "I've been feeling the same way myself." I got out, watched him drive away, then headed home.

I was walking up the stairs, thinking about taking a quick nap, when I ran into Frankie who was on the way down. He held a little man with a bruised jaw by the hair.

"What happened to you?" Frankie asked.

"Joined a punk rock band," I said. "What you got there?"

"This little fella says you know him," Frankie said. "Found him listening at your door."

I had known him long enough to know I didn't like him. On the street he was called Marbles. It was not a name that was meant to convey affection. He was a small character who lingered around the dark side of town: a snitch, blackmailer, slime-ball.

He was a man with no friends that I knew of, except for maybe his girlfriend, Nordy, and his wife, whom he hadn't seen in nearly two years. She was doing three-to-five down in Pines Correctional for some deal she made with a few old ladies. A venture that involved them giving, and her receiving.

"What's up?" I asked Marbles.

"I thought I might be able to share some information," he said.

"You give information with your mouth," Frankie said, lifted him by the hair, "not your ears."

"He banged my head into the door," he touched his jaw, winced. "I think something is broken."

Frankie turned his head, but I didn't see anything that looked like a crack, but, then again, he had a head of hair that could have concealed a small family of barn swallows.

"I don't want him around here," Frankie said, pushed him toward me. "Take him outside, get rid of him."

Marbles was smart enough not to say anything as we walked back down the stairs and outside, where we went to a table at the far side of the property.

"You said you were here to share information," I said. "What information?"

"I read your story in the paper," Marbles said. "I know the place where she worked, and I knew her a little bit. I figured I might be able to answer a question or two that would be of help to you."

"Ivy Mitchell?"

"That's right," Marbles said, looked around, nervous, like he was watching out for Frankie.

"You know what I'm looking for," I said. "What do you know about her, her job, drugs, the people she worked with, the place where she worked?"

"Yeah, great place, they call it Speed Stick T's. It's out on the Trail." Marbles broad-smiled his cooperation.

"I know that," I said. "I'm a reporter, remember? Let's just stick to what you know."

"Yeah, well about the drug thing; you know, she wasn't doing anything heavy. Just a joint now and then, some speed or acid, nothing special."

"You sure?"

"Hey, man, I knew her. She was my friend. Well, anyway, she was nice to me," he said. "She wasn't like the others. My girlfriend Nordy, maybe you know her, she buses tables there, she tells me everything about that place."

"Marbles, my contacts downtown tell me she was a messed-up kid," I said. "They say she was up to her ears in trouble, including drugs and prostitution. They say the lady was no lady."

"Well then your contacts downtown don't know shit. Man, she was a lady. I told you that." He sat forward. "Listen, she would dance, sure, she was beautiful, an angel. But no touching the merchandise. Never. And there's big money in the folding deposits. But with Ivy, no way. No serious drugs, and keep your money in your wallet, Jack. That's it."

"I've got a stack of file photos that say you're wrong."

"What photos?"

"Her on the arms of guys, mostly rich men, at society parties. I find it real hard to believe she was just window dressing."

"Man, that ain't prostitution. What happens out there on the streets, in alleys and cars, in cheap hotel rooms, that's prostitution. Sure she'd do a rich guy from time to time. So would you if you got a shot at that kind of easy money."

"I'm not following you," I said.

"That's because you, man, you live in a world of dimwits," he said. "Man, doing a quickie for a rich dirt-ball ain't nothing but smart money. Smoking a joint, that ain't a drug problem, that's the only way to survive the world she lived in. Man, you got any idea what it must be like to dance for the slobs that hang out in that place?"

"It's still drug abuse. It's still prostitution. It's still against the law."

"Look, you see things how you want, but I'm telling you, she was straight. She was the darling of the place. The baby. It would be hard to find anyone who didn't like her."

"Somebody didn't."

"Maybe it was an accident."

"You got any idea who she was with?"

"She had a roommate, Dixie Jean. They worked together. She's stuck up, but she'd talk to you," he said. "So why don't you ask her who she thinks Ivy was with?"

"I will, but right now I've got a big problem with what you're telling me."

"We gotta go through all that again?"

"Just tell me who she was with the other night."

"So she did some private numbers already. Know what I mean? But I wouldn't know who with."

"I thought you said you knew everything."

"Look, I don't know where she drew lines, or who she drew them with," he said. "I don't know."

"Please, Marbles. If you know something that can help me," I said. "It will help her."

"How's it gonna help her. She's dead, and I will be too if I, Man, if word gets around where this came from, I'm wasted. It's that heavy, Pete. Dead, gone, good-bye Marbles. You dig?"

"This is a safe place and you know it."

"Yeah, well, anyway, maybe for the kid. You know what I mean? Not because I'm scared, see, just that she was the only one would say something nice to me. Didn't treat me like dirt. Okay, so word is, Ivy spent her last night with a shadow-player, a guy with very deep pockets, and a sister who buys his women for him. She does business with Mr. Thady, direct, no middle people," he said. "They are tight. You with me?"

I told him to keep going.

"Nobody sees the guy, right? But Nordy says the girls are uptight about Ivy's death. They whisper in the dressing room, they say he is into some weird stuff," he said. "Whoever he is, though, he ain't never been at the club. None of the guys who hang out there know him. I'm sure of that. I've seen the sister a few times. Great looking chick."

"You ever talk to her?" I asked.

"No," he said, shook his head. "She might stop for a drink at the bar, shoot the shit with a bouncer, but really, she ain't a mixer."

"What's her name?" I asked.

"Yeah, well I don't know her name. But the girls call her Little Sister." He laughed lightly. "Some Little Sister, right?"

"Come on, Marbles," I said. "You can do better than that."

"No way. But I do know her brother is into 'pain,' as in shit your mama never told you about, probably never knew," he said. "Man, just, let's get off this thing."

"Something is still missing, Marbles. What else you got?"

"What else? Man, you crazy. I just gave you my life. You ask what else?"

"Marbles, if Ivy was not the only woman who worked for this Little Sister and her mysterious brother, why doesn't your girl-friend know her real name?"

"Pete, the girls are scared stiff," he said. "Like me, really scared."

"Okay, so why the hell would she sell herself to a guy like you just described if she was, like you said, straight. It doesn't make any sense."

"Come on, man. Shit, I don't know. I always figured it had something to do with her family."

"No way, I was there yesterday. They didn't look like they were endowed with anything but trouble and debts."

"I'll be damned. I never really thought about it, just always figured it had something to do with her kid."

I sat silent, the way the crowd sits when the last man in a one-second, one-point game, chucks one from the key. The ball hangs up in the rafters, suspended long enough for everybody to remember that when it comes down, no matter where it lands, things will never be the same as when it back-spiraled off those finger tips.

"What kid?" I broke the spell.

"Hey, you said you were there yesterday, at her mother's place," he said. "Didn't you see her kid?"

I shook my head. "Her mother never said anything about a child."

"Yeah, well, maybe she don't want you to know. Or, maybe she ain't living there. Maybe she is away, in a school or something. That would cost a lot, right?"

"Right." I agreed.

"Anyway, that's all I know about her."

"You sure the child is a girl?"

"Yeah."

I took out my wallet and laid two twenties across his out-stretched palm. He took the money, stuck it in his pocket.

"Do you know how old she is?" I asked as he was getting up.

He paused. "Maybe five or six. Not older than six I don't think."

"What about the father?"

"I don't know nothing about that."

"You sure?"

"Sure. But, you know, it ain't unusual for one of the girls to have a kid," he said. "Sooner or later it happens to most of them."

Chapter 12

"Yeah."

"Well, you never heard anything from me. Right?"

"Right."

It was two o'clock when I started my car. I drove a few blocks over to Belvedere Road, and turned west, headed to the Trail, to Speed Stick T's.

Chapter 13

A red light at the intersection of Belvedere and Parker Road had me cooling my heels, waiting for a splash of green so I could be on my way. Just sitting, looking around the neighborhood reminded me that Ivy's house was just around the corner, on Flamingo. A few minutes up the road.

I wondered if Dixie Jean might have been one of the women who had worked for the mystery man. She and Ivy were roommates, so it didn't seem like a stretch of reason.

The light changed and I started forward, then halfway through the intersection, I made a skidding hard right. Dixie Jean was hard on my mind. It was still early afternoon, and Flamingo was just around the corner. It was just a hunch, but sometimes good investigating was nothing more than that. Playing hunches.

I don't know what I had expected, pink flamingos or purple pelicans on a gravel or green concrete lawn, or maybe no lawn, just a yard of cigarette butts and crushed beer cans. Anyway, what I got was granny's house -- pale blue with white shutters, flower-filled window boxes, white picket fence, lace curtains flapping in opened windows. The aroma of coffee and hot apple pie had to be a regular part of this landscape.

I parked my car on the street, got out and sniffed the air. No apple pie. I walked to the fence, unlatched the well-oiled wrought iron hardware, and walked down a white pebble path that was bordered with flowers and led to a polished hardwood front door. I knocked on a brass knocker, waited, listened, sniffed the air, still believing in the cinnamon, nutmeg, and clove fairy.

I knocked again, this time a bit louder. "Hello, anybody home?" I hollered into the nearest open window. There was no answer. I was going to walk around to the side of the house, but noticed an across-the-street neighbor standing on the sidewalk with his hands in his pockets, watching me. Two little kids stood quietly near him.

I walked back to the sidewalk, and crossed the street.

"Nobody home," he said.

"You live around here?" I asked him.

"Yup." He pointed at a small white stucco house halfway up the block. It looked like a cute place.

"Nice place."

"Thanks."

"Late 1920s?"

"Close, '31."

"Wood floors, fireplace?"

"Oak in the livingroom, red pine in the bedrooms. Fireplace works like a charm when we need it."

"Sure don't make 'em like they used to," I said.

"Nothing's like it used to be."

"You know the people who live over there?" I asked, looking across the street at Ivy's house.

He shrugged. "I guess."

"Two women, right?"

"You the police?" He took his hands out of his pockets and took hold of the children.

"I'm a reporter," I told him.

"You hear about what happened to Miss Mitchell?"

"Yeah," I said. "Bad news. It'll be tough on the kids."

"Say again?"

"My report said at least two young children lived there."

"No way. No kids, just the two women."

"Well, you know newspapers screw anything up."

"Sure can."

"Lucky you happened to be around."

"I guess," he said. "What paper you say you with?"

"The News & Journal."

"Yeah, that's the paper we get, ain't it, kids?"

The children agreed, "Yes."

"What'd you say your name was?"

"Pete Krekow."

"Oh, yeah, I've seen your name."

"Hey there, little girl," I said to the older child. "What's your name?"

"Sally," the kid said.

"That's Sally and this here's another Pete, same as you, and I'm Roy Rogers," he said, laughing.

Sally kicked him playfully and said, "No you ain't, Daddy." They all laughed.

"Ouch. Now Sally, don't you do that," he said. He held out his hand, I shook it. "Just kidding. Name's Roger Filbert, Mr. Krekow."

"Say, Sally, how would you like to get your name in the newspaper?" I asked. I winked at her father. When I looked back down, she was ready to give me a good kick, so I stepped back quickly. Her foot displaced a little air.

"Daddy, he moved. That ain't fair."

Her father pulled her back. "Don't now, Sally. Be nice to the man." He looked apologetic. "Sorry, mister."

"That's nothing," I said. "Say, Roger, there doesn't seem to be anyone home over there, but the windows are open. Have you seen anyone around?"

"Sure, we were walking down on the other side of Parker when she drove off. Must have gone to the store for something. It's Wednesday, she'll be back."

"Yeah, I don't want to miss her again."

"No problem there, Mr. Krekow. She weeds and fertilizes the front lawn and window boxes every Wednesday. Be there all afternoon."

"I guess I'll take a chance."

"Well, it ain't much of a chance. She don't work Wednesday at all," he said. "And, matter of fact, we asked her to dinner tonight. The kids think the world of her. So I'm sure she'll be around." The kids smiled and nodded agreement.

"Thanks," I said. "If you happen to be around later, I'd like to ask you a few questions, also."

"Sure, ask away."

"So long, Sally."

"Say good-bye to the nice man, Sally."

The kid's fat tongue vibrating made a silly noise. Her brother laughed, her father flicked the edge of her ear with his index finger. They all laughed. I drove off.

Chapter 14

*I*t was about two-thirty when I got to the strip joint. Finding a place to park at that time of the afternoon was simple. I pulled into the space nearest the high gloss, candy-apple red front door. I didn't figure to be very long.

Inside, a quiet ballad was playing on the jukebox. There were only three people in the place. Two bouncers, Tony Mally and Bill Gnowles, who sat alone at the dark end of the bar playing poker. The bartender was Bill's brother, Marty. He was washing glasses in the sink near them.

I knew the Gnowles boys well enough to make easy conversation, but I'd only seen Tony Mally at a distance. I didn't think he knew me, which was just as well. He had a reputation of doing his job with too much enthusiasm. People got hurt when he walked them to the door.

"You lost?" Marty asked.

"Hey, Marty." I walked over to the bar and sat a few seats away from the poker players.

"What happened to you, they make you a sports writer?" he asked, laughed.

"No, I'm trying out for the fashion writer's job," I said. "I figured this would be a good place to start learning the business.

Pretty basic. I could make a pioneer fashion statement. You know, work my way from nothing to pasties, G-string."

Bill sat around the corner of the bar from Tony, facing me. He smiled while he played his hand. "Yo, Pete?" he said. "What happened to you?"

"You should see the other guy," I said.

"Yeah, I bet his hands are a mess from beating on you," Bill said. He and Marty snickered.

I moved closer to the game.

"Beat it," Tony said, without turning around.

"What's with him?" I asked Bill.

Bill shrugged. "Don't worry about it," he said. "What brings you to this neck of the woods?"

"A girl who used to work here."

"You looking to get lucky?" Bill said.

"Ivy Mitchell," I said.

Marty went back to washing glasses. Tony put his cards down and turned and faced me. He was one ugly guy.

Marty carried a tray of clean glasses to the other end of the bar.

Tony tapped me on the chest with a thick finger. "Maybe it'd be better if you stuck to questions about fashion," he said.

"Maybe it'd be better if you kept your hands to yourself." I pushed his hand away with my left, and stepped back.

Tony started to get up, but Bill put a hand on his shoulder. "Simmer down, amigo."

"Thady in?" I asked.

Tony sneered. "He's in his office. But remember, to get out of this joint, you gotta get past me. So, whatever you do, don't piss him off."

"Sure." I walked around him. "Maybe while I'm gone, you can think up a better place to stick your finger." I headed to the back room, stopped off on the way and said a prayer to the patron saint of good kidneys, then went down a short hallway to the heavy wood door at the end.

I knocked, someone inside said to come in, so I opened the door and crossed the threshold, slipping from gutter to sewer. The garbage was stacked in a plush, leather chair.

George Nicholas Thadington, Mr. Thady, was a man whose shrewd business sense, and ability to deal swiftly and effectively with problems, had earned him a title of royalty among riffraff. He was a high-class pimp with impressive spheres of influence, a businessman with a noisy, crude, money-making playground.

Yet, for those who didn't know him, it would be difficult to guess his natural social strata lay buried under piles of trash, because he sure was a dainty, little bit of a thing. A pretty boy wrapped in expensive pink and white silk, weighted with jewelry and crowned with bleached, permed curls that looked the way ads in expensive magazines promised. A cliche whose eye and lip makeup might lead the unwary to mistake him for a lean, over-dressed, amusing clown.

"Mr. Thadington, my name is Pete Krekow. I'm a reporter for the News & Journal. Maybe you remember, we played a benefit golf tournament together about a year ago."

Mr. Thady stood and reached a pale, delicate, though rather too large hand across his desk. "Of course, I remember," he said, smiling warmly. "Miller's Trace." His little teeth sparkled. His eyes sparkled. His earrings sparkled. The man was a walking advertisement for glitter. Anyway, if the hand looked frail, the grip was viselike.

"Yeah," I said. "Your company made a generous donation to the battered wife program."

He sat and leaned back in his chair, put his hands behind his head. "We do what we can." He gestured for me to sit in the chair opposite him. "What's up?"

I told him I was working a story on the Ivy Mitchell death.

"Ah, poor child. We will miss her very much." He took a deep breath. I gathered it was supposed to be a sigh. "We, I especially, tried to look after her, to help her. She was a very troubled, young lady."

He spoke like a man who couldn't decide whether he had just lost a daughter or a racehorse.

"She was a free spirit, with fancies of love. We cared for her, and it seems, though I don't like to admit it, in the end, failed her."

As I sat there listening to his babble, I wondered if he believed that a man could send a woman, a girl, off to sell her soft, sensitive body to a man who would torture her, and then really believe he was watching her carefully. I looked at this sparkling piece of garbage and figured, sure.

"I can tell you feel deeply about your loss," I said.

"Fancies of love. Love and death should never be sisters, and yet, how often one seems to go in hand with the other."

"Yeah," I said. "Anyway, I'm trying to find the man who shared those 'fancies' on the night of her death."

"I wish I could help you," he said. "But my understanding is she died alone. I assumed her death was a suicide, the result of a broken heart."

"It was no suicide, I'm sure of that. A mutual acquaintance told me you would know who she was with."

"Does our 'mutual acquaintance' have a name?"

"No."

"Pity." He shook his head. "Still, I can't help you. I have no knowledge of what my employees do when they are outside these walls. They like it that way. So do I."

"Does the name Little Sister ring any bells?"

"Should it?"

"It's a nickname for a lady who likes soliciting strippers for her brother to play with," I said.

"Most men, and many women, like to play with, or would like to play with my strippers."

"Maybe, only this guy doesn't ask for dates," I said. "He buys them, then does some very nasty things to them."

"Well, thank you for bringing this to my attention. I'll look into the matter as soon as you leave." He wrote something on a scrap piece of paper. "I certainly wouldn't want any of my ladies to fall into such a trap."

"I'm sure they'll appreciate your concern."

"Perhaps you should tell our friend," he said, "she is chirping about something of which she knows nothing."

"She?"

"Ah. Now we're getting somewhere."

"I don't think so."

"Let's conclude this discussion quickly."

"I don't believe Ivy's death was a suicide. If she died of an overdose, my guess is it was because she was filled with enough dope to keep her from stopping some very painful fun and games being played on her body by one very sick person, enough to kill her. Ivy was murdered and I'm going to find out who did it."

Thady banged his fist on the table. "How wonderful, Pete. You make me feel safe. Tonight I'll sleep with my windows open, just knowing you are out there somewhere, protecting me from evil." Thady sat back in his chair. "Still, freedom-fighter inclinations aside, you must understand, even if you are correct, all this still has nothing to do with me or anybody else in this business."

I shook my head. "If she was introduced to the man who killed her by someone here, someone who knew she was going to be physically abused, and drugged, then it has a great deal to do with your business, and with you." I took a pen out of my pocket and on a piece of paper on his desk wrote, "conspiracy."

"It has to do with conspiracy," I said, "which is a felony, which has a great deal to do with making license plates."

He drew his hands apart, rather theatrically, and held them opened in front of his face. "You are fishing dangerous waters." He put his hands on the arms of his chair.

"Meaning?"

"Don't piss into the wind." He stood and extended his hand once again. "Must get back to work now. Good-bye."

"I'm going, but I'm still sitting on a murder that I am going to prove had nothing to do with fancies of love."

"Everything has something to do with fancies of love."

"Yeah."

I headed out, back down the hall. The card game was over. Bill Gnowles was nowhere to be seen. Marty was talking on the phone, and didn't notice me as I walked past him.

Tony was standing on the customer side of the bar, looking in the mirror in back of the bar, combing his hair. I could tell by the stench of bay rum that he had just shaved. He watched me in the mirror as I passed. I didn't say anything, just left quickly. The place was making me sick.

Chapter 15

Dixie Jean Evans was weeding window boxes when I pulled in front of her house. She had on shapeless, denim, gardening pants with padded knees, an oversize sweatshirt, high-top boots, work gloves, and a large straw hat. I guess I had expected something less in the way of clothing, but as I was parking, she turned, and half-hidden under the wide brim of the straw hat, I saw the smile that got Roger walking.

She answered my "I love your garden" with a friendly nod. It was her smile that caught my eye, the shape of her mouth, the way she had of wetting her lips with her tongue after she smiled, not affected, just kind of nervous, quick. Beautiful. Her eyes were a dark brown, rich in color like the soil that held her flowers. She was very attractive.

"'Your garden,'" she said. "That sounds nice."

"You must hear that often."

"Not enough." She brightened the yard with another smile.

"You must have been raised on flowers and sunshine."

The smile faded. "Grew up in a grey and black city. My old man was a Baptist preacher who allowed only one book in our railroad flat, and believed television and radio were the work of Satan. The only gardens I ever saw were in books or magazines at school."

"What city?"

"Hell," she said. "You're a reporter, right?"

I nodded. "Pete Krekow, News & Journal, at your service."

"Dixie Jean Evans, House & Garden. Have pruner, will travel." The smile returned.

"How did you know I was a reporter?"

"Roger Filbert."

"Hope you kept a fence between you and the kid."

"Sally?"

"She's going to grow up to be the first woman placekicker in professional football."

"Yeah, well, she's a good kid," she said. "And they are the only family I know that has fun together."

"I had a feeling the whole team was on the street."

"You felt right."

"Just the three of them?"

"Yeah. Patti split some time back."

"Cable repairman?"

"Greyhound bus. Alone."

"You knew her?"

"A little. Danced to the beat of a different drummer," she said. "Know what I mean?"

"I guess."

"Married too young to appreciate a sweet guy, a fireplace, and she was wound too tight to live with Sally," she said, reflected a moment. "Everything was an argument."

"You like them, don't you?"

"Yeah, well, when I was a kid, all I ever heard was yelling and screaming," she said. "My mom and dad, my brothers, they were always at war. My sister and I spent all our time hiding from the rest of the family."

"Kind of takes the fun out of childhood."

"What childhood?"

"I hear you."

"Sure, Sally is a little out of control sometimes. But she loves her dad and her little brother. And he pulls in the reins every once in a while. No need to break her spirit. It's nice being around good people."

"As opposed to work?"

"I'll try not to take that personal, Mr. Krekow," she said. "But I'm beginning to understand how you got that sock in the eye."

"Nothing personal intended," I told her. "You should see the other guy."

"That's not the first time you've said that today."

"I guess not."

"You're solid, Pete."

"Thanks."

"As long as you asked, no, you'll never see Roger there, and I'm thankful for that. But that doesn't mean all the people who hang out at a joint like that are no good. Some are fine people, just lonely. You know what I mean? I guess they feel safe there. They know the rules," she said. "They can sit quiet and watch a woman dance without anybody disturbing them, preaching at them. Nobody to say 'you can't do this,' or 'you can't do that.' It's a simpler world."

She took a clean rag from her pocket and pushed her straw hat back so she could wipe her forehead, then slid the hat forward again. "And, there are a lot of reasons why women do the kind of work I do," she said. "And they are not all bad either. Some of the dancers really believe it's an art form. Some get up there, on the stage or bar, and all of a sudden they are in control, when the music starts and they unbutton that first button. For the only time in their lives, they are appreciated in a way other than as a maid, whore, breeder, punching bag."

"Sorry I struck a nerve."

"I want you to get it right. I want you to understand that some women want more from life than a husband who thinks the living room is a sports bar, where you live from pay check to pay check," she said. "But opportunities are limited, you know that, especially for women with poor educations."

She put the rag back in her pocket, then played with the angle of her hat some more. The afternoon sun beat strong on the brim, cut a shadow on her face so that her lower lip glowed in the light. "Pete, in a decade of dancing, if I'm careful with my investments, I'll make a small fortune doing what I do. Within the next five years, this yard garden will be swapped for a farm. That's the kind of money I make. And, no, I'm not ashamed of my work, nor of the few friends I have made there. Okay?"

"Absolutely," I said.

"You have a family?"

"Long ago."

"Any kids?"

"A daughter, but she's grown."

"Sally remind you of her?" She laughed softly.

I joined her laughter and shook my head. "But you're right about Roger, he's got the right idea about family. Does he always spend days with his kids?"

She nodded. "Yeah, he works out of his home. He's a lumber broker."

"Don't believe I've ever met one of them before," I said. "Then again, we haven't left many trees standing in the way of progress down here in South Florida."

"Well, I'm no expert, but he says his folks left him a small timber farm up in the Carolinas somewhere." She scooted a mosquito off her arm without killing it. "Apparently the lumber is furniture grade, which means he sells off small portions of the place to furnituremakers who are willing to pay a higher price for a better quality lumber. He goes up there a few times a year to check on things, but mostly he works at home, near the children."

"Sounds like a nice job."

"You bet. Anyway, you're here about Ivy, not Roger or me," she said. "So, like I told the police, we split the mortgage payment, shared a desire to live quietly. We were friends, but didn't hang out together. She had her friends, I keep pretty much to myself."

"Doesn't sound like you had much in common."

"Well, actually that's a lot in common," she said. "Think about it. We both wanted something better someday."

"What did she want?"

"What?"

"Ivy? What did she want?"

"A day without rain," she said. "That was a saying of hers."

I took my notebook out of my pocket and wrote, "A day without rain." So far, that had been my only entry in a book that should have had pages filled by this time in the interview. I put the book back in my pocket.

"I'll miss hearing it," she said.

"What happens to the place now?"

"I buy Ivy's share against her estate."

"That already in motion?"

"Yes."

"What was she like to live with?"

"We worked on it, made it easier with a strict 'no-guys-over-night' policy. If either of us felt like a run with the pack, we did it away from home."

"She run with the pack often?"

"No."

"You keep the place up?"

"She took care of the inside, and she did that very nicely," she said. "I take care of everything outside."

"Can I see how she did her job?"

"I don't think so."

"Have the police looked around."

"Of course. No, there were no surprises. So look, Pete, Ivy's death has really upset me, and it has turned this homestead upside down. This is my day off. I need this time to relax in the garden. Dig?" She smiled.

"I dig. But doors keep closing on me, Dixie Jean. I need to know two things badly. Please."

"Let's do one at a time."

"Who was Ivy with that night?"

"Sorry, I can't help there."

"You know and won't help, or really don't know?"

"Take your choice."

"Please."

Her soft mouth turned hard, "No."

"Do you know anything about someone called Little Sister?"

"Pete, you seem like a nice guy. I kind of like you. So, same question, same answer." She closed her eyes, and shook her head slowly. When she looked up at me again, there were tears in her eyes. "Leave this alone."

"Somebody else just told me that same thing."

"Good, because strike three could be a real problem."

"I keep getting the feeling that I'm out there all by myself."

"Absolutely."

"I have to go after them."

"Absolutely not."

"It cost Ivy her life."

"Keep knocking on those doors, and she'll have company."

"You frightened of this one yourself?"

"Yes, very."

"Okay, I'll let it alone," I said. "Just one more."

"That was two. So, nothing personal, but it's garden time. Bye-bye."

"Ivy had a daughter."

Dixie Jean had started to walk away, but stopped, and turned. Still, she said nothing.

"Do you know where her daughter is?" I asked.

"No."

"I need to know if she needs help, and if so, I want to help."

"Robin Hood the Reporter. Now I've heard everything."

"You don't believe me?"

"Frankly, no," she said. "But if you want to help, keep her out of this."

"Do you believe that's possible?"

"I hope so."

"I'll do everything off the record."

"I wish I could believe you."

"You can."

"Look, I didn't mind the 'I love your garden' and the 'when we were kids' stuff because it didn't hurt anyone," she said. "And who knows, maybe you really meant it."

"I did," I said. "I do."

"Great, and maybe you really believe you want to help. But if you keep after this, sooner or later, you are going to sell her out for the story. That's your job."

"That's not true."

"Pete, I don't know you, but I do know men."

"You don't know me."

"The kid is out of bounds. End of conversation."

We heard Sally holler "Dixie Jean" from across the street at about the same time her dad yelled for her to wait, and the tires screeched.

I turned in time to see a large, black car with heavy-tinted windows stop inches short of the kid, who had slipped in the excitement, and fallen on the pavement. Her father ran in front of the car and picked her up. He held Sally in his arms and brought her quickly to where we stood.

"You all right, Sally?" he asked.

She nodded, frightened.

"Pete, wait where you are," Roger said. "I'll be right over to get you. You hear?"

Pete, who looked like he was about to start crying, waited patiently on the opposite sidewalk.

Dixie Jean saw me start to move toward the big sled, and gave a quick, "Be cool, Pete."

It was the concern in her voice that stopped me. I turned back to her, and saw in her face what I had not understood. She knew the car.

"How's Sally doing?" Dixie Jean asked.

"She's fine," Roger said.

"I thought you might be trouble," Dixie Jean said to me.

We watched the car roar off.

"Now, Dixie Jean, don't blame Pete," Roger said. "Those folks are driving like fools. That isn't his fault."

Dixie Jean opened the front gate and came out and knelt next to Sally, who put her arms around her neck and began crying again.

"I'm going to get Pete," Roger said, and walked back across the street.

"It's all right, darling." Dixie Jean rocked her. "Everything is going to be fine."

Roger came back leading Pete by the arm. "With those tinted windows, you can't tell who's driving," Roger said. "Maybe we should have thought to get the license plate number."

"They're gone, Roger," I said. "Let's just be happy Sally isn't hurt."

"You're right there." He knelt next to them, and put his arm around Dixie Jean as he steadied himself. Pete went to his sister and hugged her.

Watching them together reminded me I was an outsider, so I took two of my cards out of my wallet and reached over and put one in Roger's shirt pocket, and put the other in Dixie Jean's hand, she palmed it.

"I've got to be running along," I said. "If either of you ever need help, or would like to talk to me, just call, anytime."

"Thank you, Mr. Krekow," Roger said. "You still going to ask me some questions?"

"Maybe later, Roger," I said. "Thanks."

"So long, Sally," I said. "Glad you're not hurt."

I thought I heard her say something, but her voice was muffled and I couldn't tell what it was. I stayed, not wanting to leave, but knowing I had to. I thought of Crystal, and her little sons. Family.

"Sally says 'thank you,' Mr. Krekow." Roger said.

I walked over to my car. I got in, did the seatbelt thing, started the engine, waved so-long, though nobody was paying any attention to me.

I pulled away, headed quickly north to the quiet lounge, and hopefully, Crystal.

Chapter 16

*I*t was almost three-thirty when I walked up to the bar. The bartender on duty was a short, hefty woman who was pulling the tall, brown handle of a Guinness tap, slowly filling a pint glass she held angled under the spout.

I sat on a stool near her. "Feel like drawing another one of those?"

"You got it."

"Thanks," I said. "Crystal around?"

"She expecting you?"

Her question was defensive, packed with a suitcase full of bad experiences, years of working bars where guys with banged-up faces rarely spelled anything but trouble. She was uneasy and I didn't blame her.

"I probably should have called first," I said. "But last time I was here, she said if I was up this way again I should stop in and say hello."

"I think she's in the back." She started my beer. "Just here to get her check though, one of her kids is playing ball tonight, over at the Polish Hall."

"Could you give her a message for me?"

"If she's still around." She placed my half-filled glass on a stainless steel drain. "I'll let this head settle a minute."

"Thanks."

"Who's the message from?"

"Pete Krekow."

"You got it," she said.

"Also, ah, mind if I use your phone for a quick local call?"
She put the phone in front of me.

"How about a phone book?"

"Down there." She pointed to the other end of the bar. "You get the book, I'll tell Crystal you're here."

"Thanks."

I walked to the end of the bar, opened the phone book, looked for Dixie Jean Evans. She was not listed, Roger was. I wrote his number in my notebook. I was on my way back to my stool when Crystal came out of a door at the far end of the bar.

"Well, if it ain't Pete the Singing Cowboy," she said. "Glad to see you, Pardner. Though I thought we agreed you'd call first."

"Sorry," I said.

She smiled. "Don't worry about it."

"Would it help if I said some rustlers stole my phone along with a herd of my cattle and left me with a mess of business that had to be tended to right away?"

"Looks like you might be telling the truth," she said. "What the heck happened to you? Fall off your horse a few times?"

"You should see the other guy."

"Why would I want to see the other guy? You look bad enough."

I looked at myself in the mirror in back of the bar. She was right. I did look pretty beat up. But, I didn't really feel as bad as I looked. I shook my head, "You're right, but I don't feel bad. Not as bad as the gang of thieves I hunted down like dogs, and brung to justice."

"Yeah, well I've seen worse. You like football?"

"Don't know much about it."

Harriet finished drawing my beer and placed it in front of me.

"Want to learn the rules?"

"What rules?"

"Football," Crystal said. "How'd you like to watch Farenzella's oldest ranger run over the stiffs at the Polish Hall?"

"Football?"

"Football? Of course football."

"Now?"

"Jeez, forget the beer." She took my Guinness and put it back on the drain in front of the tap. "Harriet, this one's on me."

"He didn't drink out of it, did he?"

I shook my head.

"Okay, thanks." She tossed back a third of the pint. "Grrr."

"Let's go." Crystal started for the door she had come out of, at the back end of the bar. "I'll meet you outside."

I was left alone, sitting without my beer, being watched by Harriet. "Waiting for an invitation?"

"Seems like I already got one," I said as I got up.

"Get along little cowboy," Harriet said, then drank another third of the beer and belched.

I waved back, and walked to the front door. I went outside and looked around the parking lot for Crystal. I didn't see her, then I heard the roar of a car engine and saw her drive around the corner of the building in an old Falcon station wagon. She pulled up next to me, stopped, and opened the driver's window. "Hop in the back, Cowboy."

I got in the back and looked around. On the seat next to me was a kid dressed in a green, hooded Middle Ages outfit, with sword, and a bow and some rubber-tipped arrows. He looked younger than the boy in the front, so I figured he was the five-year-old. In the front were Crystal and the older boy, who was dressed in a football uniform.

"Thanks for not saying anything in front of Harriet," Crystal said. "You are here about Ivy Mitchell?" She put the car in gear and headed out of the parking lot.

I nodded. "I brought along a couple of pictures of Ivy," I said.

"Yeah, well I'd rather talk alone," she said.

"Sure," I agreed.

"Sorry about the back seat, but it's a family rule, football gets shotgun on game day," she said. "Anyway, this is Harry, the fastest tackle in Palm Beach County. And parked next to you is Joseph, also known as Robin Hood of Sherwood, the most cunning outlaw in Merry Olde England. Okay? So, guys, this is Mr. Pete Krekow."

They said "hi" in unison, without much enthusiasm, but not without some interest.

I noticed that although the car was old and worn, the interior was clean. There were cartons, bags, folding chairs, and coolers stacked neatly in back of the back seat. Like the car itself, the things showed use, and care.

"You a football player?" Harry, the tackle, asked.

"No," I answered.

"You look like a linebacker."

"Is that good?"

"Not bad," Harry said.

"Not bad?" Crystal said. "That's great."

"It's okay," Harry agreed.

Robin Hood laughed. "You're funny."

"I've got a friend I think you would like to meet," I told the archer from Sherwood. "He is an expert in swords, sorcery, and dragons."

There was a quiet minute. I wondered if I had said something wrong.

"He knows about dragons?" Joseph was impressed. "Think he knows about Sherwood and Nottingham?"

"Sherwood, Nottingham, and probably Lichfield and Leicester as well."

"Lichfield? Leicester?" The little guy was wide-eyed.

"Sure," I said.

The kid undid his seatbelt, slid over and fastened himself in the middle of the seat, next to me. Thankfully he left his weapons behind.

"You don't have your seatbelt on," Joseph observed.

I clipped in.

"I never heard of Lichfield," he said.

"You haven't?"

He shrugged and shook his head. "Or Leicester either."

"Well," I said. "Lichfield is where Will Scarlett's brother owned an alehouse, and once Will and Friar Tuck hid there to keep the Sheriff of Nottingham from finding them."

"They did?"

"Sure, this knight, Sir Guy of Gisborne, he works for the sheriff," I said. "Have you heard of him?"

"Yes."

"Okay, so, Sir Guy hears the men, Will and Tuck, are in Lichfield, staying at the alehouse. So Sir Guy takes the Sheriff's men, and at night they sneak into the tavern where Will and Tuck are sleeping."

"They sleep in a tavern?" Crystal asked.

"Those places stink," Harry added his two cents. "They smell like smoke and beer. Yuck."

"Well, it's just a story," I said. "I'm sure they were only there because it was the only place to hide."

"How come?" Joseph asked.

"You solid with this story, Pete?" Crystal laughed.

"You want to see my books?" Joseph asked.

"Yo, guys, we're here. So hold the story, and get ready to do some cheerleading," Crystal said.

Joseph went back over to his side of the seat and started gathering weapons. About the time he had everything in his lap, we pulled into the parking lot of a rather good-sized playing field. There seemed to be a football field, and next to it there was a baseball diamond that apparently used part of the football field as its outfield.

"Here we are champ," Crystal said as she pulled into a parking place at the edge of the field. There were about forty to fifty cars parked together. "Harry, you can go on ahead and get with the guys. Pete and Joseph and I will get comfortable with the food and soda."

"Thanks, Mom," Harry said, and got quickly out of the car and ran to the place on the field where his team had assembled.

"Okay gang, we split kitchen duty," Crystal said.

We got out of the car, followed her to the back of the wagon where she opened the back door and slid two coolers to the edge.

"Pete, grab hold. Let's take this and set it on the ground at the edge of the field."

We carried both coolers, one at a time, and set them on the ground in front of the car. Then we went back and took three folding chairs out, and set them up near the coolers.

"Glad you had three," I said. "How'd you know I'd be along?"

"The green one is for my mom. She uses it when we cook out at the park."

"Why isn't she here?" I asked.

"We disagree about the football thing," she said.

Joseph, who was standing on the edge of the field, was looking like he was ready to launch some arrows at the players. "Yo, Hooded-Crusader, stow the weapons and get your tent out of the back and we'll help you set it up." He ran to the back of the wagon.

"So she silently boycotts."

"Afraid he'll get hurt?"

"Sure. And she's right. It is dangerous, even with the flag thing. They're not supposed to get knocked down too much, but they do."

"Maybe he'll tire of it," I said.

"I guess, but in a way I'm torn, because part of me feels pride, too. When he plays well." She looked out over the playing field at about the same time Harry got knocked down. She shook her head and laughed. "And I think it's good for him. Knocking around out there, with some good rules and a chance to feel what it's like to get knocked on your butt, and get up and get knocked down again. And not quit."

Joseph dragged a sack over to where we were sitting. "Not here, this is the grown-up section." She helped him drag the bag a respectable distance away, and began unpacking the tent. I walked over and watched.

"Here, hold this," she said. I took the part of the tent she handed me, and in a very short time, and with only a few more commands, the tent was up, Joseph was situated inside, and we were back by the cooler. "You want a soda?"

"Thanks."

She opened three cans of soda, handed me one, took one to Joseph and kept the third for herself. She settled in her chair.

"Thanks for inviting me."

"My pleasure," she said. "I guess you're really here to talk about Ivy Mitchell though, right?"

I shook my head. "No, I'm here because I appreciate you inviting me, Crystal." I took a sip of soda. It felt cool in the afternoon sun. "I like being here, with you and your boys," I said.

"But," she said, smiled.

"But, I'm between a rock and a hard place on this story," I said. "If you can, I need all the help I can get."

"Shoot, Cowboy," she said.

"You remembered her name?"

"I read both your story and the one in the paper this morning," she said. "There was a picture with yours."

I nodded, took the pictures out of my pocket. "Still, I'd appreciate if you would take a look at these photos." I unfolded them and handed them to her. "Is this the woman you said you knew?"

"Yes and no," she said. "She was one of the women who came in often, but she was very shy." She handed the photos back to me. "I didn't know her like one or two of the others. She was always pleasant, but stand-offish."

"Could you try to remember anything that might help. Like, who among the women she seemed to be close to? Did she ever come there with other friends, men perhaps? Did she ever seem like she was, well, acting like she was doing more than just having a social cocktail?"

Crystal nodded. "She seemed to be well-liked by all the women, though she didn't seem to have any particular favorites," she said. "That is, other than the woman who was my favorite of the group, but they weren't together much."

"Do you know who that was?"

"Sure," she said. "She was Ivy's roommate, though I didn't know that until I read the stories."

"Dixie Jean Evans?" I asked.

"Yes," Crystal said. "She and I get along really well. Something in the chemistry. We liked each other right off."

"I met her today," I said. "I agree, I liked her, too."

"They were very different," she said. "Still, you could tell, when they were together, they were close."

"Do you remember Ivy ever coming in with any men," I asked. "Perhaps the men in these photos?" I handed the photos back to her.

She looked at them again, and shook her head. "There were a few of the women who would run off to a room upstairs with a man every once in a while," she said. "But not Ivy. At least, not to my knowledge."

"How about Dixie Jean Evans?"

"Absolutely not," Crystal said. "Actually, she doesn't come to the lounge all that much. Like me, she's not much of a drinker. She can nurse a glass of red wine all evening and leave half a glass for the dishwasher."

"Sorry to push this on you, Crystal," I said, "but do you think it possible that Ivy was doing any kind of drugs?"

"I don't think it would be fair for me to say 'yes' without really knowing it was true," she said. "And I don't."

"How about any times you had a chance to talk to Ivy," I said. "I know you said she was shy, but you must have had some contact. Maybe when Dixie Jean was there?"

"Well, one time only." Crystal glanced off at the football field, watched her boy play. "But I'm really not comfortable talking about private conversations, Pete."

"Please, Crystal," I said.

She thought a moment, then shook her head. "I'm sorry, but a confidence should not show up in tomorrow's newspaper," she said. "I don't think that would be right."

"If I promise I won't use what you tell me in a story," I asked, "would you be more comfortable?"

"If you'd make me that promise."

"I do."

"Well, one time, the only time we really talked, somehow her friends went off without her. It was late, I don't remember why, but she didn't have her car, and she needed a ride home," she said. "Now, mind, I'm not in a position to run a home delivery service for patrons who could call a taxi. But that night, I got off a little early, and happened to ask where she lived. It was way across town, but I figured, 'what the hell' maybe she and her friends would remember me at Christmas or something."

"You drove her home?"

"Yes."

"Do you remember what you talked about?"

"Of course, give me a chance, Pete," she said, and frowned. "It has nothing to do with what you have been asking about, so it might not be much help anyway. Still, I don't want to see it in the newspaper."

"You won't," I promised.

She watched the play on the field as she talked. "We talked about our children."

"She talked to you about her daughter?" I asked.

"It was kind of sad," she said. "On the way out to my car, I showed her the photos of my boys. When we were in the car, just pulling out of the parking lot, I noticed she had started to cry. I asked what was wrong and she told me she had a little girl who was away at boarding school."

"Crystal," I said, "this is very important. Do you remember the child's name, and the name of the school?"

"I remember the girl's name, but not the school," she said. "Her daughter's name is Sparrow."

"Did she say anything about the school?" I asked.

"She said it was a very special place, far from here," Crystal said. "I believe it's up around Martin County somewhere. Hobe Sound sticks in my mind. I remember she said the rest of the children there were from very wealthy homes, and that at first the school had not wanted to admit her daughter."

"Did she tell you what changed their mind?" I asked.

She laughed. "Sure did."

"What happened," I asked.

"Well, Ivy said she went up there on a weekend when the headmaster's wife was out of town. That was that. Next thing she knew, Sparrow was hobnobbing with royalty."

I shook my head. "That's a sad commentary, Crystal."

"Oh, I don't know," she said. "From the way she talked, I think Ivy had an understanding of the way people work that is outside our reality."

I shrugged, not sure.

"Ivy seemed to take it with a grain of salt," she said. "I remember she said he wasn't a bad guy."

"I guess you're right," I said. "It just seems unfair that some people are born to take and others just seem to give."

"I wonder what will become of Sparrow now that her mama is gone?"

"I don't know," I said. "But I promise you and myself that I'll find out, and if I can help in any way, I will."

"You always get this close to your stories?"

"Never have." I crushed the soda can in my right hand, looked off over the field at Crystal's boy. "Thanks, Crystal."

"My pleasure," she said. "You want I should explain what's going on out there?"

"I don't think so. I'll just watch Harry. If he looks happy, I'll figure they are winning. If not, oh well."

"Good plan, only when Harry plays, he never looks happy. Until it's over, he is a mean little football player."

We watched the game. She was right. Harry-the-Tackle was a competitor. For a pint-sized player he still seemed to be near the center of most plays.

Joseph stayed out of sight for about half an hour, then he came out of the tent looking for some food.

"I'm hungry, Mom."

"Okay, halftime is coming up, and Harry might be ready for a sandwich."

"He eats in the middle of a game?" I asked.

"He's six-years-old, Pete. Don't you remember what it was like to be six? You eat, play, sleep, even in school, that's the routine, though not always in that order."

"God, it was so long ago, I forget. But you sure were right about Harry being a competitor."

"He's just like his father. Sometimes it makes me crazy."

"Is that part of what troubles you and your mom about Harry playing football?"

"Sure. It ruined his father. The belief that winning is everything."

"He been gone long?"

"Yeah. The kids were still babies when he left."

"Do they miss him much?"

"They never knew him. He left, like I told you the other night, without saying goodbye." She scratched lazy designs in the soft ground with the tip of her shoe. "I guess he woke up one morning and figured out he never would be good enough for the majors. He was having a bad year, so instead of staying and fighting for his place on the team, he turned-tail and headed home to Oregon. Back to mother's apron strings."

"You never heard from him again?"

"Nope." She took off her shoes and wiggled her toes. "And, nope, I didn't chase him for money."

"Why not?"

"Pride, I guess. And I've had too many friends let themselves get dependent on the payments. Tied them to the past too tight. Friday nights were still pay nights. I can take care of myself and my kids."

"Can I ask a stupid question?"

"Ask away."

"With what you just told me, I don't understand how you enjoy watching Harry play football?"

"I guess it's because I remember the game days when he won. The way he reacted to winning. The way he ran the bases when he hit one out of the park. Hearing his name on the loudspeaker, the applause."

"If it matters, I'm afraid I never was very athletic, and never cared much for sports," I said. "Except for riding the range, chasing rustlers."

"Like Joseph? Living in a dream world?"

"There's no harm in it."

"It's not life."

"Neither is baseball or football."

"Yeah, well, enough of me and mine, and sports. Let's hear about you and yours."

"I fell in love with the wrong woman. You met her, Officer Light-on-the-Vermouth," I said. "We had a daughter, Robin, who is now attending junior college. I've been divorced, and lived alone for a long, long time."

"Lonely?"

"Only when I run out of books."

The half ended there. Harry came running off the field, and came over to where we were sitting.

Crystal called Joseph, and began unpacking sandwiches from the cooler.

"I want tuna," Harry said.

"Guests get first dibs," Crystal told him.

Joseph said he wanted peanut butter and jelly. He offered to share his with me.

"Great." Harry grabbed the tuna, but before he could unwrap it, Crystal snatched it away from him and put it back in the cooler.

Harry looked at me with something less than affection. "You a new boyfriend?"

"Mind your ways, Harry," Crystal said.

"I'm sorry," he said to his mom. "Can I please have a sandwich?"

She leaned over and kissd him on the head, and handed him his tuna sandwich.

He turned to me without urging. "Sorry, mister." Then he ran back to the field with his sandwich. Crystal didn't try to stop him.

We watched him stand alone, then when the game restarted, he became his old, animated self. The first player to run near him carrying the ball took a nasty shot that stripped the ball free, but drew a flag and a penalty that cost Harry's team some yards. After that he settled in and played team ball.

Joseph, who was sitting next to me, finished his sandwich and handed me the empty wrapper to put in the plastic garbage bag Crystal had on the cooler.

"How do you know so much about Robin Hood?" Joseph asked.

"I'm a reporter," I said. I took out my pen and notebook. "See, I carry these everywhere I go, so if I run across a Norman invasion, or a crop failure, or an archery contest, I can write about it."

"Archery?" He looked disappointed. "Are you a sports writer?"

"No." I saw relief in his face. "I only write about archery if someone shoots something other than the target. Like maybe another archer."

"Or a football player?" Joseph said.

"Don't start, Joseph," Crystal said. She flicked a damp dish towel his way. It snapped close to one of his arms.

"Mom," he half-whined, half-giggled. "Can Pete read to me?"

"Ask Pete," she said.

I nodded. "Sure," I said, and took the book he handed me.

Joseph climbed in my lap and rested his head on my chest.

It had been a long time since I had held a small child. The last time would have been with Robin. I tried to remember, and could not.

I patted the kid on the head affectionately and began reading. I read for about twenty minutes. I hadn't noticed while I was reading, but Joseph had fallen asleep. He woke up fresh, the way only small children seem to be able to.

Crystal looked over at Joseph who seemed delighted. "It's real nice of you to take an interest, Pete."

"Hey, Mom," Joseph said. "Is Pete coming home with us for dinner?"

"Sorry darling, but I have to cover for one of the waitresses from eight to closing."

"Darn," Joseph said to me.

"Maybe next time," I said.

Crystal began packing things away.

Joseph and I went over and helped Crystal put the gear back in the Falcon. Harry joined us. He sat alone in the front seat of the car, sullen. His team had lost. Crystal ignored him until we were all packed in, then she gave him a hug, patted him on the shoulder, and told him she was proud of how well he had played.

The drive back to where my car was parked was quiet. Joseph fell asleep with some books in his lap, and Harry was daydreaming, probably replaying football stuff that I didn't understand. Crystal drove without saying anything until we got to my car.

"It was nice having you along," she said.

I told her it was nice being along.

"Seems like my little man has taken a liking to you."

"I feel the same way. He's a wonderful fellow."

"Yeah, well, you ain't too bad yourself," she said.

"How about I take you all out to dinner sometime soon?" I asked her.

"That would be nice."

"Your mom also, right?"

"She'd like that."

"Well," I held out my hand, she had a nice grip. "I'm sorry I'm not very good about the football thing."

"I'm not very good about the story thing, so maybe we'll even things out between us."

I said fine, and watched as she drove off, then I headed home.

It felt good to be home. The excitement of the last 48 hours left me exhausted. I entered my dear little apartment with the expectation of a cool bath and a deep sleep. The breeze from the open window across the room greeted me as I opened the door. Things were looking up, yeah.

I smelled the bay rum about the same time my arms were pinned behind my back and I was bent at the waist and placed in swift, forward motion. My feet barely touched the floor as I was rushed across the room and through the window.

I would have cleared the opening with room to spare, except I twisted when they let go of me, and both of my feet hit the bottom of the window frame, sending me into a spin, showered with shards of glass and wood fragments. I was airborne long enough to see a blur of ground, sky, and building as I rolled a couple of times on the way down. I don't remember the sudden stop.

Chapter 17

I breathed in the strong smell of isopropyl alcohol, felt the cool touch of a damp cloth on my forehead, listened to Cricket's voice, soothing, "There now, Pete, you've had a close call." She wiped my face.

"You're telling me," I said, felt for anything that might suggest something was broken. Nothing. I smiled in a manner reserved for those few who are fortunate enough to cheat fate -- I was sitting smack in the middle of Willie Dee's compost heap.

"Frankie's in our place with Willie," she said, used a canvas glove to brush splinters of wood and glass off my shirt. "Poor thing was working here when you fell. He did real good, getting Frankie and me out here quickly. But his nerves are shot, at least for a little while."

The scent of bay rum, followed by that quick flash of light so often followed by a shot to the head, be it knuckles or trash pile, lingered. "I'll bet there was a black car parked nearby."

"You know who did this?" Cricket asked. "Frankie went looking for them, but they were gone by the time he got out front."

I wondered at how easily a matter of being tossed out a third-story window could be. I shivered. It seemed that a near-death experience should have been more difficult to explain, more complex. It should have taken a bit more doing.

I had come very close to having my neck broken, and it hadn't taken much trouble at all. "I think so," I said, answering her question.

"Frankie'll be glad to hear that," she said. "Someone's gotta pay for this mess. Window frame, glass, labor."

I wiggled my toes and fingers. Moved my arms and legs. "Doesn't feel like anything is broken."

"You got lucky."

"I don't feel lucky."

"You want we should call the police?"

I shook my head. "I'd prefer you didn't," I said.

"I ain't that high on having them around myself. It makes tenants nervous. Happens too often, lowers rent," she said, gave me a look I thought might be a warning.

"It's not something I plan on repeating," I said.

"Have anything to do with the little fella Frankie found outside your room?" Cricket asked.

"Maybe," I said.

As I sat there, the vision of the black car with the tinted windows parked at the top of the hill came to mind. "Damn."

"What's wrong?" Cricket asked.

"I've been too careless, too long," I said.

I checked my wristwatch. It was nearly ten. I relaxed a little, knowing Dixie Jean was safe at her neighbor's house, but figured I should give her a call.

Cricket walked me to my apartment. I found Roger's number in a notebook in my pocket. "I have a call to make."

"You sure you're good enough?" she asked. "Frankie wanted me to stay with you here so he could make sure you were not hurt bad."

"Tell him I'm okay, but thanks anyway," I said. "When I find out who it was, I'll see to it they get a bill for the damage."

"Ah, I ain't really worried," Cricket said. "Insurance'll take care of most of it. We'll stick anything left over onto your rent. Frankie likes to holler."

"There's another incentive," I said, picked a sliver of wood out of my hair, "to find out who did this."

Chapter 17

I called Roger, but there was no answer.

I took off my clothes, dumped them in the trash, on top of my shirt. The pile of bloodied clothes was building.

I was stepping in the shower when I heard someone unlock my door, felt a rush of fear. "Yo, Pete, it's me, Frankie. You around?"

I told him I was showering, would be right out. As the shower cleansed me, I listened to Frankie bang away in the other room. By the time I got out and slipped into some clean clothes, the mess was swept up, and the window was boarded up.

"You okay?" Frankie asked.

"Just shaken up," I said. "It's been a long day."

He patted me on the shoulder. "Glad you weren't hurt."

"That makes two of us," I agreed. "How's Willie Dee?"

"He's doing good, but someone's gonna have to pay for all the beer I poured to get him settled," Frankie said, laughed. "You better get a second job, Pete. I'm running a tab on you." He left, I locked the door behind him.

I gave Roger another call. "Hello?"

"Roger, sorry to bother you," I said. "This is Pete Krekow."

"Sure, calling to ask me some questions?"

"Actually, I need to talk to Dixie Jean," I said. "It's important."

"Oh." He sounded disappointed. "Well I'm afraid she's not here."

"I thought she was having dinner with you tonight?"

"Supposed to," he said, "but the people she works for called her in at the last minute."

"What?"

"Yeah, they said another girl called in sick. She told me she was sorry about dinner. Sally and Pete were real disappointed," he said. "Nothing wrong, is there?"

"It's just that I have something important to tell her," I said. "If you should see her before I do, please keep her at your place. It's important. I'll stop by and talk to her."

"I sure will," he said. "See you soon."

I was bone-tired, but there was only one way I could be certain it was Tony Mally and Bill Gnowles who threw me out the window. If it was them, Dixie Jean could very well be in danger.

I knew I had to go there, right away.

Chapter 18

Speed Stick T's parking lot was crowded, busy with traffic. Groups of men shared laughter and anger born of too much drink. I passed Gnowles, who was at the center of a group where there was pushing and shoving going on. He had his back to me. I looked for Mally, didn't see him.

It was quiet at the back of the building, so I swung into a dark corner near a sizeable clump of overgrown foliage, parked. I walked around to the red front door where a girl who looked too young to have on so few clothes in a place with a liquor license collected a cover charge.

While she made change of a twenty, I took another look around the parking lot. I caught a glimpse of a big guy with a lovely blonde on his arm getting into a large pickup. It was dark, so I couldn't get a good look at him. It crossed my mind how much he reminded me of Robbie Provot. I wrote down the license plate number.

"The band is awesome," the girl said, handed me the change, stamped the back of my hand.

I nodded, stepped inside, stood in a shadowed place near the door and surveyed the main entertainment area. It was a large room, divided by a low, broken wall in the center. There were two service bars, one on each side of the wall. Most of the floor space was filled with tables, chairs, and rowdy people.

To my right, the main bar ran the length of that wall. The bar crowd was more subdued. The far end of the bar turned a corner, became the hallway that ran behind the entertainment area, and led to Thady's office. Except for the two small stages against the left wall, which were bright with stage lights, the place was rather dark. The band played on a lower, dimly lit platform set between the two dance stages.

The place was packed. I tried to spot Mally, but it was too dark and too crowded. Dixie Jean, I noticed, was not dancing on either stage.

On my left was a dark hallway with a restrooms sign. I wanted to find my way to the room where the dancers were, and thought this hallway would be a good place to begin looking for doors to open.

I walked down the hallway, passed the restrooms, and stopped at a door marked "employees only." I turned the handle, opened it. Three women were drinking coffee at the only table in the small room. There were two vending machines against the opposite wall, and doors on each side of the machines. The one on the left was marked "exit." The other, I assumed, must lead to the dressing room.

"My name is Pete Krekow," I said. "I need to talk to Dixie Jean Evans."

"Nobody's allowed back here," the nearest woman said. "Try out front."

"I'm a reporter," I said. "It's important."

"Try asking at the back bar," another woman said.

I was about to step into the room when I felt a blow between my shoulder blades that drove me into the partially opened door. I twisted, a kick hit me behind the knee, I fell. The pain in my back took my breath away as I rolled on my side, arched back in a spasm that was broken by a kick to the shoulder that drove me farther into the room. I lay near the edge of the table.

"Break's over girls," I heard Tony Mally say to the women, whom I heard quickly leave the room without saying anything.

I was holding the table, trying to get on my feet, when I saw Mally reach into his pocket, take out a large leather blackjack.

"You're a hard man to do away with," he said. "But that's okay. This is going to be a fun evening." He swung on me.

I tried to catch myself, grabbed the table to keep from falling, but it gave way under my weight and toppled over on me as I went down a second time. I rolled away quickly, expecting a blow or kick, but as I raised myself on one arm, I saw he was standing there, smiling.

I grabbed one of the legs of the table and tore it loose, but it was light aluminum.

"Whew, beat my chops," he said. "You gonna rough me up with that?"

I got up quickly, headed to the door the women had used to leave.

"I wouldn't go in there if I was you," Tony said, took a chair with his left hand and threw it on the run as, head lowered, he charged at me.

I blocked the chair with my arms. Mally came hard into my gut and drove me into the wall, just short of the door. I felt his arms lock around me, and pull me away from the door and throw me toward the center of the room. I spun away from him, looking for a way out.

I ran to the back door, turned the knob as he hit me from behind, driving me into the door. It opened with a snap, and dumped us both outside, on the ground.

I pulled away from him. We were still on the ground. "That was you in my apartment, wasn't it?" I asked, rolled and got up, backed away from him.

"Looks like I should have gone down after your solo flight," he said, getting up and moving toward me, "and made sure your neck was broken."

"Why me?" I asked.

"Because I don't like your face."

"Funny, I was just getting used to it," I said, crouched in a fighter's stance, braced for what was coming.

"We've done enough talking." He swung the blackjack in front of my face.

I timed the first blow beautifully, feigned a fall forward, then pulled back hard, grabbed his arm with both hands and twisted his wrist, cartilege and bone snapped. Things broke.

He made a pained noise. I took the blackjack away from him and cracked the side of his head hard with the weighted length of leather. He fell to the ground, didn't move. I noticed the strap of a shoulder holster, pulled his coat back, took the gun, put it in my pocket.

I went back inside just as a woman entered the room by the door that the others had left by earlier. She saw me and started to leave. I called to her, "I'm looking for Dixie Jean Evans."

She stopped. "Last time I saw you, you were on the floor," she said. "What happened to Tony?"

"He had an accident after you left," I said.

"This place is getting nuts," she said. "The kid's with Thady. I wouldn't mess with him right now if I was you."

"Thanks," I said, and beat it back to the big room. I walked down the length of the bar, headed quickly down the hall to Thady's office. I didn't knock.

Thady's face was red with anger, excitement. Dixie Jean looked frightened. She was dressed only in a robe, the shoulder was torn away, and the belt was in Thady's left hand. She held the robe closed like a frightened child. I noticed a little blood at the corner of her mouth.

Thady turned on me with a tight karate stance, then shouted, swung his arms in arcs, and snapped his legs in a roundhouse motion designed to shear my head from my shoulders.

I pointed the pistol at his face and cocked the hammer. He froze.

I closed the door and directed him to sit in the chair behind his desk. I wondered if Marty had seen me, would call the police from the bar phone. I didn't think they would want to throw the evening's entertainment into the lap of a judge. Tony would make a lousy prosecution witness.

Even if the cops weren't already on their way, I figured I didn't have time to waste. I pressed the barrel of the pistol into Thady's neck. "I want you to talk to me about why you sent Tony Mally to my apartment tonight, to kill me."

He shook his head. "I have no idea what you're talking about."

"Thady, just once more," I said, pressed the barrel tighter into his neck.

"You're not a killer, Pete," he said. "The only thing that keeps me sitting still is I'm afraid that thing might go off by accident."

I stepped back, took the gun from his neck, and quickly, before he could react, hit him hard, flat on the ear with an open left. Blood dripped down the side of his face.

"Are you crazy," he said, and wiped the blood with his hand. He started to get up.

I pointed the gun at his face again. "You stand Thady, and you're dead," I said. "Tony's lying in back of the dump. Think about that. He didn't get there because I was afraid of him, and I'm not afraid of you.

"You killed him?"

"Last time I listened he was breathing," I said. "But not too well."

Thady asked if he could reach in his jacket for a clean cloth. I shook my head, leaned forward, held the gun to his head and reached in his coat. There was no weapon. I pulled back, nodded.

"Pete," Thady said, "you are not a killer, I am not a killer. I know nothing about any assault on you. Why didn't you talk to Tony about it?"

"I did."

"Well?"

"I didn't like his answer."

Thady put his face in his hands, shook his head. "End of conversation."

"Thady," I said. He looked away. "Thady," I said again.

He shook his head. "End of conversation."

I looked toward the door, knew I didn't have the time to push him for an answer. I leaned close to him. "I'm leaving now," I said. "But I want to leave you with two thoughts. The first is, nothing can stop me from finding out who killed Ivy Mitchell. If you were involved in her death in any way, I would advise you to call me, help me, and I'll do everything I can to help you.

"The second is, I'm going to take this lady with me. In the future, if anything, anything should happen to her, like a hit-and-run, or she is killed in a mysterious break in at her home, anything -- I'll remember tonight, what I found here, and I'll track you down, and if you don't think I'm capable of killing, you will have made a deadly mistake."

Dixie Jean had stood quiet, huddled in a corner. Thady looked over at her, nodded. "You understand, this effectively ends our business relationship," he said to her.

There was a door near the corner where she stood. She said nothing, grabbed her coat and handbag from a chair, unlocked the door, and ran outside.

I followed her, closed the door on my way out. I wished there had been a way to lock it from the outside, but there was not. We were on dangerous ground. I hurried after her.

"Dixie Jean, I think it would be smart if you stayed either with me or Roger until this thing is cleaned up," I said as she took the keys out of her bag, unlocked the car door, got in.

"I'll be okay," she said, turned the key. Nothing. I quickly lifted the hood, saw that the battery cables had been torn loose.

She got out, leaned against me. I felt her shiver. "I'm frightened."

I put my arm around her. "Let's get out of here."

Chapter 19

We sat quiet as I drove. I knew that between the clash with Thady, the loss of her job, and the discovery of the torn battery cable, she was a lady on the ragged edge. I finally asked her where I should take her.

"Pete, I just want to get as far away from here as I can," she said. "As quickly as possible."

I asked if we should head to the Rainbow. "My place, or would you feel more comfortable with someone you know?"

"It's no good going to Roger's house," she said. "With the kids there, and even Roger, who is a kid himself, much as I'd like to stay with them, I can't."

"Well, there 's my place," I said.

"That's a very nice offer," she said, "but I don't think it's a good idea."

"Just put a book in my lap, and I'll be asleep in a few minutes," I said, thought about the boarded-up window, the mess my apartment was in.

"I don't know, maybe a motel," she said. "I don't know."

"I could ask my landlord if he has an empty apartment," I suggested. "Something with a bed, chair, anything to make it livable."

"That would be nice," she said. "If you don't mind, would you please stop by my house long enough for me to grab a few things and make sure windows are closed and the place is locked up?"

We turned north on Parker, swung around the corner of Flamingo and stopped in front of Dixie Jean's house. I waited while she went in and did whatever she had to do to safe the place up, and pack for a short stay away from home.

I got out of the car when I saw her coming out the front door. I walked over and took her bags, put them in the back. I got back in and drove to the Rainbow. On the way, I worried about bothering Frankie and Cricket in the middle of the night. Still, there was no choice.

We parked, and I carried her bags into the building. Frankie made my life a lot easier -- the door to apartment number one, his place, was open.

I stuck my head in, saw Frankie on the sofa watching television. "Hello," I said.

He turned, clicked the television off, motioned for me to come in. He didn't seem overjoyed to see me, but I couldn't blame him. "If you're here to tell me someone tossed you out of another window," he said, "I'm gonna toss you out of the Rainbow."

"I've got company," I said, stepped into the room.

He seemed even less happy. Then Dixie Jean followed me, stood in the doorway.

Frankie had an attitude transformation. "Whoa," he said, and the look on his face told me I was no longer in danger of getting tossed out of the Rainbow. Actually, if I had thought he could talk, I would have asked him for a rent reduction.

Cricket quickly changed that. "Okay," she said, walked quickly into the room."What's with the 'Whoa,' stuff. Last time I heard that," she said, saw Dixie Jean, stopped before finishing the sentence.

"Sorry to be a bother," Dixie Jean said, "but it seems like I have run out of friends." She stood in the doorway, began sobbing, her body bent and shaking with dispair.

Cricket hurried to her. "There, there," she said, put her arms around her, led her to the sofa.

Frankie stood near me. We watched as Cricket comforted Dixie Jean. They talked quiet while he and I stood around shuffling out feet.

Finally Cricket told Frankie, "Get her bags and take them next door to apartment two."

He nodded approval.

"Apartment number two?" I asked.

"That's the one apartment we never rent," Cricket said. "We keep it for emergencies."

"I couldn't let you do that," Dixie Jean said. "You don't even know me. What we ran into tonight could spill over into something even worse. I don't want you to get involved."

Frankie held his bare arms forward. "Miss, these tattoos was for fun, the scars was for war. I ain't scared of nothing or nobody," he said. "Cricket says you stay with us till this trouble blows over. You listen to her. We'll keep you from harm."

"I'd insist on paying you," Dixie Jean said.

"Good, that's settled," Frankie said, picked up the bags and Cricket and Dixie Jean followed him to the apartment next door. Dixie Jean said she would thank me in the morning. I shrugged, "It's nothing."

I waited until Frankie and Cricket got back.

"She's tucked in safe and sound," Cricket said.

"How about you?" Cricket said. "Should we find a place for you to camp out as well?"

"I can't imagine they could get past Frankie tonight," I said, smiled. "Thanks for everything."

"Stop by in the morning, Pete," Frankie said. "We'll have breakfast together, swap war stories from tonight." He was making a large sandwich.

I looked at my wristwatch, it was almost two o'clock. I wondered if they ever slept.

"First thing in the morning," I said.

Chapter 20

I woke the next morning to the loud music of a Florida Power & Light tree-trimming crew cutting branches and turning them into sawdust in a machine that sounded like an impatient Formula One race car.

The sound was coming from the other side of the boarded-up window. I thought about Dixie Jean, looked forward to seeing her at breakfast, thinking she would be more inclined to help me with my search for Ivy's killer. It was time for her to answer questions that she had been hesitant to deal with earlier.

If she still would not or could not help me, I determined, much as I resisted the idea, I would have to revisit an old hunting ground. I wasn't tied to anything until my meeting with Robin, which meant I had the morning and most of the afternoon to take the next important step, once again, to visit Ivy's mother.

Although it seemed unreasonable to assume Iris Mitchell would know anything about the dark side of Ivy's life, she might know a friend or friends of Ivy who could help me, or in turn, know someone else who might. I also wanted an opportunity to ask her about Ivy's daughter.

So I went down to Frankie's apartment. On the way out the door, I picked up my newspaper, put it under my arm and walked down to the first floor. Cricket was washing dishes, Frankie was sitting at the kitchen table.

He looked up when I walked in the room. "Morning, Pete. You look like you could use a cup of coffee."

I put the paper on the table as Cricket poured me a cup. I took it, sat next to Frankie, and was about to ask about Dixie Jean when I saw the headline on my paper.

"Cedar Key Man Found Dead." I gave it a quick read, learned what I might have expected as I thought back to the night before. Robbie Provot had been found in his truck, dead. The truck was at the back of a small shopping center in the western part of Lake Worth. It had been parked at the edge of a canal.

Police said the motive had not been determined. They had ruled out robbery, saying Provot's wallet was apparently untouched. Money, identification and registration were all there. I sipped my coffee, pictured Provot and the attractive blonde getting into his truck.

"That little lady in number two, she bounces back real quick," Frankie said.

"What?" I asked, thinking about Little Sister, wondering if it was the same pretty blonde.

"Your friend, Miss Evans, she's already up and out, looking for work."

"Dixie Jean is already gone?"

"Up before the crack of dawn, had breakfast, asked if someone could drive her to a car rental place at the airport, which isn't far. I took her and was back in no time," he said. "She said she knew someone in Fort Lauderdale who owned a club. Offered her a job about a year ago, so she was headed down to talk to him, see if the offer still stood."

I looked at my watch. It was just after eight. "She already had breakfast, rented a car, and is driving down to Fort Lauderdale to find a job?" I asked. "She doesn't let any grass grow under her feet, does she?"

"No way," he said. "You want cereal or something?"

I shook my head. "I better get moving," I said. "I've got a long day ahead, and tonight I have a date with Robin." I finished my coffee, headed out.

On the way to the Mitchell house, I stopped at a fast food place, got a bite, and called a friend I had at Lake Worth PD. He told me Provot had been shot at close range with a small caliber weapon.

"Don't know much else," he said. "How 'bout you, Pete? Got anything I can use?"

I told him that I had seen Provot the previous evening with an attractive blonde. "They drove off at about eleven o'clock," I said.

"How'd you know him?"

"Friend of a friend," I said.

"Yeah, give me a call around lunchtime," he said. "Maybe we'll know something more by then."

I thanked him, ate my paper-wrapped breakfast, and drove across town to where the perennial crop of dirty kids played in the front yard. They were kicking around an empty motor oil can when I parked at the edge of the property. They stopped playing when I got out of my car. One of the older children, a skinny boy with a broken-tooth sneer, shouted something that sounded like "leckin treble," then he ran into the house shouting, "Gra'maw, Gra'maw."

I was barely in the yard before Iris Mitchell came out of the house. I stopped where I was, and waited near my car. This time I left the car door unlocked. As before, Gloria was at the center of a small group of women who waited just outside, near the front door. Others inside looked out through the torn-screens and open windows.

"You kids, get along now," Iris said to the group of children who seemed anxious, pushed and shoved, eager to follow and watch "Gra'maw" take a switch to the stranger who wore shoes.

"Never supposed I'd see you again," she said to me as she crossed the yard.

I touched a swollen left eye gently. "Never expected to come back. You have a wicked right cross."

"Gone get better, you keep messing with me." She walked to the place where I stood waiting. She squinted, "Didn't know I hit that hard though."

"You didn't," I said. "I visited Provot yesterday."

Her face paled. "He beat you like that?"

"Pretty much. But I got a shot in," I said.

"You telling the truth?"

"Yes."

"You drove all the way to Cedar Key because of what I said?"

"Yes."

She reached in her pocket. I stepped back a bit, out of her reach. She took out a clean rag. "Here," she said, and came closer. She patted the rag lightly around my torn, swollen eyebrows.

"You tell him what I said?" she asked.

"Yes."

She turned to the children and shushed them off with an arm gesture, pointing at the playground of wrecked cars. They ran off. "You all go back inside now," she said to Gloria and the others, then turned back to me. "Like to walk the neighborhood?"

"I'd like that, Mrs. Mitchell."

She held out a thin, red hand. Her grip was gentle, but there was a strength in the tips of her fingers as they pressed against my hand. "You hit him a good one?"

I nodded. "Good enough to quiet him." I didn't say anything about the morning paper. I wondered if she knew he was dead.

She held my right arm as we walked on the dusty road. We walked in silence for a ways, then she asked why I came back. "You must need something bad to chance another run in at this homestead."

"Yes ma'am." I stooped and, with my left hand, picked up a rusty nail in the roadway and tossed it in a drainage ditch.

"It's painful to say, but I believe Ivy was not alone the night she died. I've been trying to find out who she was with. So far, without much success," I said. "I'm here to ask you if you can think of anyone Ivy might have known well enough to confide in. Talk with about personal matters, people."

"I see," she said.

"I know this is hard for you, but if you could think of anyone who might have known her that well," I said, "I would appreciate your help."

She stopped walking and took my elbow, turned me so we faced each other. "Then you don't believe Ivy's death was an accident?"

I shook my head. "No, I don't," I said. "I can't explain why, not yet, except to say it doesn't make sense to believe she ended her life where she did without another person playing an important role in getting her there."

I picked up a few small chunks of limerock and tossed them at a stop sign that was shot full of bullet holes.

"How about the woman Ivy shared a house with, over on Flamingo Drive. She might be able to help you."

"I hope to see her later today," I said. "I've met her twice now. The first time she didn't seem inclined to talk much about either Ivy or her work. I saw her again last night, we talked briefly, and I think she has had a change of heart. I'll find out later. Until then, I need to keep knocking on doors."

We reached the end of the street the Mitchell house was on. I saw my old friend Gerald playing in the front yard of a small frame house that looked very much like the Mitchell house, except he was playing alone in the yard. The house was quiet. We walked down an adjacent street.

"I don't reckon you know what Ivy was doing, hanging around with that sort of folks?"

"I think she put too much trust in the wrong people."

"You mean among her friends, or those she worked for?"

"Certainly those she worked for," I said. "I can't say anything about her friends. Dixie Jean Evans, her roommate, is her only friend I have met."

"This Evans woman, she seem like nice folk?"

"Yes. I liked her." I looked back at Gerald and wondered why he was in the yard alone when there was a yard full of kids just up the block at the Mitchell place. He looked lonely, sitting in the sand next to his two-wheeled trike, fidgeting with the chain.

"Ivy and me, we never talked about her work." I felt her hand tighten on my arm, then she began a spasm of short breaths that frightened me. I put my arm around her shoulder and held her close to me. I felt her gasp for air. The spell passed as quickly as it had come on, but still, she seemed shaken by it.

"Maybe we better get on back now, Mr. Krekow."

We walked silently back, past Gerald, and down the street toward her house. I was concerned that the conversation about Ivy had brought on the spasm, so I didn't say anything more as we walked. It was Iris who broke the silence.

"I knew something about what she did for a living. I didn't approve. Yet, I knew I couldn't do nothing about it. So I kept silent."

She stopped walking and took a few deep breaths. "Now I feel like maybe her death was my fault. If I had put my foot down, said I would not allow a daughter of mine to do that, that dancing business. Instead I stayed silent."

"You can't blame yourself." We began walking again.

"Sure can, Mr. Krekow," she said, softly. "Sure can."

"If I get to the person who was with her the night she died," I said, "I'll prove you share none of the blame."

"That'd be nice. But I'm too old for a miracle, and my Ivy is gone." We were next to my car when she stopped walking again. She called to the broken-tooth boy. "Peanut, you get me a glass of cold water, hear?"

"Yes, ma'am," he said, and ran into the house.

"I feel like you was hoping I would know someone could help you get to this man was with Ivy, but I'm the last would know. I'm afraid we never talked about nothing but family." In the yard the children played, kicked around an old motor oil can. She watched them for a moment. "Now, it probably won't come to nothing, but Nellis Collins might be able to help some. He ain't kin, but those two, they were tighter than tight when they was kids, and I believe Ivy kept on talking to him from time to time. Probably when she could catch him away from his home."

"Nellis?" I asked.

She spelled it as I wrote the name in my notebook. "That house back there, the one we passed with the little one alone in the yard?"

"Yes ma'am."

"That there is the Collins boy. His mama don't let him play with no Mitchells. The woman is pea green with jealousy because Ivy and Nellis was close, and when they were kids, the two of them, Ivy and Sass, that's what we call her, real name's Darlene Jones, there was the feud years back, pardon." She coughed into the rag she had in her pocket. "I don't know if Ivy and Nellis ever got together, but somehow I believe they was too close not to speak from time to time."

"You know where I could find him?"

"At work, I expect." The boy, Peanut, came out the house with the water. He brought it quickly. "There's a good boy." She took it and patted him on the head, then nudged him away, back toward the game.

"Think I could stop by where he works?" I asked. "Or do you think the feud would get between us?"

"Not if you tell him straight off that you are trying to find the man that killed her." She drank some of the water. "You can catch him over at Rip Tide Towing, out on Okeechobee, near the Turnpike. I'm told he's a good mechanic, and drives a truck if need be. He's a good worker. Always was. Always was sorry he married that white trash, Jones."

She noticed me watch her take another drink of cold water, and stopped, shook her head. "Mr. Krekow, I ain't got a bit of manners." She hollered to the boy again. "Peanut. Go on and get another of these. Go on now."

I told her I was obliged. "Mrs. Mitchell, there's another question I have." Her breathing spell had left me skittish about raising delicate subjects, but I couldn't leave without asking. "I've been told that Ivy had a daughter."

Iris Mitchell frowned, deep, that old rolling thunder was returning.

"I don't mean harm," I told her. "I just have to know what will happen to her now."

"It's true about the girl. She's tucked safely away in a private school up in Martin County. Years ago Ivy set aside a separate savings in my name for the girl. It's just for her, and I pay all her bills out of it. It's hers. I'll see to that," she said. "There's enough to keep her comfortable for many years more. You leave her alone."

I nodded. "I don't mean harm," I said. "If I can ever be of help, just call."

"I'll take care of her." The boy came along with my water. She thanked him, and handed it to me.

"If something happens to you?"

She took my empty glass. "You go on now. Tell Nellis, I send my best."

I thanked her for her help.

"Don't be a stranger, hear?" she said. As she walked back to the house, Gloria came out and walked with her.

I got in my car, started the engine, and drove over to Okeechobee Boulevard, then turned left and headed to the Turnpike.

It was nearly ten-thirty when I pulled into Rip Tide Motors. It was a large garage, six mechanic stalls, four full-service gas pumps out front, and a large back storage area that was nearly filled with cars, some of which looked like they would never see roadway time again.

I parked on the side of the building, figured it was time to check in with Barbara. I called the main number from a phone booth, and was transferred to her office.

She picked up the phone while in the middle of a conversation about where to go for an early lunch. I said, "Pete here," and told her I was "just checking in."

"Oh, Pete, hang on a minute will you?"

I said, "Sure," to an empty line.

She returned shortly, said, "Sorry for the wait."

"No problem."

"I was waiting to hear from you," she said. "The dead man from Cedar Key, is that your guy?"

"That's him," I said. "This time Robbie played with the wrong woman."

"This story is growing," she said. "I'll be out of town tomorrow, but one way or another, give me a call on Saturday, at my home," she said, and gave me her home phone number.

"You got it."

"Say again?" It wasn't a question for me. Her voice was muffled, the receiver was partially covered, she was talking to someone else. "Yeah, I've got Pete on the line. Who? Sure."

She came back on. "Pete, I'm switching you to Johnny Reilly," she said. "He has a message for you. Remember, call Saturday." I heard her click the phone button and press four numbers, there was a ring.

Before the second ring, Johnny Reilly was on the other end of the line. "Yo, Pete?"

"Si, Amigo," I said. "What's up?"

"Guy named Roger Filbert asked for you."

"He say anything more than that?"

"Wants you to call him, said you have his number."

"Got it," I said. "Thanks, Zippo. Catch you later." I hung up and searched my notebook for the page where I had written Roger's number, toward the front. I dialed, it rang a half dozen times, nobody answered. I hung up and redialed, let it ring longer, still there was no answer. I gave up and walked around to the front of the garage.

The office was to the right of the stalls, at the edge of the building. I went in and asked an old man in dirty work clothes if I could talk to Nellis Collins. He was pouring coffee from a pot into a brown-stained, white coffee mug.

"I'm a reporter," I told him. "I'd appreciate if I could have a few minutes of his time."

The old man finished pouring the coffee, then looked up at me, then at his wristwatch. "Ain't in trouble is he?"

"No. A friend of his told me he might be able to help me find someone I'm looking for," I said. "That's all."

"Anybody I might know?" He squinted, and blew into the hot coffee. "Glad to help if I can."

"I don't think so," I told him.

"He'll be on break in a few minutes," he said, and sipped his hot coffee. "Why don't you go on down to the first stall, where he's working, and ask him if he's wanting to talk to you."

"Thanks," I said, as I walked back outside.

"Don't go in the work area," he hollered, as I closed the door.

Nellis Collins was a big country boy, with greasy coveralls and a smile that went a long way towards making him the friendliest looking mechanic I'd ever met.

He was walking away from the car he had been working on when I got to the first stall. He carried an oversized insulated jug.

"Nellis Collins?" I asked.

"I'm flat busted if you're selling anything, mister," he said. "But, I'm gone sit over there and have a cup of coffee with my friends, so if you want to get out of the sun, you're welcome to join us. But I wouldn't advise you try to sell this bunch anything on their break time."

I told him who I was, and why I was there. "I sure would appreciate it if you and I could talk alone a minute."

His smile turned a sad kind of frown. He nodded and said he would be glad to talk to me. "But Ivy and me, we ain't talked in many moons. Too many. Somewhere along the line she and me, we lost touch. And I sure enough regret that, especially now that she's gone."

We sat on the ground under a banged-up shade tree. He offered me a sip from his coffee cup. I declined. "Nellis, I just left Iris Mitchell. She said maybe you could help me. I know you said you hadn't talked to Ivy in, how long would you think?"

"Months, almost a year even. Except once, a short while ago, but we didn't talk much then. Just 'hello' and 'goodbye.'"

I shook my head. "That's a long time. Still, I wonder if you remember if the two of you ever talked about her work. I'm particularly interested in the people she worked with. Especially those closest to her."

He talked between sips from the cup. "Ivy never talked to me about anything like that," he said. "She knew how I felt about her doing that kind of work. After a while we couldn't talk about it without an argument, so finally we just talked old times, then finally, we seemed to stop talking altogether."

"Iris said something about trouble between your wife and Ivy."

He shook his head. "No trouble with nobody could have stopped me and Ivy from talking if that's what she wanted. It's true about Darlene being angry about this or that, but that don't matter none, and sure enough don't have nothing to do with nothing except Darlene keeping herself all the time upset. Still, she's a good woman. She'll come around and make peace with the Mitchells."

"You don't know anything about Ivy's job?"

"Ivy was letting her life get away from her, I knew that. I went once to that place where she worked, and it about broke my heart," he said, took a sip of coffee and sat thoughtful a minute. "Once upon a time, she and me, we were like brother and sister. I'm gone miss her awful."

"How about a boyfriend who might be able to help me? Did she have a steady fellow that you know of?"

"Ivy had some personal things she cared very much about. Other than that, as far as I know, she just worked to make as much money as she could." He finished his coffee and screwed the top back on the jug. "She was smart. Loaned me money for my house. I still make payments to Iris on the first of every month. I believe there are other families doing the same. She was real good about helping her own."

"She held your first mortgage?"

"Indeed she did," he said, "and at a more reasonable rate than the banks would have. I wouldn't have a home if it wasn't for her."

"The more I hear about Ivy, the more I'm coming to believe she was quite a woman," I said.

"You're right about that," he said, and rubbed his fists against his eyes. "She'll be sorely missed."

"Nellis, my back is against a wall. Please, try to think of someone who might be able to help me," I said. "I need to find the closest friend she had. Someone who knew any important details about her life at the place where she worked. In particular, I'm looking for someone close enough to that scene, to know the name of the person who was with Ivy the night she died. I'm stuck without that name."

Nellis shrugged. "Well, only person I can think." He shook his head and sat silent a bit longer. "Can't be nothing, but remember I said I went to the place where she worked?"

I nodded.

"Well, Ivy had a roommate, Miss Dixie Jean Evans. She came and sat with me a short spell. She seemed like nice people. Maybe she could help you."

I told him I already had met Dixie Jean, and was going to see her again later in the day.

"That's it, except, well," he said, started cleaning up, "it probably ain't nothing, but when I first got there, I sat at a table way in back; not spying mind, just wanted to see Ivy real bad, but wanting to be somewhere else. There, and out'a there, at the same time. Right?"

I told him I understood.

"I ordered a beer. Four dollars and fifty cents," he said, played with the cap on his Thermos. "Looked at that bottle for the longest time, tried to get courage to ask for Ivy. Then this snot-nosed little fella come over, said, could he sit? I shrugged, wanted him to hightail it, but didn't want trouble. Then he asked if I was there for, well, you know."

Nellis was quiet a short while. I didn't say anything, just left him with his memory, hoped he could pull something out of the mist that would help me find Ivy's killer.

"Words sure are funny things," he said. "I sat there and thought about my little lost sister, a lifetime of growing up together wove it's way around that four dollar and fifty cent beer bottle."

"Do you remember his name?" I asked.

He shook his head. "Soon after, Ivy saw me at the table, come over an drove him off."

"Did she seem to know him?"

"I'd say so," he said. "Though she didn't show a liking for him."

"Could you describe him to me?"

"Sure." Nellis described Marbles.

"The name Marbles ring any bells?"

"Could be," he said. "I didn't pay him any mind."

"How long ago was this?" I asked.

Nellis stood and picked up his jug. "Well now, don't go telling Darlene, or you'll have me in the middle of a tornado. When I said I saw Ivy a short time ago, that was only a few weeks back. But we really did not talk much. I just went because I hadn't seen her in such a long time. Wondered how she was. Then, my being there, I could tell it upset her, so I sat a minute, met Miss Dixie Jean," he said, soft-smiled, seemed sad. "Then I left."

I stood, dusted the seat of my pants. "Nellis, I'm not sure I'm following why Marbles came to sit with you, or what he wanted?"

"That was the last time I ever saw her," he said, started to walk slowly back to the first stall. I walked with him. "He just seemed crazy to get me a woman. I figure that's what he does with his life."

"If we're talking about the same man," I said, "I find it hard to believe the people who own and operate that place would let him run a scam like that, something that could get them closed down, end up in court."

"Well, I don't know what you want to hear," he said. "Littla fella wasn't there long, just enough on how he bragged, him and his girlfriend had special stuff at their house."

"At their house?" I asked.

"It was about then that Ivy came over, chased him off."

"Somehow the pretext doesn't jive," I said.

"Sorry. Wish I could have been of help," Nellis said. "Now, I gotta get."

"Thanks, Nellis, you helped a great deal," I said. "Do you remember if he told you where that house was?"

"Next to City Park Zoo, on a side street. I remember him saying Saint Francis Street because it seemed funny, him living anyplace with the name of a saint. We shook hands. "I gotta get now, Mr. Krekow."

I thanked him once more, told him I might stop by again.

"That'd be fine," he said, and walked off.

I watched him go back to work, then got in my car and headed quickly back to the other side of town.

Chapter 21

It was nearly noon by the time I drove down Saint Francis
Street, and pulled into the half-circle driveway of the small,
stucco house where I saw a compact Ruster parked in the
driveway. It's tag was three months overdue, the passenger door
was caved in, and it had a fading Speed Stick T's back bumper
sticker that said something suggestive, but not very clever, about
the entertainment. I figured I was at the right place.

I walked up a short concrete sidewalk to the front door. The
windows were open. I could hear a television or radio playing
inside. I knocked. There was no answer. I knocked louder, and
waited before I called through the open louvers in the door.
"Hello. Marbles? Anyone home?"

After a few minutes, I walked around to the side of the
house where I thought the noise came from. There was a large,
untrimmed hedge blocking the view of the room that, because of
the glow from a television screen, I figured was the living room.
"Marbles? Nordy? Anyone home?"

Nobody answered. I pushed into the hedge to see through
the louvers, which were cracked, but not wide enough to get a
clear look inside. I thought I saw someone sitting in a chair in
front of the television, but wasn't sure.

I went around to the rear of the house. The place backed up to the zoo, and was landscaped with some old, generous shade trees. It was very private. There were no signs that the people who lived there got enjoyment from it. There was no outdoor furniture, the lawn needed mowing and raking. The flower beds were overgrown with weeds, flowers long gone.

I went to the back door and knocked. There still was no answer, so I tried the door. It was unlocked. I opened it and went inside. "Hello?"

The kitchen was small, too small for the mess.

The sink overflowed with dirty dishes. Boxes and cans, opened and unopened, were stacked on the counter next to the sink. The stove was decorated with grease and food-caked pots and pans, and the garbage was stacked in brown paper bags next to the refrigerator.

The refrigerator door had been left open. I wondered why? I noticed condensation on a pitcher of tea, or whatever it was, on the top shelf. It had not been open long. Still, it was not cool in the room. It was hot, sick.

I went into the living room and found Marbles sitting in an overstuffed chair in front of the television. The louvers had not distorted my original perception. He was, for the most part, comfortably seated. Except his face was resting on the back of his left shoulder.

He was barefoot, with cut-off shorts and a floral-patterned shirt that was buttoned at the throat. The shirt did not show rips, or snapped buttons. His face did not show the kind of trauma associated with a beating. His body was twisted slightly, as though he may have reached back, startled, when someone twisted his head, broke his neck.

I used the phone on a stand by the front door to call the police. I wondered, remembering the open refrigerator door, if Marbles and I were alone in the house. As I talked, I kept an eye on the short hallway that ran left from where I stood.

Next, I called my office. I asked the desk person who answered to transfer me to Latham.

"What you got?" he asked.

I told him, said the police were on the way. As I stood there listening to Latham, I noticed Marbles' screwed-up face. In a way he reminded me of a dog we had when I was a kid. If you scolded him, he would lean down, turn his head sideways, his eyes kind of glassed over, tuck his tail, and whimper. Marbles' whimpering days were over.

I told Latham I needed Cooper to back me up, to file the first day Saint Francis Street death story so I could move ahead with what I was working on. He began to get cute. I reminded him, "I'm sure you've been advised, I am on a special project." I said, "Gotta go, Amigo." I hung up the phone before he could answer.

I began looking around the place, careful not to disturb anything, but remembering the refrigerator door. It seemed a sure bet it had not been left open by Marbles.

There were two rooms down a short hall. One left, the other right. The door to the one on the left was open. There was nobody there. It must have been the one Marbles and his girlfriend slept in. The room was nearly as messy as the kitchen. The bed was unmade, clothes were tossed around. It needed a housekeeper, but other than that, it wasn't out of the ordinary.

The door to the second room was closed. I didn't want to mess up a crime scene, but I wanted in the room. I pushed gently against the door, hoping against hope the old hardware had failed to click in place the last time the door was closed; also, praying there wasn't somebody on the other side, somebody with a resume that included an expertise in neck breaking.

I pressed. It held. I pressed a bit harder, and felt the latch begin to slip. I pushed harder. The door opened with a soft click.

I remembered Marbles had said something to me about "shit your mama never told you." From where I stood in the doorway, I knew this was the sort of thing he was talking about.

The police were going to spend a long time in this room.

The camera stood on a tripod at the foot of the bed, looking very much like the conductor of an orchestra of slime. The bed was against the wall to the right of the door where I stood. In case I missed it the first time, a ceiling mirror above the bed reflected the dismal state of the linen. Gadgets that looked like weight training apparatus were bolted to the ceiling, anchored at points where holes had been drilled in the mirror.

The windows were boarded on the inside. Light came from one bank of track lights above the door that someone had left on. There was a track light strip on the wall opposite the bed, and a dozen various sized spotlights stood on stands and tripods throughout the room. There was strip lighting above the bed.

Magazines that complemented the ambient theme littered the floor. A small pile of photographs was stacked on a two-drawer file cabinet in the far corner of the room, across from the bed. The floor around the cabinet was covered with photographs. Both drawers were open. I guessed somebody had been going through the photo files.

As I crossed the room and stooped over the cabinet, I wondered if I would find any pictures of Ivy, or perhaps the blonde I had last seen with Provot. Whoever it was, whatever they had been looking for, it had been important enough to kill Marbles to get.

I knelt, and using the blunt end of my pen, moved the photos on the floor around enough to satisfy myself that Ivy was not in any of them. I was looking at the pile of photos on the cabinet, when I heard a car pull in the driveway. I left the room quickly and went to the front door, ready to let the police in.

I was in the living room when I heard the key in the lock click. It had to be his girlfriend. "Nordy?" I went to the door quickly. "Nordy? Please don't come in," I hollered.

The door started to open, then, when I called her name, it shut with a bang.

I went to the door, was about to go out when I heard her shout to somebody. Another car had pulled up on the street. I looked out the louvers of the front door, saw two policemen get quickly out of a patrol car. Nordy pointed to the house, shouted. The policemen drew their guns.

"My name is Pete Krekow. I'm a reporter for the News & Journal," I shouted. "I'm the person who called 911."

The taller of the two policemen shouted, "Open the door and step out with your hands on your head, Mr. Krekow."

Chapter 21

I turned the knob and opened the door a crack, then put my hands on my head and opened it the rest of the way slowly, with my foot. I stood in the open doorway with my hands on my head as Nordy came running toward the house, shouting to her boyfriend.

"I don't think you should let her go in the house," I said to the policemen, but it was too late for them to stop her. She rushed past me, and in back of me I heard a scream. Then, while the first policeman watched me, the second came up, ran around me, and into the house.

While I stood there, a second patrol car pulled in back of the first. I recognized Higgins. He got out and walked over to the tall policeman.

"I know him," Higgins said to the policeman. "You call this in, Pete?"

I nodded. "Yes."

"What's inside?" he asked.

"The guy they call Marbles," I said.

"I've run into him," Higgins said as they walked toward me.

"His girlfriend just went in there," I said to Higgins. "You might want to get her out."

"He's dead?"

"Broken neck."

"Let's go in," Higgins said to the other policeman, and the two of them rushed into the house.

As I stood outside, I saw Cooper pull up and get out of his car. Inside Nordy still made loud, hysterical noises. I could hear the police try to calm her.

"What the hell did you let her in here for?" I heard Higgins shout. "Hawthorne, take her outside, and stay with her."

Cooper and I exchanged informal hand slaps as he walked up to me. "Yo, Pete, what did you say to Latham? What you got here? Man, I missed lunch." While he talked, he looked around the outside of the place.

"You know a street snitch named Marbles?" I asked Cooper.

Hawthorne and Nordy interrupted us as they walked by. He took her toward one of the patrol cars, but she dropped sobbing onto the lawn, and would not be moved.

Cooper and I both lowered our voices as we talked. A small group of people had started gathering on the sidewalk.

"What's his problem?" Cooper had his notebook out and was writing while we talked.

"Neck broken."

"For real?" Cooper walked closer to the open front door. I went with him. We could see Marbles from where we stood. "Looks like his keyhole days are over."

"Cooper, I think this murder is tied to the story I'm working on."

"Sure enough?"

"Yeah." I put my hand on his writing hand. "Stop writing for a sec, will you?"

He stopped and looked at me. "What's up?"

"I need to get next to that woman." I indicated Nordy by glancing in her direction.

"She Marbles' wife?"

"Girlfriend," I said. "She may know a name that is very important to me. I need you to help me get next to her right away."

"Right now?"

"Yeah. I want to talk to her while she's still upset."

"You want I should go ask the cop something to distract him?" Cooper put his pen and notebook away.

"That would be grand," I said, and we walked together over to where Hawthorne was standing next to Nordy, who was still sobbing on the ground. She seemed to notice nothing of what was going on around her.

As Cooper and I walked, I noticed the crowd growing on the street. In back of us, Higgins called to Hawthorne and told him to keep bystanders back.

"I'll stay with Nordy if you'd like," I said.

"Okay if this guy stays with the Mrs.?" Hawthorne asked Higgins. While he talked, he began watching people gathering on the street and sidewalk. "Stand back, please," he said to the few who stood at the edge of the front path.

Higgins nodded. "Just keep an eye on her. I don't want her walking away," he said. "Pete, don't get lost. I need to talk to you about this."

"I'm gonna get inside," Cooper said.

I waved him off, turned my attention to Nordy. I knelt by her on the ground, touched her on the shoulder. "I'm sorry about this," I said. "Your man was a friend of mine."

She looked at me in wonder. "Marbles?"

"Yeah, he was a great guy." I prayed Saint Peter didn't keep a list of lies told to comfort strangers, and elicit much needed information.

She broke into more tears, then turned to me again. "Please tell them to let me go back inside." She started to get up. "I want to see my Marbles."

I put my hand on her shoulder. "Nordy, the police won't let you go in." I heard a siren in the distance. I knew when the ambulance got there, the emergency crew would take over for me. "Who would want to hurt him, Nordy?"

She shook her head and cried. "I don't know."

As we sat together, I thought of the photos I had seen on the floor. There was no doubt Nordy had not been camera shy, she had been one of the women in starring roles.

I heard the siren getting closer.

"Nordy, I think the person who did this to Marbles may also know something about the death of Ivy Mitchell."

She shook her head. "Little Sister wouldn't hurt my Marbles." She looked up, her face drained of color, drawn, her blue eyes were wet with tears that left small paths down her cheeks.

"I'm not talking about Little Sister, Nordy," I said. "I think it was her brother."

"Who are you?" she asked. Her eyes showed caution. "I don't know what you're talking about. Leave me alone." She turned her head and began sobbing again.

"Nordy, I'm just trying to help you."

"Marbles never told you anything about that."

"Marbles and I go way back, Nordy." I looked up the street for signs of the ambulance. "He trusted me, and so can you."

"I don't know what you're talking about," she said, and reached up with one hand and pushed against my chest. "You get away from me."

I wanted to go easy, but as I knelt next to Nordy, I remembered the way Ivy looked the last time I saw her, floating dead on the rocks. I could see Iris Mitchell standing in the yard, surrounded by grandchildren, tears in her eyes.

And I thought of the child, tucked away in a boarding school, who would never see her mother again because a guy whose pleasure was hurting women got more than his share of the fun.

"Nordy, don't play cute with me. I've seen your little playroom in the back. I've seen your bare-butted acrobatics on the pictures that somebody tossed all around the room, and it's just a matter of time before the boys in blue come out and begin to ask you to explain your acting career." I reached over and turned her face toward mine. "Somebody broke your boyfriend's neck, Nordy, and if you don't help me now, whoever did that to Marbles will come back and break yours."

She tried to pull away, but I held her, made her face me. "Tell me who was with Ivy Mitchell the night she died, and I'll do my best to get to him before he kills you, too."

"Doc," Nordy said, and began a new round of hysteria.

"Who the hell is Doc, Nordy?" I turned her to me again. The ambulance was nearing. "Please."

She wiped her face and looked over at the crowd. The people were watching her. She turned back to me. "Why won't you let me see my man?"

I heard the ambulance coming down the street. Higgins came outside and shouted to me. "Pete, when the ambulance gets with the lady, I want to see you inside, pronto."

I nodded, then turned back to Nordy, who had slipped again into a state of mild hysteria. "Nordy, please tell me his real name."

"Who?" She looked up at me, confused. "Who are you? Why won't you let me see Marbles?"

The ambulance jumped the curb, and parked on the sidewalk, close to where we were sitting. Higgins was back in the doorway when the first attendant got out of the passenger side of the vehicle. Higgins pointed to Nordy.

I stood and walked toward Higgins. I checked my watch. It was nearly two. I wondered if there was time to catch Kay at home before she went on duty. I looked around for Cooper, didn't see him. "Higgins, mind if I run off long enough to make a quick call? It's important."

"I guess," he said, and looked at his watch.

"Thanks," I said.

"You see the room in back?"

I nodded. "Yeah."

"I thought the zoo was on the other side of the fence."

"If you collect autographs, one of the stars is on the front lawn," I said.

"His wife?"

"Girlfriend."

"Jesus." Higgins shook his head. "You didn't touch anything in there?"

I shook my head. "You know better than that."

"Sure." He watched the medics try to comfort Nordy, who was sobbing. "Strange world we live in."

"Strange world she lives in," I said. "The homicide folks are going to be in that room the rest of the day," I said.

"Longer maybe," he said. "Better them than me."

"Me too. I'll be right back," I said.

"We'll be here."

I walked past Nordy and the emergency guys, drove around the crowd and headed to the nearest shopping center, a half dozen blocks away.

Chapter 22

The public phones were in front of a supermarket. I parked and checked my pockets for quarters. None. I went in the place, changed two dollars at the service desk, which took more time than it should have because the store manager was twitting with a cashier who looked young enough to be his daughter and old enough to be trouble. She finally giggled her way over to me and counted out eight quarters.

By the time I got back outside, both phones were in use. While I waited, I chatted with a guy who was taking a break from his job cleaning the sidewalk and curb with a blowing machine that didn't really clean anything, just blew dirt into the parking lot, where the wind would blow it back. Built-in job security.

Still, he seemed like a nice enough guy. I knew the machines were loud, I told him I thought it would be wise for him to wear some kind of hearing protector. He shrugged. Maybe he didn't hear me. I excused myself when one of the phones came available. He went back to work.

I looked at the person who had just used the phone and wished I had an alcohol swab to clean the mouthpiece. I wiped it carefully on my shirt, and dialed Kay's number.

She answered on the third ring. "Hello?"

"Sorry to bother you," I said. "It's Pete."

"I know who it is." She sounded stressed. "You're not cancelling tonight with Robin?"

"Of course not. It's business."

"Well, make it short," she said. "I was just on my way out the door."

"Does the name 'Doc' ring any bells?"

"About fifty," she said. "Why?"

"I'm looking for a high roller who likes to hurt prostitutes. One of them recently died while in his loving care," I said. "So far, he's been nameless and invisible. But I just got this nickname, and I wonder if you've heard it kicking around the corridors at work?"

"Not really," she said.

"Could you just think back to anything you might have heard?"

"You're going to have to give me a little more to work with," she said. I could hear the television in the background. I wondered if the ambulance chaser was home. "There are two cops I can think of called 'Doc.' There's a bartender, there's the guy who sold us the wagon, the greenskeeper where we golf, not to mention real doctors."

"I hear you," I said. "Thanks, anyway."

"Sorry," she said, and sounded like she might have meant it. "Let me kick it around the place tonight. If I get anything I think might be of help, I'll give you a ring."

"Thanks," I said.

"Sounds like you're riding a good story."

"I am," I said. "From here I go back to a crime scene that may be at the heart of the investigation."

"Crime scene?"

"Yeah." I told her about Marbles getting his neck broken.

"How does that tie to the nickname you're tracking?"

"I'm not sure," I said. "How about the name Little Sister? Does that ring any bells?"

"That's it?"

"Yeah," I said.

"I don't think so," she said. "I'll ask around."

"Thanks, anyway," I said. "I'll call you tomorrow, and tell you how the meeting at the college went."

"Remember, you're not there to make friends," she said.

"Got it." I hung up the phone, then checked my notebook for Roger Filbert's phone number. I called and let the phone ring. There was no answer. I hung up, and dialed again, making sure I dialed correctly the first time. Still, no answer.

Next I called my friend at Lake Worth PD. He told me he had just talked to the investigating officer on the Provot homicide, who passed along a 'thank you' for the information about Provot and the blonde.

"Actually, that's the only new stuff we've had today, Pete," he said. "Wish I could tell you more, but I can't."

"How about the name, Doc," I asked him. "I'm looking for a very bad boy with a heavy wallet who uses that nickname."

"Can't say it rings any bells," he said. "That's all you got on him?"

"He likes hurting prostitutes," I said. "Maybe girlfriends, or a wife who has filed a complaint?"

"Can't think of anyone."

"One more," I said. "How about someone called Little Sister?"

"An adult?"

"A very naughty adult," I said.

"Sorry," he said.

I thanked him, said I'd call back in the morning.

"I'll keep an eye and an ear peeled for you," he said, hung up.

I tried Roger and again, got no answer. I checked the time. I did not want to be late for the meeting with Robin. I figured the thing with Higgins might take longer than expected. That sort of thing often did. But I was excited about Nordy slipping me the new nickname, and was anxious to track down it's owner. If I used my time well, even after a little extra duty with Higgins, I still might be able to knock on another door or two before having to call it a day.

I stopped at a fast food place and got something for Cooper to chew on. By the time I got back, the crowd had grown enough that it spilled from the sidewalk onto the street. People stood in small groups, some sat on the bumpers of their cars. The people who stood around were still generally quiet, but it felt like carnival time could take over any minute.

Police, emergency, and private vehicles jammed both sides of the street. I turned around in a circular driveway about halfway down the block, and drove back, parked a block away. I walked to the house. When I got there, I had to push my way through the crowd.

I noticed Nordy sitting in the back of the emergency vehicle. A policeman stood near her. He didn't look like he was there to comfort her. She sat quiet, looked at the crowd without showing any reaction to the stares and whispers.

The police had tied the yard off with yellow band tape and barracades. I told one of the policemen in the yard that Higgins expected me. He nodded, and I stepped over the tape line, crossed the front lawn and went in the house which now was filled with blue uniforms. I looked around for Higgins, but didn't see him. I saw Cooper coming out of the dirty room.

"Yo, Pete. What a circus. What a place. You catch a look at the fun room in the back of this place?" Cooper was wired. "I haven't had anything to eat since last night. My stomach is making more noise than Columbus' crew when they first sighted land."

I noticed somebody had covered Marbles. He was the reason everybody was there, but nobody was paying attention to him. Most of the traffic was to and from the room with a view.

"Here's a present," I said.

"Oh, Pete, baby." He grabbed the bag of food and caressed it. "Bless you, my son."

"You see Higgins?" I asked him.

"Yeah, last I saw him he was out back talking to Scirrano."

"Scirrano?"

"Yeah."

"I kind of figured Flowers would be working this one," I said. "He filed the first report, notified the family."

"I don't know," Cooper said. "I haven't seen him."

"Enjoy the food," I said, and walked around to the kitchen, and went out the back door, where I found Higgins, and Joe Scirrano, a first-class homicide detective, standing together, talking.

"Higgins tells me you called this in," Scirrano said.

"That's right." We stood under a great shade tree. A light breeze made being outdoors a blessing, especially compared to the house, which reeked of garbage and death.

"It's been a while since we worked together." Scirrano said.

"Almost a year," I said. "The Bentley-Riley murder."

"Bentley-Riley. Has it been a year already?" Scirrano shook his head and picked a leaf that had fallen from the tree from the shoulder of his coat. "What brought you to this place, Pete?"

"I'm working on the Ivy Mitchell case. The dead guy in there, the one they call Marbles, he read the first story I wrote, the one from the night when Ivy Mitchell was found dead. He thought I might be in the information market. He came by my apartment," I said.

"You knew each other well enough for him to look you up at your place," Scirrano asked, "rather than catch you at your office?"

"As far as I know, he didn't do business in offices," I said. "He was an alley snitch, nothing more."

"Nothing more?" Scirrano wore a nice three-piece suit, a conservative tie. He was a man who liked to dress well. He stood with his hands at his sides, never stuck in his pockets.

"We weren't friends, if that's what you mean," I said.

"Maybe you broke his neck?" Scirrano said.

"I'm not in the neck-breaking business," I said.

"I dunno, Pete," he said. "You look like you could be a pretty dangerous character to me."

"Yeah," Higgins agreed. "Who you been mixing it up with?"

I wondered just how much of what I knew I should volunteer about Iris Mitchell, Robbie Provot, Tony Mally, and the late-night war over the custody of Dixie Jean Evans.

I had had an eventful few days, and figured a detailed explanation of each of the incidents could chew up the rest of the afternoon. I didn't know if Thady & Company, Tony Mally and whoever had reported my activities of the night before to the police. I assumed if they had, Scirrano and Higgins would have said something. If not, I would be opening another can of worms best left closed.

I wouldn't withhold information that I thought would be critical to a police investigation, but I didn't want to volunteer more than I felt necessary. I decided to hold back and see if they were interested enough to follow with good questions.

If they weren't on the Ivy Mitchell investigation one-hundred percent, I was, and I didn't want to get sidetracked in a pile of paperwork that would accomplish nothing more than keep a file clerk in a job.

"Would you believe somebody's grandmother," I said.

"Grandmother?" Scirrano said, laughed. Higgins joined him.

A young officer came out the kitchen door. "Yo, Hatch," Scirrano said.

"Yes, Sir."

"See if you can find three chairs inside that the dust-up people are finished with, and bring them out here."

Hatch responded with enthusiasm, hurried back inside.

"Maybe we should find out what this counter-punching grandmother was up to when the little guy was getting his neck realigned," Scirrano said.

I shook my head. "Marbles changed channels for the last time within the last hour, not much more, probably less. I know where she was during that time. It was a long way from here."

"What makes you think it happened that recently?" Scirrano asked.

"When I first got here, I went in the back way, through the kitchen. The refrigerator door had been left open, and there was still some condensation on a pitcher of tea, or soda, or whatever it was. The room was too hot for it to have stayed cool very long."

"Why do you think the refrigerator door was open?"

"I don't know," I said. "Maybe the killer was here when I pulled up in front, and slipped out the back door in a hurry. I guess he forgot to shut the door, or didn't give a damn whether it was open or not."

"You see any cars in the driveway or on the street that seemed out of place?"

I thought for a minute, pictured my drive down the street. "Nothing caught my attention," I said. "Then again, I've never been here before."

"How many cars were in the driveway, or nearby on the street?"

"Just the one with the banged-in door. Other than that, none that I remember." I looked around the yard. At the back of the property there was a chainlink fence that separated the zoo property from the houses at the dead-end, west end of the street. "Maybe he jumped the fence and went through the zoo? Parked on the next block, and walked through the back way."

"That makes sense." Scirrano nodded as he looked at the back of the property. "You want to make a guess who twisted his head?" Scirrano asked.

"Not yet."

"You think this killing is tied to the Ivy Mitchell death?" Higgins asked.

"It seems likely," I said. "Marbles spent a lot of time at the place where Ivy worked. His girlfriend, Nordy, the woman you saw out on the front lawn, also worked there."

"Speed Stick T's?"

"Yeah," I said.

"You think there's any way the little back room inside is tied to the fun and games at Speed Stick T's?" Scirrano asked.

"I don't know. Maybe," I said. "If you haven't already noticed, his girlfriend was not a stranger to the camera."

"We noticed," Scirrano said. "Did you toss the photos around on the floor, Pete?"

"I didn't touch anything," I told him. "You found them in the same place I found them."

"I didn't really figure you would spoil a crime scene."

"There was a stack of photos on the cabinet," I said.

"Yeah?"

"Think I could get a quick look at them?"

Scirrano shook his head. "Sorry."

"Could you tell me if Ivy Mitchell was in any of the photos?"

"She wasn't," Higgins said. "But the cutie doll out front sure spent some time under the lights."

Hatch returned with another officer and three chairs. Scirrano thanked them and scooted them back inside. We settled in the chairs.

"What did Marbles give you?" Higgins asked.

"A name."

"What name?"

"Little Sister," I said.

"She work at the strip joint?" Higgins asked.

"No," I said. "That would be too easy."

"So?" Scirrano said.

"So, Marbles told me that Thady was into more than just paying dancers to dance," I said.

"That's no surprise, Pete," Scirrano said. "How does this Little Sister fit in the picture?"

"Marbles said Thady and Little Sister did business."

"So, she's into women?" Higgins asked.

"No," I said, shook my head. "Marbles said she's into soliciting for her brother."

Scirrano began writing in his notebook. "This is getting very weird, Pete."

Higgins put on his best cop-face, leaned forward in his chair. "What about the brother," he said. "You got a name on him?"

"I didn't," I said. "That's why I came back today."

"Didn't, don't," Scirrano said. "No games, Amigo. You got a name, or no."

"When I was in the front yard with Nordy," I said, looked at Higgins. "You said it was fine for me to be with her."

Higgins nodded. "So?"

"So, she let slip the name 'Doc.'"

"Doc?" Scirrano said. "That's it?"

"That's a start," I said. "It's more than I had an hour ago."

Both Higgins and Scirrano wrote in their notebooks.

"So, how about it guys? I'm doing all the talking," I said. "How about a two-way street here. I give the name, now it would be nice if you could tell me if this nickname fits anywhere that you can think of."

"The name doesn't do anything for me," Higgins said.

Scirrano agreed. "Popular nickname, but connecting it with anything like this," Scirrano said. "I really can't think of anyone I've busted over the years with that name."

"Sorry, Pete," Higgins said.

"An everyday name," I said. "Now, all of a sudden, nobody wants it."

"We'll keep trying," Higgins said.

"Meanwhile, what about the strip joint?" Scirrano asked. "You talk to anybody there?"

"Of course," I said. "I talked to Thady first, then one of the bouncers who thought grandma shouldn't have all the fun, and who trashed my ribs and cheek bones a bit."

"He got a name?" Higgins asked.

"Tony Mally," I said. "We mixed over a dancer who wanted to leave without his permission."

"Who was?"

"Ivy's roommate."

Higgins checked his notebook. "Dixie Jean Evans?"

"Yeah."

"So what happened."

I shrugged. "I convinced him she should leave with me."

"That's it?"

"That's it."

"What about the guy with the broken neck?" Scirrano asked. "You think he would have given more names? Maybe a face, or an address?"

"That was my hope," I said. "I came here to try to convince him to quit playing games."

"Maybe he played a game with the wrong person today?"

"Looks that way."

"Pete, you seem to be a step ahead of us on both deaths," Scirrano said. "Mind if I make one more pass on some of the things you've told us before you split?"

"No problem," I said. "But I doubt I'm ever ahead of you on a murder investigation, Joe." I smiled.

He nodded a 'thank you' for the complement. "So, Marbles told you Ivy was in a money triangle with Thadington, someone called Little Sister who solicited for her brother, and a brother who doesn't like publicity, who calls himself Doc?"

"That's right," I said. "Except, Nordy gave me the brother's name, not Marbles. And she was hysterical when she let it slip. I don't know how much we should rely on it."

"Doc was with her the night she died?" Higgins asked.

I nodded. "All my energy is pushing me in that direction," I said.

Higgins flipped pages in his notebook. "So the only people who would know him are Thadington, his own sister, and Ivy?" Higgins asked.

I shook my head. "No, I don't think so," I said. "Thadington may just have known the sister, not the brother. Although I have a gut feeling Tony Mally figures somewhere in this mess."

I sat facing the back yard, and as we talked, I noticed two children at the back of the property. Carnival time was at hand. "There's trouble," I said. Higgins and Scirrano turned and saw the children.

Higgins jumped up, "You children, run along home," he said. He walked to the back of the property.

"Higgins," Scirrano said. "How about you go in and get somebody to dust that fence before it gets spoiled."

Higgins nodded and went quickly into the house.

"Let's walk back there and keep it clean while we talk," Scirrano said.

"Sure." We walked slowly to the back of the property. The children were gone, but neighbors were standing in yards on both sides of us. But the yards were large, and we were far enough away that they would not overhear our conversation.

"Penny for your thoughts, Pete," Scirrano said. We stood near the fence.

The sun was full in my face, hot. I missed the cool shade of the old tree. "Sure," I said. "Something about this bothers me."

"Shoot," he said.

"Let's say Thadington set Ivy up for a night of pain," I said.

Scirrano reached down on the ground and picked up a small, dry twig. He broke it into pieces. "So?"

"He did that for money."

"Keep going."

"Then, why would he kill the little guy inside?"

"To shut him up once and for all," he said. "To get some photos."

"I don't think so," I said. "Thady would just demand the photos. If anyone got stupid, he'd put one of the bouncers on him. Break his fingers."

Scirrano tossed the broken pieces of wood away. "Or his neck."

"We know from the photos that his girlfriend is close with what's going on," I said. "If she thought Thady had killed Marbles, she would be either furious or frightened."

"Rock and Roll, amigo," Scirrano said.

"So how about we put this in the puzzle." I wiped my face with a handkerchief. It came away from my forehead dripping wet. I wished Scirrano would suggest moving back into the shade.

"Before I came here, I talked to an auto mechanic, a cousin of Ivy, who told me he went to the strip joint a few weeks ago to see Ivy, to try to get her to quit her job," I said. "Anyway, he told me when he was there, Marbles tried to hustle some action. He said Marbles made some heavy claims about the women he ran, and what they could do to make you happy."

"Then, maybe it was this guy, not Thadington, who did business with this Little Sister," Scirrano said.

"Now we're thinking alike, " I said. I patted my forehead lightly, thought a minute. "I think that little weasel almost took me out of the game by putting me on Thady, when it was him I should have been after all along."

He nodded. "Hard to argue with."

"I just never saw Marbles as being anything more than a two-bit snitch," I said.

"I'll bet you never saw him as a film-maker either," Scirrano said.

I shook my head. "It must have been this guy Doc, or his sister, who came around here before me, and made sure that Marbles would never be able to finger him or his sister."

"Always said you should have been a cop, Pete." Scirrano opened his notebook, brushed through a few pages.

"So after Ivy died, this guy sees an opportunity to blackmail Doc and his sister," I said. "He figures there is plenty of money around."

"He underestimates the brother, sister duo," he said, "and ends up dead."

"Very," I said.

I felt the sun burn into my clothes, felt sweat soak my shirt. "You up for another story?" I asked. "Only this is just between you and me. Okay?"

He nodded. "Unless it's against the law."

"It's against the law, but I haven't pressed charges," I said.

"Now I'm interested," he said.

"Last night, I came home rather late, two people were waiting for me. They threw me out my third-story apartment window," I said. "I assume they wanted to kill me."

"Is that how you got banged up?" Scirrano asked.

"No, I was lucky enough to land on a pile of leaves and cuttings the gardener had piled under my window," I said. "That broke my fall."

"What does it mean to you, Pete?" Scirrano asked.

I shook my head. "I'm not sure. Perhaps somebody thinks I'm getting too close," I said. "Except that's the way my investigation has been going, I don't see myself as a threat. Unless I'm closer to something than I realize."

"Do you have any notion who they were?"

"I know one was Tony Mally. I don't know who the other person was," I said. "Something in me says when I find that out, I solve the mystery. Meanwhile, I hope we don't get any more surprises like the one inside. I feel like I should have thought to come here with questions for Marbles sooner, and maybe he would still be alive."

"We both feel that way," he said.

"He was a little jerk," I said, "but I don't like to see anyone get that kind of treatment."

Higgins and a technician with a finger print kit interrupted. "You want this fence dusted, Lieutenant?" the technician asked.

"Yeah, we think someone jumped it. If they did, they might have grabbed hold of that rail," Scirrano said. He pointed to the round galvanized crossbar.

"You got it, Lieutenant."

"Sorry to break in," Higgins said. "But the troops are starting to walk into each other. Maybe you could go in and get them moving with a purpose."

"I'll be right in," Scirrano said.

"Also, the crowd is getting a little rowdy," Higgins said. "You want me to put some pressure for quiet?"

"No, leave things on the street alone unless it looks like somebody is interferring."

"Okay," Higgins said. "See you around, Pete."

I nodded, turned back to Scirrano. "Thanks for the therapy session, Joe."

"Watch your back, Pete," he said. "Tony Mally bothers me mucho. If you have mixed with him twice and walked away, I wouldn't advise you to look for it to happen a third time. Don't turn your back on him."

"I hear you," I said, and thanked him. "Got to get moving, hellhound's on my trail."

"Don't leave town without giving a goodbye party," Scirrano said.

"Thanks again, Joe," I said as I walked around the side of the house, jumped the yellow ribbon and walked quickly back to my car.

Chapter 23

I drove away from the crowd, relieved to be leaving behind the dark world of dirty little rooms, dirtier lives and death. Instead of heading home, I turned south, headed to the zoo. I passed a crowded school bus that was just leaving as I pulled into the parking lot. There was a ticket booth at the far end of the lot. I saw a uniformed security guard near the booth working on paperwork. I parked, walked over to him.

I said, "Hello," told him I was a reporter. "I hope you can help me. I'm looking for a man in an expensive car who would have been parked here only a short time, between eleven and noon."

"How expensive?"

"Very," I said. "Something in the Mercedes, BMW price range."

"I don't think so," he said. "I only remember seeing two cars in and out of here around that time. Both came in just after the school bus, the one that just left. I'm always extra careful when kids are here. Don't want any problems with them messing with visitors, or visitors messing with them. If you know what I mean."

I told him I did. "Could you tell me about the people, and the two cars that were here?" I asked.

"Sure can," he said. He put his work aside. Put his pen in a plastic shirt pocket protective sleeve with the name of his security agency printed on it. "Elderly couple in a green Tercel, came at about ten-thirty," he said. "And a young woman, quite a looker, drove a white Mustang, was here about a half-hour. Left about the same time as the Tercel."

"Could you describe the woman for me?" I asked.

"Sure could," he said, broad-smiled the memory. "She was a nifty blonde, with tight-skirted wiggle enough in her to get her arrested."

"Sounds like she could have had you," I said, "if she played her cards right."

It was a short time before he got the joke, then he laughed for more than it was worth. "That's a good one," he said. "She sure could have," he laughed and winked at me.

"You said a white Mustang?"

"Yeah," he said, lit a cigarette. "I'd say it had some miles on it though."

"What makes you say that?" I asked.

"I don't know," he said. "I guess because she was such a sharp dresser, but the car was dirty as all get out."

"Good observations" I said. "I didn't catch your name."

"Charlie," he said, blew smoke over his shoulder. "Charlie Sloat. Been a security guard here for nearly seven years. Never had a bit of trouble on my shift."

"You log license plates?" I asked.

"Sorry," he said, "not if they don't cause trouble, or park in a fire zone."

"One more question if you will, Charlie?"

"Sure." He leaned forward, watched me write in my note-book. "That's right. You're a good speller."

"Thanks."

"Wife calls me Slow Boat," he said, and laughed.

"About the elderly couple, could you describe them?"

"Somewhere in their sixties. Man had a walker, and she helped him some. I believe he'd had a stroke of some kind," he said. "My dad had the same. Still, he lived thirty years beyond."

"The Tercel?"

"Old, but clean as a whistle," he said. "Now if that's about all, I need to get back to my paperwork."

I told him that was all, and thanked him for his trouble. I went back to my car with the name "Little Sister" on the edge of my tongue. I thought about the "nifty" tight-skirted blonde with a wiggle. In a white Mustang. There was something to think about.

I drove over to Flagler Drive, where the trees swayed gently in the light Atlantic breeze, and the open waters of the Intracoastal sparkled in the afternoon sunlight.

I drove north, to the place where the investigation had started, the place where Ivy had been left: alone, dead, or perhaps near death, soon to die.

As I drove, I tried to think of the reasons someone would have left Ivy where she had been found. Given the unusual nature of the place, I thought if I could figure out how she got there, I might be able to hunt the killer in reverse: from the rocks at the edge of the seawall, backward, to his deadly boudoir. That left me with either sky, land, or sea as choices.

It seemed illogical to spend time trying to develop any kind of a passing airplane theory. On land, she might have been brought there by a car, however, the car would have had to double-park on Flagler Drive, someone would have had to take her body out of the vehicle, carry it to the seawall, and dump it over the side. If someone was going to dump a body from a car, there was no shortage of darker, quieter, safer places from which to choose.

If she had died nearby, in a neighborhood house, it seemed appropriate to apply the same reasoning. This was an affluent area, where everyone owned at least one car. It did not seem likely that someone would chance getting caught carrying a dead body around the neighborhood.

With sky and land eliminated, I was left with water. Nothing else seemed reasonable. I was looking for either a very small boat, or a very large one. Or both.

Given the geology of the place Ivy was found, a small boat seemed most logical. However, it did not seem reasonable to assume anyone had planned an evening of pleasure, given the nature of the pleasure, in a small, open boat floating around the Intracoastal.

In the final analysis, I determined my best bet was that a rich guy named Doc, who owned a yacht, had had the best time of his life with a young stripper until he found out that sometimes people die when you abuse them. And if they die on your watch, things can go wrong in your life as well -- even if you are rich, spoiled, and sick.

Doc must have panicked, felt he had to get the body off his boat immediately. He put her body in an open tender, covered it with a tarp, lowered the boat into the water and looked around for the nearest, darkest place to get rid of the body as quickly as possible. I remembered a nearby street light had been out the night we found Ivy. Maybe that was what attracted him to that spot, the nearest, darkest place he could find.

If I was right, my next step would be to find the marina or wherever the yacht was, or had been, tied.

I slowed to a near stop when I reached that stretch of seawall where this investigation had started. There were a number of marinas on both sides of the Intrcoastal that could accommodate large yachts. The nearest I could see from where I was on Flagler, was on the Palm Beach side of the waterway, near the bridge over the Intracoastal. I decided to begin my search there.

I drove to the bridge and turned right, onto the east ramp that would take me into the privileged world of Palm Beach society, where Old Money and New Money did its best to ignore the fact that much of the world had no money, and where, occasionally, a rodent was to be found gnawing at the threadlike infrastructure of superiority.

As I drove across the bridge, I passed the small building where the bridgetender kept watch. It had open views of the Intracoastal on both north and south sides. I looked down the coast, and saw the place were Ivy had been found.

I turned right, off the bridge, drove past yacht brokers on the left and a small, manicured waterfront park on the right. I pulled into a parking space. I was looking for a night-crawler named Doc, and I hoped he and his boat were close by, that there was someone around who knew where he was tied.

The marina was quiet. The only person around was a young fellow in a uniform with the name of a ship on the sleeve of his white shirt. His pants were white, and like his shirt, pressed sharp. He was scrubbing the side of one of the yachts. He worked with a long-handled, short-bristled brush, pail of suds, and a hose of running water.

I walked over and stood next to him. "Lotta boat for a brush," I said.

"Yeah." He kept working, turned his back to me.

"Sorry to bother you," I said. "I'm looking for a fellow I've been told might have a yacht tied up here."

He turned and looked at me in a way that made me feel self-conscious about my, it's-been-a-long-day, wrinkled clothes.

"My employer frowns on my making the acquaintance of people walking around the docks, asking questions." He pointed at the marina office. "If the guy in there was doing what he gets paid to do, rather than watching a tennis match, he would be asking you what you are doing here, or calling the Palm Beach Police, and letting them ask you."

I looked over at the small building. I could see a man sitting back in a chair, feet on a table, with his back to one of the two large front windows. A television screen glowed at the back of the room.

"It would be a wasted call," I said. "I get paid to ask questions."

"You a cop?" He dipped the brush in the pail of water.

"I'm a reporter."

"Daily News?"

I laughed. "Do I look like I work for the Shiny Sheet?" The Palm Beach newspaper that featured coverage of Palm Beach society, celebrity fund-raisers, charity balls, that sort of thing.

He shook his head. "Not really."

"My name is Pete Krekow." I showed him my newspaper identification.

"The answer is still the same. Especially when I have this uniform on. I can only tell you that 'My employer frowns on my making the acquaintance of, etc., etc.'"

"Sure." I looked over at the office. "Maybe the fellow who majors in tennis will be more cooperative."

He shook his head. "I don't think he will be."

"Why's that?"

"Because he likes his job," he said. "Like me, he's paid to serve and protect."

"Then we all want the same thing," I said.

He put the brush in the pail and wiped his wet hands with a dry cloth. "This yacht you're looking for have a name?"

I shook my head, told him I didn't know the name of the yacht. "I'm looking for a fellow whose friends call him Doc," I said. "I'm told he owns a yacht that he ties up at one of the marinas in the area."

"The people who own these floating mansions don't spend much time walking around the marina introducing themselves to the folks who wash them," he said. "Even so, I've never heard that name around this marina, or any other."

"Thanks just the same," I said.

"Sure," he said.

I started to walk away, then stopped. "How about the name of a yacht?" I asked.

"Doc?" He scratched his head. "Tied around here, eh?"

"Please," I said. "Can you think of any boats with that name?"

"Well, we just got back from a run around the Riviera yesterday, so I don't know if they've been around lately." While he talked, he picked the brush up and worked it in the bucket, standing sideways to me. "I can think of three."

He stopped working the brush, looked off over the water. "There's one from Westport, Connecticut, called Here Comes The Doctor. I don't know that I've ever seen it this far south. The boats I know best are Doc's Girl, she's from somewhere on Long Island, Montauk maybe, and there's one from Portland, Maine, called Doctor Midnight. That's it."

"Thanks," I said.

He went back to his scrubbing. I crossed the asphalt parking lot, then the soft lawn of the lovely little park. I walked up the sidewalk that led across the bridge. When I got to the small building where the bridgetender kept watch, I found the door partially open.

I knocked and stuck my head in. "Hello?"

It was a one-room structure with a small console that I assumed operated the bridge spans on one side. On the other was a small table with a lamp, some assorted magazines and books, and a telephone. A hefty man wearing a grey cowboy shirt with the sleeves rolled loosely above his elbows, was sitting in a wood chair by a far window, reading a book.

"Sorry, my friend," he said. "I forgot to hook that chain. I'm not allowed to have anyone in the building."

I stayed outside. "That's no problem," I said. "I'm a reporter for the News & Journal."

He brightened, stood and walked over to the door. "Doing a story on bridgetenders?"

"No, actually, I'm working on a story about the young woman who was found dead Monday night," I said, and pointed across the bridge, south to where we had found Ivy's body. "She was found against the seawall, over there."

"Yeah," he said. "I was on duty that night. I remember the commotion. I was real sorry to hear someone died there."

"Well, she didn't die there," I said. "Somebody killed her, then dumped her there."

"That right? Don't remember reading that in the paper," he said.

"You will," I said.

"I'll be damned."

I held out my hand. "I'm Pete Krekow." We shook.

"Al Salta, friends call me Rusty," he said. "What can I do for you?"

"Well, Rusty, first of all, I'd like to ask if you saw anything suspicious Monday evening. I'm thinking about a small boat that you might have noticed spending time over there, by the wall. Or a large one that left later at night than one might expect."

"That's a tall order," he said. "I don't know that I can help you there. I mean, there's nothing unusual about a small boat being out at night. It's well-lighted, safer than being in a car. As for a big one, no, I don't remember anything unusual, but again, they run all sizes, all day and all night."

"I understand you keep a record of boats that you raise the bridge for," I said.

He walked to the console and patted a large book next to it. "Every boat I open for goes in this book."

"Well, if I asked a few names," I said, "think you would know if they were around Monday night?"

"For sure." He opened the book, and turned the pages.

I got out my notebook and read the names, "Here Comes The Doctor, Doc's Girl, and Doctor Midnight."

He shook his head before he finished. "Not on my watch," he said. "Felix and Maria cover the other shifts. You want to give me a minute I could check a few days."

"I'd appreciate that," I said. "How about Friday through Tuesday?"

"No problemo," he said, and scanned pages quickly. "There aren't really so many that it would be hard to spot any of the boats you named." He turned pages for a minute or so, then shook his head.

"Nothing?" I asked.

"Not a thing," he said. "You're looking for the name 'Doc' in there somewhere, right?"

"That's right," I said.

"That's what I guessed," he said. "Nolo boato. Sorry."

"That's okay," I said.

"Listen, why don't you give me your office number," he said. "I see or hear anything, I'll call right away."

"I would appreciate that very much," I said. "How about, would you let me go through the last few weeks and write down the names of any boats I think might fit the bill for the craft I believe I'm looking for?"

He shook his head. "I don't think I can do that. I've never had anyone outside state or federal employees see my books," he said. "I'm real nervous about this, and frankly, the only reason I'm doing what I am, at least without clearing it with a phone call to my superior, is that you're a reporter working on the death of a young woman.

"I'd sure hate for anybody to come back to me later and say her killer got away because I followed rules too closely, made that call, found out you have to get a court order to see these records."

I told him I appreciated the position he was in.

"How about, I'll look through the book," he said. "I can search a couple of weeks in no time. That's the best I can do right now."

"Would you mind if I waited around while you looked?"

"Well, I'd prefer you didn't," he said. "Where you parked?"

"Down by the park," I said.

"Look, you take a slow walk down there, look in a couple of store windows, then drive slowly over the bridge," he said. "I'll know by then. If I see anything that looks like the name you're looking for, I'll flag you down. If I don't, you can call the office, it's listed under Florida, comma, State of."

"Sounds like a good game plan," I said.

"Don't tell anyone we talked, okay?"

I told him I wouldn't, and started walking slowly back down the bridge.

I took my time walking back to my car. I did like Rusty suggested, and looked in the windows of a yacht brokerage office. They displayed lovely boat models. I walked down, past the marina, then turned and came back to my car.

When I got to my car, there was a short guy with a marina shirt leaning against it. He gave a surly look. "Your lucky day, Bruiser."

"That's the second time somebody said that to me recently," I said.

"Yeah, what happened the first time?"

"The guy tried to break my face," I said.

"Looks like he didn't do bad," the guy said.

"I guess, only right now, his eyes are closed swollen enough so he don't know that," I said.

"I'll bet," he said. "I could'a towed your car you know."

"Just waiting for Doc to get here with the girls," I said.

"What are you talking about?"

179

"I met a guy named Doc at a joint last night," I said. "He told me he had a big boat tied up here. Loaded with booze and broads. Said I should come on over for some action."

The guy shook his head. "You got the wrong marina. Nobody here named Doc," he said. "No booze, no broads."

"Look, I'm sure he told me here," I said.

"And I told you, no," he said. "So hit the road, Jalapeno."

I considered doing brain surgery with my fingers in his nose.

"I work for the newspaper," I told him.

"You sell subscriptions?"

"I sell trouble," I said. "I'm a reporter."

He lightened up a little. "So, what'da'ya want here?"

"I want to know which boat my friend is on," I said.

"Same answer," he said. "I know everybody here. There's nobody named Doc, and nobody who would be hanging out at a joint over there. The folks that live on these boats don't see fifty cent pool tables as being society."

I nodded, but didn't say anything. I got in my car, backed out and drove away without looking back. I drove slowly up the bridge. There was nobody behind me, so I stopped next to the bridge house.

Rusty came out, and stepped off the curb. I reached over and rolled down the passenger side window.

"Sorry," he said. "Nothing."

"Thanks for the effort," I said, and drove away before the cars I saw heading up the bridge behind me began honking.

Chapter 24

*I*t was nearly three-thirty when I pulled into the Rainbow
Apartments parking lot. Somehow it seemed like it should
have been later. I was bone tired. My meeting with Robin
was still three hours away, which meant there was time enough
to make a few phone calls, and maybe take a nap, before I had to
get showered and head to the junior college. I wanted to leave
early enough so that I could stop off and see Roger Filbert.

I had stopped at a Cuban restaurant on Belvedere Road,
bought a sandwich that sat in a brown paper bag on the seat next
to me. It smelled great. I was starved. The windows in my car
were open, and I felt the breeze from the ocean cool the warm air.
The hibiscus that edged the parking lot were in bloom, swaying
gently.

I cut the engine, and got out. I figured I owed myself a few
minutes of peace and quiet in the yard. So I took myself and my
sweet-smelling sandwich to a fine wooden lawn chair that sat
under a great shade tree.

I took the sandwich out of the bag and unwrapped the wax
paper around it. I was about to take my first bite when I heard a
rasping, clucking sound next to me. I looked to my left, saw an
old grackle walking back and forth. I threw him a piece of bread,
then took a large bite. It was great.

In a short time, my sandwich was reduced to crumbs. I said good-bye to my new feathered friend, who was working the crumbs, left him in the yard to wonder when I was going to make the next sandwich run.

I walked up the stairs to my apartment, where I found a note from Frankie taped to the door. It had "urgent" in big letters across the top, and Dixie Jean's name at the bottom. There was a Fort Lauderdale phone number.

I hurried into the apartment, went straight to the phone, dialed. The first ring seemed to take an eternity. Finally a woman with a soft voice answered, "Brave New World."

I wondered if that was the name of the strip joint Dixie Jean had driven down to, to look for work. I asked for Dixie Jean Evans. The soft voice asked my name.

"Just one moment, please," she said, and put me on hold.

After a long minute, Dixie Jean came on the line. She sounded out of breath, winded, or excited. "Pete?"

"Are you all right?" I asked.

"She was here."

"Who?"

"The woman you're looking for," she said.

"Little Sister?"

"In person," she said.

"Where are you?" I asked.

She said she was at a "new age dance club" where she was auditioning for a job. I wrote down the name, address, and directions on a note pad by the phone.

"I'm sure it was her," she said. "I only saw her once before, about a week ago. She was at a corner table with a little jerk who calls himself Marbles."

"We've met," I said.

"I remember because one of the dancers, a girl named Sheila, who was standing next to me said, 'Stay away from that table if you know what's good for you.' I asked her what she meant, but she had to go to work, and I forgot to ask later."

"Dixie Jean, I want you to be careful," I said. "You are dealing with a very dangerous woman."

"You're sweet to worry," she said. "She left about a half hour ago, and won't be back until around five."

"How do you know that?"

"I talked to her, and God almighty, was I scared," she said. "At first I thought she was trying to pick me up. Then I told her I was here to audition for a job as a dancer. She asked me where I lived, and I almost slipped and told her. That would have been curtains."

"What did you tell her?" I asked.

"That I just moved to Fort Lauderdale from Orlando. That was pretty safe, because there are some great joints up there," she said. "It turned out, or she hinted, she was interested in finding out if I had any friends who were blondes. Isn't that creepy?"

"Dixie Jean, stay away from her," I said. "I'll come down right away, but until I get there, be careful."

"I'm fine," she said. "I'm in a great mood. This place is clean, no crapola. They offered me a job that pays so well I'll only have to work three nights during the week, and every other weekend. The crowd is businessmen, no rednecks, no beer throwing."

"Sounds wonderful," I said. "Just stay put."

"I'll be here," she said.

"Dixie Jean, it just occurred to me," I said. "I think I know what she looks like, but I'm not sure it was she."

"I'll point her out when you get here," she said. "She doesn't know you either, right?"

"And I'd like to keep it that way," I said. "Is there any place close enough to the club that I could use to watch the front door. You could meet me there, point her out from a safe distance."

"Yeah," she said. "When I drove down this morning, I had breakfast at a little diner directly across the street. We could meet there in about an hour."

"I'm on my way."

I called Robin, but her tape machine answered. I didn't leave a message. I would get down to Fort Lauderdale sometime after five. I would make a few phone calls from my stakeout location. I was supposed to meet Robin and her friend in the college cafeteria at six-thirty. I could call her there, and make my excuses.

I changed quickly into clean clothes, took some extra cash from the little box I kept hidden in back of one of the drawers. I locked the front door and headed out.

I got to the diner in record time. Traffic had been light on I-95, and the place turned out to be near the north end of the county, not more than a hop-skip-jump from the highway.

Dixie Jean had been right, the diner was a nice little place. It had the kind of trendy pastels and chrome decor considered chic enough to bump the price of a meal twenty percent or so. There were only a few people seated. The lunch crowd was gone, and the dinner crowd had not yet arrived.

I looked around for Dixie Jean, but did not see her. I sat at a window table that had a neon flower in a polished wood vase, and a good view of the building where I expected Little Sister to make an appearance. I checked my watch; it was just ten minutes shy of the hour.

Brave New World had the ambiance of an upscale lingerie boutique, and was about the size of a department store. Dixie Jean was right, it had nothing in common with Thady's place. There was no red lacquered front door at this place. Instead, there were varnished hardwood doors and polished brass hardware. There was a doorman in uniform, and a valet station with young men in white Bermuda shorts and Hawaiian style shirts.

The only thing that would keep the after church crowd from pulling in for Sunday brunch was the sign above the varnished doors that touted a "Brave New World of New Age Dancers." There were two small murals of scantily clad ladies, one on each side of the sign. Given the nature of the entertainment, they were in rather good taste, more American impressionist than neo-smutist.

I took the menu from a waitress who chewed gum and had a faded, home-etched tattoo of a peace sign on the back of her right hand. Somehow she didn't fit in with the pastels, though the red neon played nicely on her yellow and green polished fingernails.

I ordered coffee, and told her that I was "waiting for a friend I expect along any time now."

"Your friend a foxy brunette named Dixie Jean?"

"Why on earth would you make such a guess?" I asked, felt my stomach muscles tighten.

She reached into an apron pocket and took out a folded piece of paper, and handed it to me. "She came by about fifteen minutes ago, told me to watch for a big guy, 'kind of beat up, but not bad looking.' That's just what she said. Also said you'd probably sit by this window."

"Thanks," I said, and took the paper. "Is that what she said?"

"The 'beat up, but not bad' stuff?"

I nodded. "Yeah."

"That's it," she said, winked, and walked away. As I watched her, I thought about Crystal, wondered how she saw me, how she would have described me to the waitress. I was pleased with what I had heard.

I unfolded the paper. Dixie Jean had written in a precise hand that she was sorry not to be there to meet me, but had agreed to do two or three sets before she headed back to West Palm Beach. She wrote, "You can call me here. If I can't come to the phone, leave a message with Sandy. I know a way to get you in and out without being seen. I go on break at six, DJE."

The waitress came back with my coffee. "Name's Wanda," she said, set the coffee in front of me. "You still waiting, or do you want to order something?"

"Wanda, I'm not sure," I said. "Give me a minute, okay?"

"Sure," she said. "I ain't leaving any time soon."

I was looking at the menu, wondering what meatloaf, fries, and gravy would be like in a diner that had neon flowers on the tables, when, out of the corner of my eye, I saw a white Mustang pull up to the valet station, and a young lady with blonde hair, and a tight-skirted wiggle get out. Charlie Sloat had been right, if this was she, that wiggle was about to send her to jail.

I watched her say something to the doorman, who smiled back, then she disappeared inside.

I took out my notebook and made some notes. I didn't see the license plate, but figured I would get that when I walked over with Dixie Jean.

"You a private dick or something?" Wanda asked.

I jumped, hadn't realized she was behind me. "Something like that," I said.

"Not allowed to say, right?" She walked around and stood next to me. "You look like a tough guy."

I shook my head. "I'm not very tough."

"Yeah, sure," she said, smiled. "I'll bet you're working for our friend."

"Wanda, how about an English muffin?" I asked. "Our friend can't get away until six, and if you don't mind I'd like to hang out here."

"Don't mind a bit," she said, wrote my order down and walked away.

I was anxious to get the show on the road. Knowing she was across the street really had me hot wired. "Beat up, but not bad," ran through my head. It sounded nice. I thought about that, wondered if it meant I should stay beat up.

I saw a public phone not far away, in a corner of the room that was near another window with a view of Brave New World. Wanda was standing next to the cash register, near the front door. I walked over and told her I had a long distance call to make, and needed some quarters.

"No problem," she said. "You want I should hold the toast until you're through making calls?"

"I've just got one to make right now," I said. "But thanks just the same. I appreciate you thinking of me."

"You got it," she said.

I took the quarters, thanked her, and went to the phone.

I called Roger Filbert, who answered while in the middle of a shouting match with Sally.

"Roger," I said. "This is Pete Krekow."

"Oh, Mr. Krekow hold on, please," he said, and half covered the receiver. "Sally, just run in the other room with your brother and watch television, and we'll go for a walk after this call." There was a bit more incidental conversation before he returned his attention to me.

"I'm returning your call," I said. "I tried a couple of times earlier, but you weren't home.

"Thanks, I appreciate that," he said. "Actually, there are two things I think might interest you. The first is, I haven't seen Dixie Jean since yesterday afternoon when she had to cancel dinner with me and the kids. She wasn't around this morning.

"The other thing is, and I hope you don't think I'm a snoop, but this morning I noticed a woman walking around Dixie Jean's place. Actually, I think she was trying to force open the back door when the kids and I walked around back and disturbed her. She seemed more than just a bit angry, left in a huff, without ever saying a word."

"I'm going to guess she was an attractive, well-dressed blonde, driving a white Mustang," I said.

"Sounds to me like you already know who I'm talking about," he said.

"Yes," I said. "Do you remember about what time that was?"

"Between ten-thirty and eleven," he said.

"Thanks, Roger," I said.

"Do you know where Dixie Jean is?"

"She had some trouble at her job and is staying with some friends of mine for the next few days. I'm sure she will be calling you as soon as she can."

"Well, that's it, I guess," Roger said. "If you see her before I do, please tell her I hope her troubles work out."

"I certainly will," I said. "So long, Roger."

I returned to my seat, and Wanda was efficient enough to have a hot buttered English muffin and a fresh cup of hot coffee in front of me in a matter of minutes. I said, "Thanks."

"My job," she said.

I munched the muffin and reread the notes in my notebook. The wait had begun, and I was, once again, learning patience. It's hard when you want to get moving, really, flat out running, to sit and watch, wait, praying the noose slips over the right neck, and doesn't come up empty once again.

Chapter 25

"I never could stand the little squirt, but I'm sorry to hear he died like that." Dixie Jean picked at some lettuce leaves in a bowl of tossed salad. "You really think she did it?"

"Yes," I said, kept an eye across the street while we talked, watched for a deadly blonde to come out, and slide into a white Mustang. "She parked her car in a parking lot around the corner, walked to Marbles' house, jumped his back fence, and went in through the back door. Then she broke his neck."

"She seems so delicate," Dixie Jean said. "I didn't know a woman could do something like that."

"Marbles was relaxed, he was in a chair, watching television," I said. "They must have known each other well enough for him to be comfortable with her being in back of him. He didn't offer any resistance. Apparently she simply grabbed hold of his head and twisted real hard, real fast."

"What time did it happen?" Dixie Jean put her fork down, and wiped her mouth with a napkin.

"Sometime between eleven and noon," I said.

She looked at me with concern. "I don't know, Pete," she said. "It was sometime around one-thirty when I first met her, down here."

"I drove down in just under an hour," I said, "She had plenty of time."

I watched people park their cars near the valet booth. Business was picking up across the street. "Dixie Jean, I just talked to Roger. He told me she was at your house sometime between ten-thirty and eleven."

"My house?"

"He said she was at the back door of your place. It looked to him like she was trying to force her way in," I said, toyed with my pen, nervous about frightening her. "He said she left in a huff when he and the kids disturbed her."

"She went from my house to Marbles, where she killed him?"

"That's right."

"I don't like the sound of that," she said.

"I don't either," I said. "And I'd like to know why and how she showed up at Brave New World the same day as you."

"It had to be coincidence," she said. "I stayed at the Rainbow last night, remember? And my decision to come here was a last minute thing. Frankie drove me to the airport and I drove here directly from there."

"Maybe she followed you here this morning, then drove back to your house," I said. My pen was in pieces on the table. I wondered how Dixie Jean would react to the name Doc.

"Why would she?" Dixie Jean asked.

"She could be looking for something," I said. "I don't know, not yet anyway."

"How would she know I was at the Rainbow?" she asked.

"Almost anyone at Speed Stick T's could have told her what happened," I said. "It was no secret we left together. She or Doc could have spent the night watching the Rainbow. In the morning when you left, followed you."

"Who in god's name is Doc?" Dixie Jean said.

I was relieved she seemed surprised. "According to Nordy, he's the brother of the lady we have been discussing," I said. I explained briefly what had transpired between Nordy and me. I told her that I believed Doc had killed Ivy. "Now he and his sister are covering the trail that leads from Ivy to them."

"Killed Ivy?" She looked pained. "Why? And why go to this much trouble to follow me. I was Ivy's roommate. That's it."

"That's quite a lot. Plus, you worked together," I said. "Maybe someone believes you were too familiar with what Thady and Marbles were up to with Little Sister."

"Thady and Marbles?" Dixie Jean said. "Pete, I don't know who took you for that ride, but I can tell you, without doubt, Thady, who is a royal slime ball, still had nothing to do with Marbles. Marbles was lower than slime."

"You're sure of that?"

"Thady wouldn't even have talked to that little jerk, much less have done business with him," she said. "No way."

"I was told that Thady found employment for some of the dancers. Ivy among them," I said. "And that Little Sister was her last employer."

Dixie Jean looked annoyed. "Pete, who told you that?"

"Marbles told me Thady was pimping some of the women," I said. "I put Marbles in the stew myself."

"Well, you're talking different recipes, I assure you," she said. "I know Thady offered extra pay and dancing bonuses, gifts, time off, things like that to women who would work off the books now and then. I don't believe Ivy was part of that."

"Maybe you're letting your emotions get in the way of your judgment," I said.

"No, I would have known," she said. "The girls talk all the time in the dresssing room about what they do, where, and who with. If Ivy was part of that, I would have known."

"What did they say about Little Sister in the dressing room?" I asked.

"What could they say? Nothing. Nobody knew her," she said. "Like I told you, I saw her once with Marbles, and Jeanie Karain told me to watch out. But I'm certain she meant that Marbles was known to be trouble, and whenever anyone saw him with a woman, there was a feeling like 'too bad for her.' I never guessed she was a predator."

Wanda came by and asked if there was anything we needed. I shook my head, Dixie Jean asked her to take her salad plate away.

"How about a little bread pudding?" Wanda said to Dixie Jean. "It's good for the tummy."

Dixie Jean declined at about the same time someone at another table gestured for Wanda to head over there.

I waited a minute for the tension to diffuse, then asked her to tell me what she knew about Tony Mally.

"Tony Mally went to work for Thady about a year ago," she said. "He's just supposed to be a bouncer, but in the past few months, he has made a lot of people very nervous about the way he has gained control of the management slots at the club. We lost a good floor manager, and two good assistants, and each time he was at the center of the controversy that drove them away."

"Why would Thady put up with that?"

"I think he's frightened," she said.

"Do you think Mally would have been doing business with Marbles and Little Sister," I asked.

"Could be. I think maybe I've heard Nordy say something about Mally being at their house, but I've never been there, and can't picture the three of them sharing a pizza and sitting around watching videos," she said, then frowned. "Well, let me rephrase that: sitting around watching videos that normal human beings would enjoy. Who knows, maybe Nordy, the little slut, entertained the troops. I don't know."

"There was a room in Marbles house where some nasty business was going on. Did you ever hear anything about that?" I asked.

"I've heard about it," she said. "You really saw it?"

I told her I had and gave a brief description of the room.

"Pete, I hope you're not heading toward saying that Ivy had anything at all to do with that scene," she said, looked a bit angry. "Ivy wasn't perfect, but she certainly was not involved with that dirty room, or with Nordy, or Marbles. And I have a hard time believing she would have had anything to do with this Little Sister or her brother."

"Somehow she ended up in a very strange relationship with this fellow Doc," I said.

Dixie Jean looked increasingly upset. I didn't want to say anything that would drive her away, back across the street. That would be dangerous for her, and leave me without information I needed.

"Dixie Jean, please, I need your help," I said. "I can't avoid talking about certain truths, and making you understand how important it is that you level with me about the lady everyone seems to agree was an angel. She ended on a pile of rocks in the Intracoastal waterway. There's no way that was an accident."

"Fine, just prove it," she said, tears in her eyes, got up and went quickly to the rest room.

While I waited for her to return, I watched the valets in the pretty shirts getting a run for their money. The traffic at Brave New World was all one way, in. I stirred more sugar in my coffee, more cream from the small chrome pitcher that had been wet with frost when Wanda first put it on the table.

Dixie Jean returned shortly. She sat quiet, with her head down. Her makeup was wrecked. Still, she was very lovely.

"I'm sorry I upset you," I said after a few minutes wait. "I was frightened you might walk away from here and underestimate the danger. It was probably a dumb way of saying I'm worried about your safety."

She didn't say anything, but looked up and soft-smiled.

"Last night you went to work because somebody called in sick," I said. "Who called you Dixie Jean, Thady?"

"Tony Mally," she said. "They were setting me up, weren't they Pete?"

I said it sure looked that way. "I thought Thady was involved because when I first entered his office last night, and saw you there," I said. "I thought you were in danger."

"I believe I was," she said. "Sometimes he's a real meatball, thinks he should get free samples. Usually you only have to slap his wrist. This time that didn't work, so I slapped him. He hit me back.

"That was when you came in. I'm glad you did. He was nuttier than I've ever seen him. You're right, I think he was going to hurt me. Still, that's the price you pay for motor conveyance."

"I don't get you," I said.

She tried a slight smile. "Last year, I took time off to travel in Europe. Get away from this. I was in Ireland, in a tiny village when I got a flat tire. There was only one man around. He was both adorable and ancient. So I changed the tire myself. While I changed it, he stood by his horse-drawn cart, and kept saying over and over, in a charming brogue, 'Price you pay for motor conveyance.'"

"What if the horse gets sick?" I said, laughed.

"Price you pay for horse-drawn conveyance," she said. "Which leads to your next question, right? If Ivy was a good girl, how did she end up with the man who killed her?"

"If you could help," I said, "I'd appreciate it."

"I'll try," she said. "I know that you know where she came from. Well, I came from that bad. And I wanted to get away as bad as anyone I ever knew. Anyone except Ivy. She worked harder than anyone, even me.

"She dreamed of something that was so far removed from where she came from that you couldn't measure the distance. She was a kid with a fever for something that, I suppose, may have been unattainable. She wanted what she couldn't have -- Palm Beach.

"She would pay almost any price to get there. Do you understand that Pete? The need to be someone other than yourself, so badly, to wake up one morning and be a princess."

I told her I did, though I wasn't sure really. To want to be a princess badly enough to die for it was to enter a realm of fantasy too far removed from my reality to grasp. I did not share my thoughts with Dixie Jean, though I had a feeling she would have agreed with me.

"She liked to tell of the time when she was a child, she and her mother went to a festival over on Flagler Drive. They sat on the seawall and looked across the water at Palm Beach, at the mansions and the yachts. You have to understand that was like going to Paris, London, Rome." Dixie Jean took a deep breath, let it out slow, "Did you know when she was in school, she won awards and scholarships?"

Chapter 25

I nodded, but said nothing. I thought of the Easter dress, the trophies, and I felt a hate swell in me as I looked across the street at the fancy strip joint, thought of Little Sister watching other young women, some perhaps reminding her of Ivy.

"When she was a child, she worked hard at her studies, thinking that was the key to opportunity, to a better life for herself and her mama. Then somewhere in time something happened, she never said what, but it ruined her vision of youth. Maybe you know what it was?"

Again, I nodded, remained quiet.

"She lost the dream of scholarship. She quit school, and replaced the dream with a need to earn money, a lot of money. She was still very young when she began dancing. Maybe as young as fifteen. I don't know how she pulled that off because the authorities are very careful, tough about that. Still, somehow, she beat the system.

"She was the best dancer I have ever seen. She had a routine she called her Sparrow Dance. It was beautiful."

Dixie Jean stopped talking. I thought she was going to leave the table again. Instead, we sat quiet while she fidgeted with her spoon, then squeezed lemon into her tea and stirred it slowly.

"Her fatal flaw," Dixie Jean looked at me, there was pain in her eyes. "She was attracted to wealthy men. As it turned out, they, in turn, were delighted to be seen with her. But never with the same understanding about the relationship. For her, it was a ticket to Camelot. For them, a chance to play with a beautiful, exotic dancer. For the most part, they used, then discarded her.

"Not long ago, I noticed a change in her. She must have come to realize that men from Palm Beach don't propose marriage to dancers. Not outside the ballet anyway. But she also understood they would pay plenty for a private Sparrow Dance. So if they wanted her, they would pay. And pay they did. You have no idea what a rich man will pay for an evening with a stripper."

"I'm only interested in what one of them paid," I said. "Though I suspect he still has not paid enough."

"Sometimes that's life, Pete."

"If there's any way," I said, "he'll pay for what he did."

"And Little Sister is the key?"

"You got it," I said. "She's still inside, but she has to come out sooner or later. I'll be here."

"Last time I saw her, she was settled by herself at a small corner table, watching a dancer called Harley Steele do her thing," she said. "Her routine is kind of rough around the edges, but I met her in the dressing room before we did our numbers, and I liked her."

"Is she a blonde?" I asked.

"Jesus, I forgot all about that," she said. "Is she ever. Bleached nearly white. Though not like Little Sister, who is bleached a little too blonde, if you know what I mean."

"I'm not sure I do," I said. "You saying she isn't a natural blonde?"

"She's a little toooo blonde for a natural blonde," she said.

"That's interesting," I said. "You said she hasn't tried to make small talk with you again. Did you notice if she talked to Harley Steele?"

"I didn't notice, but I doubt it," she said. "Steele keeps constant company, that is outside the dressing room and the stage, with two guys who, well, how can I say, complement her stage persona."

"Rough around the edges," I said.

"You could say that," she said. "Leather, chrome, chains, knives, nose rings." She laughed, finally.

"Sounds like they can take care of her," I said, and returned her smile.

"I have no doubt," she said.

"Anyway, I wish she would tire of watching the bumping and grinding, and head home so I can find out who she is, and where she lives."

"Pete, let's get this straight," Dixie Jean put her spoon down, raised an eyebrow, and pointed an index finger at me. "I don't bump and grind. Get it?"

"I get it."

"I dance. I dance with my clothes on. I dance with my clothes off. Either way, clothes on, clothes off, I am dancing," she said.

196

She softened her voice a little, lowered her finger. "When this investigation is finally over, my friend, you are going to come with me, across the street, and you are going to sit your butt down in front of what actors, musicians, and dancers call a stage. And I am going to dance just for you."

"Sounds good to me," I said.

"You're blushing," she said, and smiled. "That's so cute."

I shook my head. "No, I'm not."

"You are, too. And you did it last night, but I dismissed it at the time, thinking it was just the bad light in the alley," she said. "There you stood, you had just beaten the crap out of the meanest son-of-a-bitch in the valley, you were all busted up, bleeding, you were in the process of rescuing me from the devil, and when my gown came apart, you blushed."

"I guess I did," I said, lowered my eyes.

"You're a hard man to figure, Mr. Pete Krekow."

I shrugged. "I like you, Dixie Jean," I said. "I like the way you talk, and the way you care about people, children, and about your garden. I like that you are very pretty, and yes, I guess I am intimidated by that."

I noticed Wanda standing next to me. "That's the best line I ever heard," she said. "You watch out for this one. He's a heartbreaker."

"I think you could be right," Dixie Jean said.

"Speaking of lines," Wanda said, "get a load of the curves on that blonde."

Chapter 26

I looked out the window and saw the white Mustang parked by the valet station. Little Sister was just closing the car door.

"Here goes," I said, as I headed for the front door. Outside I had to force myself to walk to my car. I wanted to run, but didn't want to attract attention.

I backed out, pushed my gear shift into forward and spun the tires as I crossed the parking lot and pulled into the street. The Mustang was a few blocks ahead, but thankfully, had not disappeared. I jotted down the license plate number.

I did my best to follow at a safe distance, but, the rush hour traffic didn't allow me to give the kind of buffer I would have liked. After a series of lefts and rights, I was tossed into a sea of brake-screeching, tailgating, honking vehicles. All I could do was stay as close as possible, and hope she didn't notice my car.

I had been following her for about twenty minutes when she turned into a huge fashion mall. She pulled into a multi-storied garage connected to one of the department stores and drove up a spiral drive to the fourth, and top, floor.

She parked in a corner space. I parked at the other end. There were not many cars on the top level, so I waited until I saw her disappear into the garage elevator, then I got out, and went to the railing, looked down to the pavement below. I watched her exit the elevator and walk to the department store.

I thought about sticking with the car, then the notion that she might be meeting someone, her brother, for instance, decided the issue. I ran to the nearest stairway, and hustled down the steps.

I hurried through the front glass doors and looked around. I was in the men's clothing section. She was nowhere in sight. I walked quickly to the central part of the first floor and tried to determine from the departments where she might have gone. I saw sections for cosmetics, perfume, women's shoes. As I looked around, I saw her reflection in a three-story wall mirror on the opposite side of the escalator. She was just getting off the escalator on the second floor.

I went to the escalator and rode it to the second floor. The entire floor seemed to be women's clothing. There was some kind of sale going on, the floor crowded with shoppers, and tables and racks of clothing. I saw her on the far side of the floor, casually holding up dresses in a mirror. I hid myself behind a tall rack of dresses, looked at price tags, read laundering instructions, tried to look inconspicuous.

After about fifteen minutes of walking around, looking at dresses, skirts, jeans, blouses, looking at herself in mirrors, she had gathered an armful of clothes, and took them to a fitting room. I waited what seemed hours, until finally she emerged, empty handed.

I supposed either the clothes had not fit, or she just did not like the way they looked, whatever. She came out, walked to the other side of the floor, and began looking again.

I went back to reading tags. She went back to holding clothes up to the mirror. After a short while, she began talking to another customer, a young blonde girl, whom I judged to be in her mid-teens. I was too far away to hear what they were talking about. Whatever it was, they giggled often. Finally, they shook hands, she patting the girl's hand affectionately. The girl walked away.

Soon after that, she walked to what turned out to be a corridor. From where I stood, all I could see was a "rest rooms, lounges" sign, and an arrow that pointed away from the shopping area. I waited around the corner a minute or two, then walked around to the long corridor, which was active with sale shoppers who were taking breaks in the lounges or cleaning up, getting ready for another run at the tables and racks.

I walked to the end of the corridor. There was a dead-end T, with the men's room on the left and the ladies' room on the right. There was only one other door, and that had a large, red-lettered sign that warned it was an alarm that would go off if the door was tampered with.

I walked back to the open floor, and waited for her to return. I relaxed a little, knowing she was safely tucked somewhere where she could not run away. There was only one way out, and I was standing at the end of it.

About twenty minutes passed. I used the cover of a small group of people to walk back down the corridor. The alarm door was still locked. I went back to the open floor, collared a saleswoman who was walking by, and told her my sister had been in the rest room a long time, and I was worried about her.

"I'll check and make sure she's all right," she said.

"I'd appreciate if you didn't tell her I was worried," I said. "She thinks I'm overprotective, you know. She might be angry with me for sending you to look for her."

She smiled in a patronizing way. "I won't say a word, I promise."

I waited.

She came back rather quickly. Her face showed concern. "Are you sure your sister went to the rest room?"

I shrugged. "I'm sorry," I said. "That's where she said she was going."

"Well, the ladies' room is empty," she said. "Would you like me to page her on the intercom?"

"No, thank you," I said. "I'll go back down to cosmetics. She's probably there, waiting for me right now."

"Well, if she isn't, come back here, and I'll take you to customer service. I promise, nobody can hide from customer service," she said, and laughed. "They sure know how to hide from customers, but you can't hide from them. So, if she's not there, come see me. I'm Brenda, we'll find her for you."

I told her I appreciated her concern, and walked to the escalator, went back to the first floor, out through the men's clothing department, and up to my car. When I got there, I was not surprised to see that the white Mustang was gone.

I knew that she must have concealed a dress and hat somehow, changed in the women's room, put her hair up under a hat, and walked right past me. She was very good. I wondered how she had spotted me, had known I was following her.

I got in my car and turned the key. Nothing. I raised the hood, and saw that the spark plug wires had been cut. I was grounded.

I went back to the store, headed to the nearest public phone, which was on a wall just inside the front door, next to an elevator. I called Kay, got a dispatcher. I told him who I was, asked for Kay, said it was very important. He told me she was on the road.

I gave him the phone number, asked him to have her call as soon as possible. He said, "Will do." I hung up, waited.

The ring back was quick.

"Yo, Salleee." The voice had a nasal, bouyant twang.

"Pardner, you got the wrong number," I said.

"Yo, Pacho, don't gimme that shit, just put'er on," he said, his voice no longer nasal, more like the sharp edge of a piece of broken glass.

"This is a public phone," I said, read him the number, and hung up.

In a few minutes the phone rang again. "Kay?"

"What's up?" She cop-voiced an attitude.

"I need you to run a plate for me," I said.

"Run a plate? You're supposed to be with your daughter," she shouted. "Where the hell are you?"

I gave a brief explanation. "This plate is critical."

"Shoot."

I gave her the number, waited.

"White Mustang?"

"That's it," I said.

"It's a rental," she said. She told me the name of the rental agency. "Anything else?"

"Yeah," I said. "Listen Kay, I need you to run by the agency, use your badge to get me the name and address of the person who rented the car. Please."

She was quiet a moment. "How long before you're back at the Rainbow?"

"I'm not sure," I said.

"I'll do my best," she said. "I'll run by the school, get a message to Robin."

"Thanks, Kay," I said. "How about having her meet me at my place? I should be home by the time her class is over."

"Sure," she said. "If she still wants to see you."

"I'm doing my best," I said.

"Sure."

I called Dixie Jean, and told her what had happened. I told her the name of the mall and the department store. She said she would be over as quickly as possible.

"I'm sure somebody here will be able to tell me how to get there," she said. "It can't be very far."

"Thanks," I said. "I'll wait by the parking lot entrance."

"You sound really down, Pete," she said.

"I feel like an idiot."

Next I called the toll-free number on the back of my automobile association membership card. I told the association operator that my car had been disabled at a mall in Fort Lauderdale. I gave her the license plate number, make, and color of my car. I told her the name of the mall, and where my car was parked.

She was swift about locating a garage nearby that could help, but said there might be an hour wait, maybe more. I told her I had made other arrangements to get home, and if she would just give me the name and address of the garage that was going to tow, and repair it, I would pick it up in the morning.

She said she was sure that they wouldn't do repairs without a written authorization, and besides, I had to be there to give them the key. I told her I couldn't wait around, so I would leave the key on the front left tire, and go by the garage in the morning and see what needed to be done -- so much for the car.

Chapter 27

We turned onto the north ramp of I-95, and rounded the cloverleaf. "I have no idea how she knew I was following her," I said, noticed Dixie Jean drove fast. I checked my seatbelt, made sure it was tight.

"You're sure she's never seen you before?"

"Where could she have seen me?" I asked. "For god's sake, I just found out what she looked like a few hours ago myself."

"Okay, Pete," she said. "I'm on your side, remember?" She roared onto the highway, crossed two lanes of traffic, and cut ahead of an eighteen-wheeler.

"Yeah, I remember," I said, watched the city speed by. "Sorry."

"Where to from here?" Dixie Jean asked.

"When we get to West Palm, let's drive by and see if Nordy is back in the Saint Francis Street house yet," I said.

"Good idea," Dixie Jean said as she cut to the first, inside lane, and raised the speed. "She's got a pea for a brain, but if you tell her what you told me, maybe this time she'll be more anxious to help."

"If we should catch her there when we go by, I think that having you along will help put her at ease."

"Who knows," she said. "She's probably at work."

"Her boyfriend was just killed," I said. "She won't be at work."

"I suspect Nordy will make a quick recovery," she said.

"You don't like her, do you?" I asked.

"No, I don't," she said. "I'm a dancer, she's a little whore. We both work at the same place."

"You're an elegant lady," I said. "You'll never have to worry about having people confuse you with Nordy."

"Yeah?"

"Yeah," I said.

"Anyway, after we stop by Nordy's, if you have a favorite tavern near the Rainbow, we'll stop there," she said. "I need a drink, and I surely do owe you one as well."

"I wish I could take you up on that offer, but I have to head right home," I said, told her about missing my appointment with Robin, that they may be at my apartment, waiting for me.

"You don't sound thrilled," she said.

"I'm not," I said. "Her mother thinks the guy Robin is with is getting ready to steal her off to California. That's what the meeting is really about. Kay asked me to get together with them, and try to keep that from happening."

"How do you feel about it?"

"If Kay is right, I don't like it," I said. "But, between you and me, I'm not sure it's any of my business. And I don't even know if it's true."

"Well, if young love is involved, good luck, Pete," she said.

I shrugged, checked my seatbelt again. "Yeah."

She changed lanes. "I'm not driving too fast am I?"

"No," I said, figuring I had finally experienced what an F-16 pilot must feel on takeoff.

Dixie Jean came up fast on a slow-moving station wagon, she down-shifted, fishtailed as she changed lanes. I felt the rear start to slide, and watched her turn the wheel into it, hit the gas and roar out of danger. "Relax, Pete," she said, pulled in front of the wagon. "There we go." She hit overdrive.

I checked my seatbelt, put my feet forward, braced against the front wall under the console.

It was not long before the signs for our exit began to appear. Two miles, one, one-half. Dixie Jean changed to the outside lane as we approached the ramp. We pulled off the highway and drove directly to dear old Saint Francis Street.

The street was quiet. The police cars and emergency vehicles had vanished. We pulled into the driveway. The car with the sticker was gone.

"That's odd," I said, half to myself.

"What's that?"

"Doesn't look like a crime scene," I said. "There is nothing left to suggest that a few hours ago the police were all over this place, looking for a murderer. No crowds, no yellow tape."

"The place gives me an eerie feeling," Dixie Jean said.

"Yeah. I wondered how soon Scirrano and his men would be done here," I said. "If they would let Nordy return."

"Well, I don't know anything about police procedure, but I do know that this is Nordy's house," Dixie Jean said.

"Nordy owns this place?"

"I don't know if she owns it, or rents it, but she was here a long time before Marbles showed up on the scene," Dixie Jean said. "He moved in after his wife was busted. I remember because they made a big deal about it at work. Had a party, which we all thought was pretty tacky. I don't think many people showed up."

I got out, went to the front door and knocked. There was no answer. I walked around to the side of the house, but didn't see any light. I walked back to the car.

"It doesn't look like the police have locked her out," I said. "They must be finished. Anyway, time to head home."

We drove quickly across town, over to Flagler, and home to the Rainbow Apartments.

Chapter 28

Sheldon Lennox had a friendly smile. "Shell," he said, absently brushed strands of long black hair out of his face, rested his elbows on the wood table. "That's what my friends call me."

"Shell," I said. "Glad to meet you."

Robin hovered nearby, lit candles while Willie Dee tied ribbons around cut flowers he had placed in a large vase on the table.

We were at a quiet edge of the property, where Willie, who had a cache of emergency candles in his apartment, had taken Robin and Lennox. He had been talking to a night blooming jasmine next to the parking lot when they arrived.

Robin had introduced Lennox. When she noticed my car wasn't there, she told Willie about her mother coming by the school and saying they were to meet me at the apartment.

Willie had used good judgment, told Robin, or perhaps the jasmine, which, in turn, told Robin, that my apartment was minus a window and in a bit of a mess. He suggested they might better, "Plunder the brave knight's pantry," noting that a bottle of beer or two would be a welcomed addition, "and spread a feast yonder, at the edge of the kingdom."

Dixie Jean and I had arrived only a short time later. While introductions were going on, Robin and I had hugged, discussed the battered condition of my knocked-about face, then she introduced me to Lennox.

I heard Dixie Jean tell Robin, who had invited her to join the party, that she was going to take a bath and change.

"I'd like to thank you for this opportunity to meet you," Lennox said, blowing gently into a mug of steaming instant coffee that Robin had made. "Robin never tires of talking about you, in fact sometimes I wonder if I don't know more about you, than I do about her."

"There's a boring prospect," I said, pleased to hear that my daughter talked about me. "Robin tells me you're an actor." I opened a bottled water that was next to a basket of sandwiches that Robin and Willie had made and brought down.

"My students are the actors," he said.

I looked over at Robin, who was helping Willie Dee with another bunch of flowers. They laughed as he tied a ribbon around the stems, put them in a second vase. "How about Robin?" I asked.

"She has the talent," he said. "But acting is an iffy business. The greatest success often comes to those willing to dig in for the long haul."

"Can't there be a price to pay," I asked, "'for the 'long haul?'"

"Sure," he said, nodded agreement. "Sometimes it's too great a price. Sometimes it's best to walk away. I wish I knew how to teach that. I don't."

"How about you," I asked. "Bright lights? Pats on the back?"

"I'm always up for a pat on the back," he said, "but no bright lights. I don't try to sell the 'you could be a star' thing. Not to anyone, not even me."

"Sounds a bit cynical," I said.

"It's reality," he said. "Once upon a time I had dreams of fame and glory. Even went so far as to take a stage name. Looking back, that seems like a silly thing, but at the time, it seemed important.

"Then I woke up one morning and found I had to make a choice. I decided I needed security more than I needed dreams. It was my choice. I've never regretted it. Not yet, anyway." He smiled, showed nice dimples.

"You have a family?"

"Had," he said, "a wife." He stirred his coffee.

"Divorced?" I asked.

He shook his head, stayed with the spoon. "Drunk driver."

"I'm sorry," I said.

He looked up. "I was one day too late for my first AA meeting," he said. "I've been sober eight years."

"I admire that," I said.

I liked Mr. Sheldon Lennox, however, he seemed too sure, and as I looked at my daughter, she seemed too young, innocent. I wondered if Kay might be right, for the wrong reason.

"My dad raised me. He was a carpenter, a cabinetmaker. He and I spent weekends and summers working together from the time I was old enough to hold a hammer. He was my best friend," he said. "When I was a senior in high school, I lost him. Nothing of my youth was quite the same again. I left town, went away to college. At first I was lonely as hell. Then I discovered set building and design. It was a natural. I've been at it ever since."

"You teach set design?" I asked.

"Back home I do," he said. "Here it's only a small part of the introduction to theater. They think of it as an afterthought. The University of California has allowed me the latitude to include set and costume design as specialties. I got interested in costume when one of my colleagues said something stupid about real men not being interested in it. I've never liked statements like that. I began researching the history of costume, got hooked, if you don't mind the pun, and have been at it ever since. I teach both, but the smell of wood still thrills me most."

"Where in California?" I asked.

"Davis," he said. "It's a great campus for the arts."

"You're a long way from home," I said.

"I'm here for a semester," he said. "The chairman of my department is a friend of the president of Palm Beach Junior College. He asked me if I'd be interested in swapping positions with a staff member here. I said sure."

"What keeps you teaching if you don't believe your students have a chance at stardom?" I asked. "Why not point them in other directions?"

"I believe in theater, in art," he said. "I believe that from the study of acting, writing, painting, music, poetry, one gains a sense of the world and of one's self that is impossible elsewhere."

"Art for the sake of art?"

"I would have thought you would approve."

"I usually do," I said, looked at Robin. "Except when my daugher's future is part of the discussion."

"You prefer she go into medicine, law, business administration?"

"Yeah," I said. "A business office sounds better to me than a dingy New York apartment. I'd rather think of her having lunch with colleagues than skipping meals."

"I wouldn't argue with that," he said.

"Shell, maybe I've misunderstood something along the way," I said, watched Robin walk away from the table, head back to my apartment. "I was told you were encouraging Robin to return to California with you. Her mother is concerned. So am I."

"We've discussed the program at Davis," he said, sipped his coffee. "I'm a teacher, and that's part of what a teacher does, tries to get the best students to the best schools."

"Somehow, I think there's more to your relationship than that," I said.

"You're uncomfortable with that?"

I nodded, watched his eyes.

"I've never been in a position like this before," he said.

"That's a good start."

"I suppose if I were in your shoes," he said, "I would be uncomfortable also."

"Why don't you tell me about it," I said.

"Robin and I have become very close," he said, still stirred.

I was losing patience. It seemed to me that if Sheldon Lennox wanted my daughter, he should quit the shucking and jiving, and talk to me. Still, I kept my composure.

After a long silence, just about the time he seemed ready to continue, Robin came back, looked angry. "Mother is on the phone," she said.

I excused myself, went up to my apartment.

"Hello?" I said.

"It's me," Kay said. "What's he like?"

"I'm still trying to find out," I said.

"I hope you're not being wishy-washy," she said. "Just tell him to leave her alone."

"Did you find out who owns the plates?" I asked.

"Yeah, but I'm afraid it won't help," she said.

"Why not?"

"It's a corporate rental," she said. "I had one of the computer people at the station run it through the computer. Came back with a Connecticut address. He cross-indexed it, found it's a smudge."

"I'll take it anyway," I said, wrote the name and address of the company in my notebook.

"So what has he told you?" Kay asked.

"Kay, from the look Robin just gave me," I said, "I think you better let me go so I can explain why you called."

"Fine," she said. "Just remember, she's not going to California with this guy. That's final."

"Gotta go," I said, hung up, and walked back to the yard and directly to Robin, who I could see was about to let loose on me.

"Daddy," she shouted, stomped her foot on the ground. "How could you?"

Lennox, I noticed, continued to stir his coffee, stay out of the way. Willie finished a bottle of beer, opened another.

"The call had nothing to do with you," I said, walked to her and put my hand on her shoulder. "Your mother was running an identification check on a license plate I called her about just before I left Fort Lauderdale."

"This isn't something you and mother cooked up?" she asked.

"I just had my car destroyed, Robin," I said. "That's why I missed your performance, and was late getting here. Your mom was helping me find out who did it."

"You promise?"

I noticed how quickly she calmed. She was a lot like her mother that way, quick to anger, quick to settle back on soft smiles. I had always found that difficult to deal with. I looked at Lennox, who was watching his student closely. I wondered what he was thinking.

"Shell, you're about to stir right through that cup," I said.

He stopped the spoon, took a deep breath, said, "I've never seen Robin angry before."

"That was nothing," I said, laughed.

"Daddy, don't start," she said. "Shelly doesn't know when you're kidding." She looked at him with one of those innocent, "do-with-me-what-you-will" looks reserved for first love, and memory. I turned my head away, embarrassed to intrude on my daughter's romantic desires.

I looked toward Dixie Jean, who had just returned. She winked, sat near Willie at the other end of the table, opened a bottle of water.

"Robin never told me what a lovely lady you had, Pete," Lennox said.

"I never knew," Robin said with a sly smile.

"She's just a friend," I said.

"Some friend, Dad," Robin whispered. "She's dynamite."

I took a plate of sandwiches Dixie Jean passed down to me. "Thanks."

"Let's sit together," Robin said, sat next to Lennox.

Dixie Jean brought her water and an apple over and sat near me, motioned Willie to join us, but he hurried off.

"Interesting fellow," she said, Lennox nodded agreement.

"Willie Dee," I said, "is a gardener whose best friends are his flowers."

"Sir Willie," Robin said. "Gardener par excellence."

"Willie's an all-Ivy scholar with graduate degrees in medieval literature and language," I said, filling in some gaps. "He gave all that up to be a gardener."

"All-Ivy?" Lennox said.

"And if you don't believe us," I said, "you could ask his flowers." I heard Robin giggle.

"Wouldn't want to interrupt them," Lennox said, smiled.

Chapter 29

"She's still a kid, Sheldon," I said.

"I don't think so," he said, finally looked me directly in the eye. "I don't want to cross swords with you, Pete. But I have to say, your daughter is a woman now. She's no longer a little girl."

I shook my head, kept close with his eyes, leaned forward. "Shell, she just graduated from high school. She just packed away her senior prom dress, and closed her school yearbook," I said. I wanted to say more, but felt an anger rising that I knew wouldn't go anywhere, wouldn't accomplish anything. And really, he looked hurt, and that bothered me.

"There is nothing unique about a college student studying at a university in another state."

"There is when it involves shacking up with her teacher."

We were quiet, picked at our sandwiches. Finally Lennox said, "Pete, I want you to know, I really like Robin very much. I wouldn't do anything to hurt her. I don't think you're right, but I'll think about what you said."

I thanked him, and meant it. "I appreciate that."

Robin and Dixie Jean giggled as they walked toward us, across the yard. They were lovely together.

They rejoined us at the table, Dixie Jean took a sandwich from the platter "Yum," she said. "This is delish."

"Hope it wasn't impolite of me to slip out for a minute," Dixie Jean said. "In the last twenty-four hours I've gone to work, been assaulted, been rescued, been fired, been hired, danced a few sets. I've been up since dawn. I'm exhausted."

"There's no harm done," we agreed.

"Dad, you didn't tell me Dixie Jean is a dancer," Robin said, enthusiastic.

"Actually, I haven't had a chance," I said, noticed Dixie Jean seemed pleased with Robin's attention.

"I'd love to see you dance," Robin said.

"I'd like that too, darling," Dixie Jean said. "It may take you to drag your daddy along."

"You really haven't seen Dixie Jean dance?" Robin asked.

I wondered if Robin understood the nature of the dance business that we were talking about. "No," I said, smiled. "But I will, we will, if you'd like."

"Absolutely," Robin said. "And Shelly, too."

"And Shelly, too," I said, pleased that Robin and Dixie Jean were getting along so well. I admired the way Dixie Jean mixed easily in a group of very different people, few of whom she had met before that night. I watched her do that wonderful thing with her tongue as she ate, caressed the sandwich gently before putting a small piece in her mouth.

"Where do you perform?" Lennox asked.

Dixie Jean's answer began a cycle of conversation that drew them together with a series of questions, answers, and wide-eyed "Really's?"

While we talked, I watched Willie Dee, who had returned to primp the flowers on the table. I couldn't quite make out what he was wrapping around a mixed bunch of wild flowers, but it looked like a gold chain.

Lennox noticed my interest, and turned to see what Willie was doing. "Lovely," he said, sat forward, looked across the table. "Rather fancy for flowers, no?"

Willie was shocked. "We are not 'flowers,' sir," Willie said.

"Well said," Lennox answered.

I got up and walked over to Willie. "And he drapes his Lady Fair in the finest gold." As I got closer, I noticed the chain had a medallion on it. "Where findest thou this treasure, Sir William?"

Willie calmed some, "Below the window of a brave knight," he said. "We found it hidden amongst lost treasures of the forest."

"You found that in the compost heap?" I asked.

"We did, indeed, Sir Knight," Willie said.

"The one below my window?"

"The very same," Willie said.

"It looks real," Robin and Dixie Jean, both of whom sat closest to it, said.

I touched the medallion with my finger tips, tested its weight. "Mind if I take a closer look at this?" I asked Willie.

"Your pleasure, sir," Willie said, and handed it to me. "Alas, I fear you will find that a link in the chain, no metaphor intended, has been broken."

"Do tell," I said, turned it a few times, looked at the back. "This is gold, and the woman on the front is pretty."

I handed it to Robin, who was next to me. She looked at the back first. There was a gold stamp and an inscription "Alwen's Clew."

"Wonder what that means?" Dixie Jean asked.

"I wondered that myself," I said.

"Willie?" Robin asked.

"No clue," he said. "Though, a clew is a thread that guides one out of a labyrinth."

"A what?" Dixie Jean asked.

"A puzzle," I said. "A place where you can get lost, can't find your way out without help."

"One might better say, a maze," Willie said.

"Or a person," I said, took it from Robin, turned it over and noted a low relief profile of a young woman. The sculpting was exquisite, the woman lovely. I looked carefully at the face, at the smooth cut of the cheek, nose, chin. The long hair fell over her shoulders in ringlets.

I handed it to Dixie Jean, who took a deep breath when she saw it. "Pretty lady."

"Willie Dee found it in the compost heap below my window," I said. "The compost heap that broke my fall last night."

"Interesting," she said.

"You ever notice this on Tony Mally?" I asked.

"This isn't his style at all," she said.

"You're thinking this ties to your fall?" Dixie Jean asked.

"How many ways could a solid gold medallion end up on a compost heap below my window?" I said. "I wondered if that face rang any bells?"

"I figured that's what you had in mind," she said, thought quiet for a moment. "It's just an engraving, but it looks a lot like her."

"That's what I thought," I said. "If it is, it fits the puzzle."

"What puzzle is that?" Robin asked. "Is that the fall you mentioned when I first got here?"

I told her it was, and one of the people who might be responsible, "Though I can't be certain, this looks very much like the woman Dixie Jean and I saw this afternoon in Fort Lauderdale."

"The one who trashed your car?" Robin asked.

I nodded. "If it is, it means that I accidentally tore this from her neck when she and another person threw me out my window," I said. "Maybe when I twisted, it got tangled up with me."

"That would explain how she knew you were following her tonight," Dixie Jean said. "You had already met, though you didn't know that."

"I'm rather lost," Willie said, stood up so he could see the medallion again.

I told him that I believed this might be, indeed, probably was, a woman who sent someone to her death.

Willie reached over and touched the engraving lightly, like it held static electricity. "Imagine this pretty thing getting into that kind of mischief."

Dixie Jean and I looked at each other and smiled.

"In the last twenty-four hours," I said, "she has assaulted me, tried to break into Dixie Jean's house, broken Marbles Rydall's neck, and led me on a wild goose chase all over Fort Lauderdale, then trashed my car."

"May I see the medallion?" Lennox asked.

"Indeed," I said, handed it to him.

We watched as he took a small magnifying glass out of his pocket, looked long and close at both the front and back of the piece.

"This was made by Cartier," he said.

"You're sure?" I asked.

He nodded. "It has their imprint and a serial number. Actually, I've met the manager of the Palm Beach store a few times. We share an interest in late Victorian jewelry," he said, smiled. "Fin de siecle."

"Afraid my French is a little rusty," I said.

"End of the century," Willie Dee said.

"There you are," Lennox said. "Great time for theater and costumes and jewelry. I've been working on a paper on that. Really, Oscar Wilde and his pals left enough on the subject to fill an encyclopedia or two."

"Then your friend at Cartier would have a record of who the medallion was made for?" I asked.

"Oh yes," he said. "That's what the serial number is all about. Though, I'm not sure how forthcoming he would be with that kind of information."

"That's my job," I said, looked at my wristwatch. "How well do you know him?"

"Not well enough to call him this late at night," he said.

"Too bad," I said. "Any chance you could meet me at the store in the morning?"

"Be glad to," he said.

"I'd like to talk to him as soon as possible," I said. "I don't suppose the store opens until ten?"

"Ten sounds right," Lennox said, tried to cover a yawn with his hand. "However, I'm certain he'll be there a good deal earlier than that."

"What's 'a good deal?'"

"Eight," he said. "Eight-thirty at the latest."

"Why so early?" I asked.

"They lock nearly everything away when they close," he said. "They have to put it back on display every morning, which, I have a hunch, takes a bit longer than it does to put it away at night."

"Excellent," I said. "How about you meet me there at eight."

"In front of the store?" Lennox asked.

"It might be better for me," I said, "if we meet in the parking lot around the corner, on Lake Avenue."

"I know where it is," Lennox said, tried to hide another yawn. "It's getting late. We should head home."

Robin leaned against him, agreed.

I fought back a frown, thanked him, shook his hand. "See you in the morning."

"How about I give you my home phone number," he said. "If you should want to call, for any reason, feel free."

I thanked him, took the number that he wrote on a piece of scrap paper, and slipped it into my wallet.

I hadn't expected it, but Robin threw her arms around me and gave me a hug and kiss on the cheek. "Oh, thanks, Dad," she whispered in my ear. "Mother and Grant have been totally unreasonable. But I knew you would be on our side."

"All I want is for you to be happy," I said.

"Oh, you're so sweet."

"We better get," Lennox said. "Goodbye, thanks for everything. Dixie Jean, it was nice meeting you."

Chapter 30

We were alone.

"I don't know about you," Dixie Jean said, "I could do with a quiet walk."

I agreed, wanted to take her hand, but did not.

As we walked toward the water, thoughts of Dixie Jean and Crystal filled a page of recent memory: a collage of warm-toned smiles, of a lovely garden, a picnic at a football field, a partially open robe, brown hair with streaks of grey.

"Mind if we go to the place where you found Ivy?" Dixie Jean asked.

"Not at all." We crossed the street and headed slowly toward the Intracoastal. "You sure it won't upset you?"

She shrugged. "I don't know if this is the right time," she said. "Maybe there never is a right time." She wrapped her arm lightly in mine.

"Seems like the right time to me," I said, felt a rush of warmth.

"I'm angry with myself," she said. "I'm not a woman who plays games. I don't giggle for attention. I've never liked women who tease. I suppose, at first, I didn't believe you were different. So for the first time in my adult life, I got cute."

"Dixie Jean," I said, "you've been a lady in every way."

"Perhaps, but I want you to know that I regret embarrassing you," she said.

"I don't understand."

"Things like kidding you about blushing when my robe came open," she said, "and talking too much about my dancing, getting you in the front row to watch me, things like that."

"That's nothing," I said.

"I guess," she said. "It happened by accident, but I could have closed it with more determination. Instead, I watched you, wondered if the brave knight would act like the others, try to get his hands in my robe quicker than I could close it. Turned out he wasn't like them after all."

I looked at her as we walked, she looked up at me, we smiled. "I'm glad you feel that way," I said.

"Last night, before work, I was really upset about everything. I almost never stop off for a drink, but I felt like, with Ivy gone and nobody to talk to, I needed a drink and a friendly smile," she said. "So I stopped off at a place that is convenient to work, had a short martini and talked with a friend I have there."

"You met Crystal?" I asked.

She nodded. "She was anxious to talk about, 'this great man I met,' who went with her to the park to watch her kid play football," she said. "She really likes you."

"Thanks," I said. "It's nice to hear that."

"Pete, I've pulled your strings, and you've remained a gentleman. I appreciate that in you," she said. "You're a rare breed. An honest guy, with a heart that beats steady, and hands he keeps to himself. So I'd like you to know, I also really like you a lot. I don't know where I fit in the puzzle, but I do know if I'm there, I want to be there like Crystal, because I'm honest with you, not because I can take my clothes off faster." She put her head against me as we crossed Flagler.

We stepped onto the sidewalk and walked south, toward the place where Ivy had been found.

"I don't know what to say," I said, put my arm gently around her. "I would like you to know, when I think of you, I think of you like the first day we met. I remember the way your eyes and your smile reflected the bright colors of the flowers in your yard. You were beautiful."

We were soon at the place where I had found Ivy. "This is the place," I said.

We stood quiet, watched the current run, watched small waves wash over the rocks, heard them brush against the sea-wall. And somehow it seemed to me that Ivy became part of the silence, drew us together. I held Dixie Jean's hand, felt the coolness of her palm against mine.

"Is this a bad time to ask about Roger?"

Her eyes softened in the shadow carved from the light the streetlamp cast across us. "Roger's a sweet, naive guy," she said, "and a good friend. And there have been times when the idea of settling down with him seemed like a desirable alternative to dancing the best years of my life away. Spending up all those years working, saving, investing for a lovely old farmhouse, where I'll probably end up walking alone from room to room, wondering what my neighbor and his family are doing that night."

I turned her so that we faced each other, took her hands in mine. "If it upsets you to talk about this, please don't," I said.

She gave my hands a soft squeeze, and looked away, over the water. "Then I wonder if I might spend all my time trying to be the new mother, fill the vacancy left by somebody else. Never quite making it. And I wonder how long I'd be happy doing little more with my life than deciding where to walk the kids, what to cook for dinner, what to watch on the television -- I don't even own a television."

She pulled away from me a bit, enough so I could turn away from the water and sit on the seawall. She sat close, leaned against me.

I put my arm around her. She turned toward me, and I saw a smile. I put my arms around her, and we hugged soft, and long.

Chapter 31

I don't know what jarred my troubled sleep, cars racing on Dixie Highway, a freight train rumbling through town, or perhaps a yacht whistle; whatever, I awoke with a start. The first thing I saw was the boarded window. That didn't help settle my nerves.

The nightmare had been a surrealistic walk through the little house of death on Saint Francis Street. It had been peopled with an assortment of characters: villians and victims, innocents and not-so-innocents, people I knew, and one I did not know, who moved, always faceless, just out of my reach, in the shadow of others.

The luminous arms on my old windup told me it was four o'clock. I knew I wouldn't get back to sleep, so I turned on the light. I had left the medallion on the table by my bed. I picked it up and looked at it once again. I knew it was time to find Alwen.

I went to the closet and slipped into some clean clothes. As I pulled a shirt off a hanger, my hand bumped something hard in the jacket I had worn the night of the fight at the club. I reached in the pocket and took out Mally's pistol. I had forgotten about it, and thought about putting it in a dresser drawer, then changed my mind. I put on a clean jacket, tucked the pistol in my belt.

I called a cab and had it take me to a car rental place. It was only a short time before I was headed back to the zoo parking lot. I turned in without knowing what to expect. A white Mustang, perhaps.

What I found was a large, black car, with tinted windows. I drove past it, turned, and headed out.

I drove to Saint Francis Street, cut the lights and the engine at the top of the hill, coasted down. I rolled past Nordy's place. There was a car in the driveway, lights were on in the living-room. I took a deep, nervous breath, let the car come to a stop next to a fence at the end of the street.

I was near the house, but far enough away not to have alerted anyone inside. I wiped the palms of my hands on my pants, took a deep breath.

I walked to the house. It was quiet on the street. I could hear light traffic from Parker. Up the block someone opened and closed a car door. I waited while they backed out of a driveway and drove off.

As I walked quietly toward the front door, I felt light drops of rain on my face. I listened for sounds of a television or radio, but didn't hear anything until I got near the front door, then heard what sounded like angry shouts from inside.

The rain came a little harder, and I used the cover to sneak around to the place where I had first seen Marbles seated in front of the television. I pushed into the same large hedges, and looked through the louvers.

This time, instead of a little fella with a broken neck, I saw hairy-chested Tony Mally wearing only a pair of boxer undershorts, a silver whistle around his neck, and a bandaged-cast on his right wrist. He was running after Nordy, swatting her on the legs and butt with a small switch.

Nordy wore a skimpy shirt, and skimpier panties, her legs and buttocks showed a few welts. She hooted and giggled as Mally chased and swatted her.

I watched as she used the chair that Marbles had died in as a barrier, ran first one way, then the other, around, and finally jumped on and over the chair, only to be caught, and swatted once again. Then they ran into another room.

For a few minutes I didn't hear anything. I stayed where I was, in the hedges, wondered if either of them gave any consideration to the fact that their playground was a crime scene, a place where a murder had recently taken place.

While I stood there, I thought about the back room, and hoped Nordy wasn't feeling like getting her picture taken. I didn't know anything about the smut business, but figured if Mally started the camera rolling, it might be a long time before either of them came up for air.

I pulled my coat collar up against the rain, looked through the louvers about the same time Nordy came back into the room. This time, she had the switch, and was chasing Mally. All in all, it was a pathetic sight.

I left the hedges and went around to the back. The kitchen was dark. I tried the door, found it locked. There was, however, a large rip in the screen, and the louvers were opened enough to slip one of the glass panes out of the track. I reached in and unlocked the door.

I slipped the pane back and quietly entered the dark kitchen, closed the door, and looked around. The place was a mess. I stood in the darkness near the refrigerator, and listened to the noise in one of the back rooms.

It was a few minutes before they came running back up the short hallway. By a strange circumstance, Nordy made a left, came running into the kitchen, and ran smack into me before I had a chance to get out of the way. I put my hand hard over her mouth and watched Mally run by the door.

She stood frozen, wide-eyed with fear. I kept one hand over her mouth and the other held tight on the back of her neck. I nudged her toward the door. It was only a short distance before we were in the doorway. Mally saw us and froze.

I took my hand off her mouth, and pushed her into the room. She stumbled toward Mally. He ignored her.

"Cute shorts," I said to him, opened my jacket enough so he could see the gun in my belt.

He pointed to a pile of clothing on the sofa. "Mind if I get dressed?"

"I'd like Nordy to show me you don't have another one of these in your jacket," I said, put my hand on the gun.

"I wondered where that went," he said.

I didn't answer him, just watched as Nordy looked to him for traveling orders. He moved his chin toward the sofa, she went over, picked up the pants, shirt, jacket, shoes, and brought them to me. I gave them a careful once-over, then let him get dressed.

As he dressed, I realized my first mistake. He had been more vulnerable in his shorts. I should have kept him that way.

"Why don't you sit on the sofa," I said to Nordy, "while Tony and I talk about Alwen."

Mally's reaction, a quick hard glare, told me I was on the right train. "Never heard the name," he said.

"Me neither," Nordy said, smirked.

Tony gave her a smack on the chops for her effort. "Do like the man said, get over there and shut up."

Nordy took it like someone who was used to being knocked around. I was beginning to feel sorry for her when she let fly with an ashtray. I hadn't seen her lift it, she probably snatched it when she was getting the clothes.

The missile missed my head by a few inches. She told him to run for it, but he watched as it sailed past me. Apparently he didn't have much confidence in her throwing arm.

I had made my second mistake in as many minutes. Not a good start.

Mally smiled, looked like he was going to say something, then changed his mind.

"How about you sit together on the sofa," I said. "That way I can keep an eye on you both."

"Can I get dressed?" Nordy asked.

"Where are your clothes?" I asked.

"In my room," she said, gave a coy tilt to her head. "You could help me get dressed."

I shook my head. "No thanks."

Tony cuffed her again. "Shut up, you little tramp." He pushed her toward the sofa.

Chapter 31

I could see the rain beating against the outside edges of the slightly opened louvered windows in back of them as they moved to the sofa. The windows covered most of the wall, let in a nice breeze.

Then, along with the breeze, came mistake number three as I watched Tony lift a table lamp, tear the cord free, and hurl it at me. I raised one arm in front of my face, blocked it, and ducked to one knee with the gun drawn. I figured he'd either charge me, or bolt for the front door. I was wrong on both counts.

From that crouch, I watched as Mally lifted Nordy like a child, tossed her over the sofa, and into the windows, which broke in a shower of glass. He jumped over the sofa, through the opening, and ran across the yard, to the fence.

I followed him through the window, stepped over Nordy, who had not made a sound as her body splintered the glass. I jumped the fence and ran after Tony, who had crossed the road, and climbed the high fence that bordered the zoo.

I followed across the road, hit the fence at a good clip. My hands clawed the chain links as I pulled myself up, dug the soles of my shoes into the wire mesh, gave a hell of a kick, and was over in a driving motion that would have made my old drill sergeant proud.

A bunch of scrub brush broke my fall as I swung over the top and dropped to the ground. I rolled with a tucked shoulder, and came up running.

As I ran through muck and heavy brush, I heard footsteps hammer heavily on a wood deck. I'd taken Robin to the zoo enough times when she was young to know he was on the nature trail boardwalk that ran through a preserve of wetlands vegetation.

Although Mally had a good start on me, there were no lights in the area, and the moon was a sliver. It was too dark, and slippery-wet with rain to make a flat-out run across the zoo property.

I sloshed, ran as best I could through the heavy muck, toward the sound. I reached the boardwalk, felt the tug of muck on my shoes as I pulled myself up on the walkway that was on pilings about four feet above the wetland.

I ran down the boardwalk, toward the entrance to the nature trail that I knew could not be far off. As I ran, I heard a shout, and was close enough to hear wood splinter and snap, then a thud as I rounded a slippery corner.

In the short time it took me to get to the place where I found a wood rail broken, Mally had disappeared into the darkness. I could hear his footsteps on the asphalt path that wound through the zoo.

I stopped just long enough to stand by the split rail, look down and see that there was a uniformed guard on the ground. He had caught Mally on the boardwalk side of the trail entrance. Now he was on his back in the muck. I called to him, but he didn't answer. I tore off a four-foot length of broken two-by-four, and took off after Mally.

I headed in a direction I hoped Mally had taken, to the central area of the zoo, where a sporadic placement of low-level, blue-hue lights gave a soft, blue-green tint to the vegetation close to them. Most everything else was left in near darkness.

I heard another thud, a curse, then what sounded like someone hitting tin, or sheet metal. A commotion began: first a chorus of monkeys, then scattered sounds that haunted the zoo with mysterious bellows, screeches and whoops. I followed the sounds. It wasn't long before I found out that Mally was having more trouble than I was in the darkness.

In his haste, he had fallen over a low, black, metal rail that bordered a canal near the center of the zoo. There was an aluminum boat turned over on the shore. I figured he must have fallen on it. I looked around, cautious. He couldn't be far ahead of me.

I ran toward a low, yellow light on the other side of the park. That was the only beacon around. I guessed it might lead me to the main entrance of the zoo, and to the parking lot.

The commotion on the monkey island died down. I rushed around a large open pit that I remembered was a place where gators kept the company of anything they didn't want to munch on. I rounded the pit, and on the other side, saw Mally pass a small snack shop that had a blinking red neon light in its window. He limped and his right shoulder seemed slumped.

I ran across the deck in front of the take-out window, then jumped over a round wood table, landed near the center of the small food service area that was closed on three sides by bamboo fence. Mally turned, cornered.

"Time to talk about Alwen," I said. I charged full speed, juked right, then feigned a low, shoulder-driven body blow. I went in fast, shifted the piece of wood rail to my left hand, and used my right arm to block with.

He had expected me to hit low, into his midsection, so he held his left arm high, fist balled, brought it down, but my right arm broke the full force of the blow.

I turned quickly and hammered my splintered wood club into his right shoulder. He hollered in pain, grabbed at his shoulder. His legs wobbled. I shifted the club to my right hand, was careful to miss his hand, hit him hard again, close to the same place. I felt something shatter. Then, he went down.

I was about to begin the interview when I felt a crack across my right arm. The wood club went flying. I grabbed my elbow, turned and saw a young guard with a night stick.

"Both of you," he said, "hold it right there. Freeze." He stood in a tight karate stance, twirled the night stick in his right hand.

"This guy is dangerous," Mally said, got up on one knee.

"I said freeze, you sorry som-bitch," the guard said, patted the handle of the gun in his holster with his left hand. "You two clowns just rode into the wrong town for this kind'a shit."

"He's got a gun," Mally said. "He's a killer."

"Son of a bitch," the guard said, hit me low on the back before I could explain that he was making a big mistake.

The sharp pain arched me back enough so he could reach in my jacket and grab my gun. He pointed it at me, was about to say something when I heard the first blow to the back of his head.

I saw the look of disbelief, confusion as the blow staggered him. The second caught his forehead as he turned to face Mally. Still he didn't go down. Mally hit him a third time, and if that didn't finish him, the shot that his face took as he hit the concrete, did.

The gun was on the ground. I kicked it hard enough to knock it across the floor. Mally started to run after it, but I tripped him. He turned in a rage, swung, I ducked under the swing, which was awkward because he was not much good with his left hand. He body-blocked me into the fence, but the impact seemed to cause him as much misery as it did me.

I used the heel of my shoe to hammer hard on his instep. He hollered, swung wildly at my head, hitting the fence. I banged my forehead hard into his nose. He pulled back in a shower of blood. My right arm was coming back to life. I pushed him and he fell backwards into the center of the serving area. He landed on his bad shoulder, moaned in agony.

I walked over to where the pistol had stopped it's slide. I picked it up, pointed it at his face. "Time to talk about Alwen," I said, again, softly.

He laughed. "All this was for nothing, you jerk-off," he said, raised himself on one arm. "She's gone."

I kicked his arm out from under him. "Wrong answer," I said, picked up the two-by, hit him hard with the flat side.

"The next one will be worse," I said.

"I'm telling the truth," he said, whined. "Her and her brother left town late last night."

"They left in his boat?"

He shrugged. "What boat?"

This time I hit hard, near the shoulder. "Wrong again."

He cried in pain. "I'm telling the truth," he said, tried to roll away from me, but was in too much pain.

I pressed my foot on his ankle. "Tony, this is going to be a long interview if you don't get your act together, and tell me where she is, because I'm not playing games with you," I said. "I want both of them, and you're going to get me to them."

"I don't know nothing about nothing with those two," he said. "She paid me to help toss you out a window, that's all I know."

"Strike three." I drove the heel of my shoe hard into his ankle. He cried enough to make me believe he would tell the truth. "I know it was you, not Thady, who set Ivy Mitchell up to die," I said.

His voice sounded pained, far away. "Jesus, I didn't know her brother was a psycho," he said. "I never did anything like that before, but she laid some heavy money on me."

"Right now, I don't give shit about any of that," I said. "I just want you to tell me how to get to them." As I talked, I slipped both my hands through his belt, and with the last word, picked him up enough to run him into a stack of folded metal chairs that leaned against the fence. He hit head first with a crash. He didn't make a sound.

I was afraid I had broken his neck, but finally he groaned, groggy, then said, "I swear, I don't know where she is."

"What's her brother's name?" I asked.

"She never talked to me about him," he said.

I rested my foot on his other ankle, pressed. "Nordy told me his name is Doc," I said. "Now you're going to give me a complete name."

"She told you that?" Mally said, pain-shouted.

"Yeah," I said.

"That little tramp," he said, tried to raise himself again. I pressed on the ankle and he dropped back.

"What's his name, Tony?" I said.

He began laughing, laughed in a hard gut roll that caused him to wince in pain. "That stupid little tramp," he said, forced back the spasms into grotesque little grunts of pain and anger. "I thought they might be up to something behind my back."

"Who's 'they?'" I said.

"Who knows with them, maybe all three," he said. "Nordy must have done a job for them."

"You mean like the one that killed Ivy?"

"Yeah, only Nordy, man, she's as crazy as this guy you call Doc. And here I am getting myself busted up." He fell quiet a short time. "Maybe she's not so crazy as she seems?"

"Congratulations, Sherlock. So, it's all on your shoulders," I said. "What's the name of their boat, Tony? Don't make your answer too cute."

"I didn't know they had a boat. Why should I? Do you think if they had one, they'd invite me over? What for, a ride? A cup of tea?" he said. "She talked to me like I was dirt. Why the hell am I taking a beating for them?"

"How do you know they're gone?"

"She paid me off," he said. His words were coming hard. "She came by the club late last night, said that was that. Told me if I said anything about anything to anyone, she'd see that I was erased from the planet."

"Was her brother with her?" I asked.

"I've never even seen him," he said. "But her, she's a tough cookie. You should be happy they're gone, man, you don't want to catch those two."

"Do you have any idea where they are headed?" I asked "When they might be back?"

He groaned without further provocation. "I'm telling the truth. They're gone. Neither one of us will ever see those two again."

"They can't hide forever," I said.

"They don't have to hide," he said. "They've got the weight to drive away, fly to another country. Man, you're not getting it, are you?"

"Tell me about it."

"Man, she must take her nut-case brother all over the world, looking for kids like Ivy," he said. "I mean, if they can get away with murder here, what do you think they could get by with in places where life is really cheap?"

"Murder a young woman, and just sail away?" I asked.

"You got it," he said.

"I don't think so," I said, lifted a pair of cuffs from the guard's belt, and clipped one of his arms to a steel roof support that was anchored in the concrete floor.

"Not on my shift," I said, and walked away.

If Tony was telling the truth, they couldn't have gone that far yet. But they were leaving a wake. I would have to work fast, and have a bit of luck if I was going to nail them.

Chapter 32

*I*t was still dark when I got back to the car. I noticed two big guys in white coveralls carrying Nordy on a stretcher, taking her to the back of an ambulance. Inside the house I could see two policemen, one on the phone, the other staring out the broken window, a fast food coffee cup in his hand, yawned.

I slipped into the car with as little fanfare as possible. The last thing I needed was to attract the attention of the police. The way I looked, I knew if they spotted me I'd spend the next few hours in the back seat of a patrol car. Meanwhile, Alwen and her brother would sail off into the sunrise.

The engine sputtered, stopped. The cop with the plastic cup looked my way. I felt a chill, prayed to the saint of car rental agencies, coaxed the car to life. The next sputter was either an answer to my prayer, or a miracle of good carburation. No matter which, I pulled out slowly and drove up the hill.

At the top of the hill I pulled into a driveway, and cut my lights. I waited about ten minutes, finally the ambulance drove by. I pulled out, followed.

It was just beginning first light when they turned into the emergency room entrance at Memorial Hospital, stopped in front of a pair of sliding glass doors. I drove past, parked in the visitor parking lot.

I went to the emergency room. On the way in, I passed the medics who hurried out, jumped in their ambulance and sped off with lights flashing, siren wailing.

Inside, I looked around, didn't see Nordy. I went to the front desk, where a nurse with an armful of clipboards and a frown darker than dirt slid one in front of me, said, "Fill this out. Make sure you put your insurance company and policy number in the upper right corner box." She pointed. "The one in red."

"I'm here to see Nordy Nichols," I said. "The ambulance just brought her in."

"She's on her way up to the operating room," she said, stacked the clipboards neatly on the left side of the desk.

"You know how badly she's hurt?" I asked.

"The doctor will file a report as soon as he's finished treating her."

"Any idea how long that will be?"

"No telling," she said. "You a relative?"

"A close friend." I wondered, with Nordy out of immediate reach, and Doc and his sister ready to leave town, if it might be time to tap Joe Scirrano.

I gave him a call, told the desk sergeant who I was.

"Pete!" Scirrano was on the line in a flash. "What the hell is going on out there?"

"Come again?" I said, surprised at the anger in his voice.

"In less than half an hour my men have filed reports of assaults on four people, at two different locations, three of whom are either already at, or on their way to the emergency room," he said. "And one of them says you put'em all there."

"Joe," I said, fought back a feeling of sickness, felt the investigation slipping away. "You got it all wrong."

"Maybe, but one of my patrol cars just answered a 911 from the zoo, and what he found was two park security guards who had been assaulted. One is in critical condition," he said. "He also found Tony Mally cuffed to a pole, apparently with some broken bones. Mally says you went on a rampage, beat him and the guards, and that you used a gun while threatening him and

Nordy Nichols at her house. He swears you threw her through a window."

"That's not true, Joe."

"I'm all ears," he said.

I told him what had happened, that Mally had been the one who threw Nordy through the window, and knocked the guard unconscious.

"That would fly better if the other guard hadn't said you knocked him through a fence in the nature walk," he said.

"Mally did that, Joe," I said. "It was dark. The guard must have gotten us mixed up."

"Whatever," he said. "I need you here right away."

"I can't do that," I said.

"Pete, I'm about to put an all-points out for your arrest," he said. "Armed and dangerous."

"Come on," I said, "you don't want to do that."

"Did you break into the house, and threaten Tony Mally and Nordy Nichols with a firearm?"

"Joe," I said, "I'm a reporter, not an armed robber."

"Did you assault Tony Mally, and break some of his bones?"

"Joe, it's me," I said. "You know who and what Tony Mally is. And you know I wouldn't hurt Nordy Nichols."

"Then you did bust Mally up?"

"Yeah."

"Did you threaten them with a gun?"

"Joe," I said, "I didn't threaten anyone."

"Then you do have a gun?" Scirrano asked.

"I didn't threaten anyone."

"Listen, just get your ass in here now," he said. "No, wait! Stay where you are. Don't move. I'll send a patrol car for you."

"Sorry, Joe," I said, "but there seems to be trouble on the line. I'll call you back."

I hurried back to the car, turned the ignition key. The engine sputtered, stopped. I tried again, and again, frantic to get it started, but this time neither prayers nor miracles did the trick. I heard the sound of sirens around the corner.

Back inside, I dialed Frankie's number and was surprised when Dixie Jean answered. I asked her where Frankie was.

"They just went to the store," she said.

"Dixie Jean, I don't have time to explain, but I need your help," I said. "I need a change of clothes and a car quickly." I told her where I was, and that I would wait for her in the car. "Just grab a shirt and pants from Frankie's bedroom," I said. "I'll explain to him later. Please hurry."

"I'm on my way," she said.

I looked around, noticed the front end of a police car parking at the corner of the building. It was just out of sight, though I could see the flash of lights reflect off the front row of cars in the parking lot.

I hunkered down about the same time another patrol car raced around the corner, slid-stopped next to the other.

I sat quiet, counted the minutes, waited for Dixie Jean.

Chapter 33

"The nurse at the desk said Nordy is on her way to room 312," Dixie Jean said. "She told me they picked out a lot of glass, but none inflicted serious damage. Still, they're keeping her overnight."

"Overnight?"

"That's what she said."

"Well, I'm glad to hear she wasn't hurt badly," I said. "Given that, I would have preferred to hear she was on her way home."

"What's next?" Dixie Jean asked.

I poured water from a bottle onto the corner of a towel and scrubbed myself, grateful that Dixie Jean had figured that I might need a couple of towels and some water to go with my change of clothes. The shirt and pants were on the floor beside me. "Nordy holds the key that can unlock this case, Dixie Jean. I've got to find a way into her room right away."

"Pete, the place is crawling with cops," she said.

I slipped into the pants, pulled the shirt over my head, played with the collar. "I have to take a chance that the police are still around because they have reports to finish on Mally and the security guard, not because they're looking for me."

I peered out the window, noticed that there was no police activity nearby.

"There's an entrance on the other side of the building," I said, wrapping the pistol in the dry towel. "Let's drive around to the other parking lot. That way we won't have to walk past the emergency room."

"You got it," Dixie Jean said, opened the door, and we changed cars.

I slid the towel-wrapped gun under the passenger seat, slouched down while she drove around.

She parked in a space close to the building. We went in the side entrance, walked down a long hallway to the elevators. We got in the first one that opened, pressed the third floor.

The doors opened, and we started to step out, but I pulled Dixie Jean back when I spotted a policeman lounging in front of one of the rooms. We went on to four.

"I need for you to see whose room that cop is guarding," I told Dixie Jean.

As she headed back down to three, I walked to the end of the hall, looked for a stairway. I found one at the end of a far corner. I returned to the elevator, where Dixie Jean was waiting.

"He's hanging around 318," she said, "waiting for them to bring Mally and the security guard from the operating room."

"He told you that?" I asked.

She nodded.

"Great," I said. "Did you notice Nordy's room?"

"Sure, it's on the far side, toward the end of the hall," she said, pointed in the direction of the stairway.

"Looking good," I said, took her hand and headed toward the stairway.

"I wonder if you could get the guard to turn the other way long enough for me to get in Nordy's room?"

"I think so," she said. "What are you going to do if she's got a roommate?"

"I don't care if the whole Mormon Tabernacle Choir is in there," I said. "Nordy knows where Alwen and Doc are, and before I leave, I'll know as well."

"I know you will," she said, smiled, patted my cheek, then walked away.

I hung back, waited until I heard her ask the guard a question. Dixie Jean laughed. I was about to make my move, when I was startled by a tap on my shoulder and a loud voice behind me. I turned to see a small, grey-haired woman.

"Say," she said, "you know when they're bringing breakfast trays around?" She played with her hearing aid with one hand, and her skimpy hospital gown, tried to get it right on her thin body, with the other.

I shook my head, talked quiet, hoped she would follow my example. "I'm just here to visit a friend," I said.

"Say again?" Her voice trailed off as her hearing aid kicked in.

"I'm sorry, I don't know," I said.

"Well, I'm not supposed to be out of bed," she said, "but that damn nurse light isn't working, so if you see one, I'd appreciate if you'd tell her I'm hungry."

"I'll do that," I said, smiled.

"There's a good boy," she said, walked off, disappeared into a darkened room.

I could still hear Dixie Jean and the guard talking. I moved quickly, slipped around the corner, and ducked into room 312.

I stood just inside the doorway and looked around the room. There were two beds. Nordy was in the farthest one, next to the window, her eyes were closed. She seemed to be sleeping. The other bed was empty.

I took a couple of steps into the room, then froze when I heard the guard say something about checking on the woman in 312.

The bathroom was to my right. I ducked in and closed the door behind me.

I stood in the dark, listened, wondered about Nordy, wondered how she would react to having been thrown through a window by her new boyfriend. I wondered if the shock might knock her off the tracks, change her way of seeing the world.

I thought about Marbles, the way he had had his residence shifted from a hot little house to the morgue. Nordy Nichols was up to her ears in betrayal.

A minute or two passed, then I got a break when someone in the hallway shouted, "Harrison, I have to leave, so park yourself in 318. On the double."

Harrison answered that he was on his way, and I breathed a sigh of relief. I stepped out, walked over to Nordy's bed. On the way, I pulled the curtain around the end of the bed, blocked the view from the hallway.

As I got close, her eyes opened, though she remained quiet. Her face was scratched, her arms bandaged. She looked real bad.

"Nordy," I said, softly, "I'm real sorry about what happened."

As I stood by her, I watched her expression change. Her eyes seemed slightly glazed as they shifted from hostility, to curiosity, to caution.

"I thought he was my friend," she said, winced as she moved her bandaged arms, tried to sit up.

I took one of her hands, helped her up, said, "Sometimes it's hard to know who your friends are."

"He told me if I wanted to stay at the club, he'd see I had a future there," she said, her gaze shifted from me to her bandaged arms. "Something better than waiting tables, having customers laugh at me."

I didn't say anything, just watched as she blew her nose, wiped her eyes, took a few deep breaths. Nordy Nichols was one banged-up lady.

"He said I could be a star," she said, put her face in her hands and cried softly.

There was a chair next to the window, I slid it to the side of the bed. "If you work at it," I said, "I'm sure you can."

"For sure?" Nordy allowed a smile to slip through the clouds.

I nodded, noticing her words were slurred. I wondered if the drugs they had given her in the operating room were still working.

"The nurse at the front desk said that you weren't hurt badly," I said. "I'm glad for that."

Her eyes teared again. "This doesn't look hurt bad?" Nordy lowered her hospital gown, turned enough for me to see that her shoulders and her back, as far down as I could see, also were bandaged.

"Yeah," I said. "It looks bad."

She pulled her gown back up. "I can't believe he did this to me," she said, looked past me, out the window, sat for a minute without moving. She was far away.

I was quiet. We were getting along.

Finally she came back, said, "Even so, with what he done, I can't help you hang Tony. I just can't."

"That's all right," I said, slid the chair closer, tried to talk as softly as possible. "I'll let you deal with him any way you think right."

Nordy blinked hard at me, didn't say anything.

"It's still about Alwen," I said, wondered if we were dancing in the same ballroom.

"You don't give up, do you?" She lay back slowly, her face showing pain. "You're gonna get us both killed."

I shook my head. "That's not likely," I said, and took the medallion out of my pocket. "Alwen lost this the other night when she and Tony threw me out of my third-story apartment window. They tried to kill me. They blew it. I walked away stronger for it."

"Tony's got a thing for throwing people out windows," she said, laughed, her eyes grimaced with pain.

"Nordy, you want to deal with Tony in your own way, that's fine with me. I want to deal with Alwen," I held the medallion near her, turned it slowly so she could see the front and the back. "You do recognize this?" I asked.

She nodded. "She's a very dangerous lady," she said.

"I can take care of myself," I told her.

"She treated me like dirt," she said, her voice was getting softer, her eyes heavy, like she was about to nod off.

"And her brother?" I asked.

"He's not like his sister at all," she said, moved her tongue at the edge of her lips, tender, like her mouth was dry.

There was an aluminum water pitcher and plastic glass on the table near me. I poured a little water in the glass, held it while she drank. She reacted like a parched flower.

"Thanks," she said, licked her lips again. "Maybe a little more."

"Sure," I said, gave her another drink.

"That's nice, thanks," she said, took a deep breath, let it out slowly. "He lets me dress up in nice clothes, wear expensive jewelry."

"On the boat?" I asked.

She nodded, said, "He's my friend. Okay?"

"Sure."

"You're just after his sister," she said, "ain't that right?"

"That's right. We'll leave him out of this. Let's just talk about her."

She looked relieved. "He's going to take me with him," she said, drifted. "We're going to stand on the deck, and all the people will be jealous as they watch us go by."

"It must be nice to have a captain and a crew to wait on you," I said.

"No crew," she said. "Just me and Doc."

"That's a lovely picture you paint, Nordy," I said. "I'm certain everyone you know will be pea green with envy."

"Bright red," her voice trailed off, "in the sun."

I was afraid I was losing her. "Tony told me that wasn't going to happen."

"What?" Nordy said softly, turned her head on the pillow so she faced me, her eyes opened slightly. "Tony said what?"

I took out my notebook. She watched while I flipped through the pages, found the section where I had jotted down some notes while waiting for Dixie Jean to bring my change of clothes.

Tony Mally was at the top of one of the pages. His name was underlined twice and had a star next to it. "They're gone. She paid me off," I read aloud. "She came by the club late last night, paid me off, and said they were ready to leave in the morning. And that was that."

I looked at Nordy, and was frightened by the way her eyes had opened wide, seemed to strobe, like a light. Her breath came fast, in bursts. She tried to sit. I tried to calm her.

"I'm sorry," I said, felt her pull, try to twist away. "Nordy, maybe he's wrong. He did this to you, he's probably a liar. I'll go to the boat right away and tell Doc what happened to you. I'll tell him to wait for you."

She grabbed me, put her arms around me and cried in pain. "Please, please," she said, "don't let him go without me."

"I won't," I said. "He's docked in Palm Beach, right?"

"Sure, near the bridge," she said. "Bright red in the sun."

"Is that the name of the boat?" I asked.

She shook her head, "No, silly," she said, cough-laughed, "It's named Labyrinthine Lady."

"Thanks Nordy," I said, settled her gently back. "I'll go there."

She held me, said, "Yes," seemed about to say something more when the curtain was pulled back with a sharp snap.

"Time out lovers," a nurse said. She was a young woman, dressed in a starched white uniform that hugged her generous body. She had black hair tied in a tight bun, dark eyes, and a round Slavic face. Not a beauty, but attractive.

"I don't think this is what the doctor had in mind when he wrote 'rest,' and 'quiet' on the chart," she said, walked to Nordy's side, looked across the bed at me. "Please, I need to attend to my patient. If you'll just step outside, I won't be a minute."

"I was about to leave," I said, started to walk away when Harrison hurried into the room.

"Say Kathy, my guy is complaining something is wrong with his traction," he said. "After you're done here, would you stop by and see what you can do?"

Kathy said she would be there in a minute.

I recognized Harrison right away. We had never spoken beyond a simple greeting, a nod, a hello. He was a cop who had made traffic or crowd control assignments a career. I had seen him at more than a few crime scenes I worked over the years. He knew me.

Harrison raised his right hand, palm forward. "Please stay where you are Mr. Krekow," he said, "and put your hands behind your head. Leave them there until I get my orders."

"What the hell's a cop doing in my room?" Nordy shouted. "You gonna arrest me for getting thrown out my own window?"

Harrison didn't answer because he was already busy with his two-way phone. He watched me, eyes cautious, like, if he played this one right, my arrest might bring the promotion his wife had nagged him about for the last twenty years.

"Hey you, dip shit, I'm talking to you," Nordy was fast-wired, the drugs anger-burning out of her system. This was the kind of distraction I needed. I wanted everything possible to hit the fan, and splatter.

Nordy looked back and forth between us. I measured the distance to the door as she pushed the nurse, who tripped over a chair and fell back. Harrison grabbed for her, tried to break her fall.

Nordy reached for the aluminum water pitcher. I had a pretty good hunch what she had in mind, prayed she was more accurate with that than she had been with the ashtray. I made my move as she let fly with the pitcher, hitting Harrsion dead between the eyes.

I passed him and the nurse as they tumbled together, slipping as water splashed over them. I was out the room before he could recover, headed to the stairway, hurried down.

The first floor was quiet at the far end of the hall, near the stairway entrance, where I stood with the door opened a crack. I stepped out, listened for the kind of activity that a police alert might bring.

I figured Harrison's support would have come from the troops gathered around the emergency room, though, if they were still there, it seemed like they should have been pushing elevator buttons, closing exits, by then. Instead, all I saw was a news crew loading equipment on an elevator, heard one of the men say, "three," as the doors closed.

I hurried to the exit, went directly to Dixie Jean's car. She was waiting for me. I got in on the passenger side, said, "I'm sure glad to see you."

"That makes two of us," she said, started the engine. "I was beginning to worry about you."

"I came close to giving you good reason," I said, glanced around. "Let's get out of here."

"You got it," she said. "Which direction?"

"Back to where it all started," I said, fastened my seatbelt. "I know where Doc and Alwen are, and I know they plan to leave this morning. I have to get there in time to cancel those plans." I checked my watch: almost seven. It seemed later, a lot later. I thought of them under sail, and my stomach tightened, sickened.

"Sounds good to me," she said, backed up, drove down a line of parked cars, turned right, and headed out of the lot.

As we turned onto the street, the sound of sirens blended with the music that played on the car radio. I saw them in the distance, two police cars with lights flashing, turned into the hospital entrance. I ducked down.

"They looking for you?" Dixie Jean asked.

"You bet," I said.

We turned left onto the street, drove north. "Does this make me an accessory to anything it's better not to know about?" Dixie Jean asked.

"I hope not," I said, brought her up to date, told her briefly what had taken place.

We stopped for a red light, waved off a drunk with a cardboard sign that had, "will work for food" penciled on it.

"Sounds like you're running close to the razor's edge," Dixie Jean said.

"I'm sure I'll be able to straighten this out if I can catch up with them. Otherwise I have a real problem," I said. "Still, it's nice to have a friend along in case I slip."

"Glad to be along," she said.

"Nordy said the boat is tied close to the bridge," I said, took out my notebook, turned to a blank page, wrote Labyrinthine Lady across the top, underlined it three times. Under that I wrote "Bright red in the sun," underlined that twice.

Dixie Jean pulled in the left turn lane at the intersection of Dixie Highway, stopped for a light.

"I hope we're not going to catch every red light between here and Palm Beach," I said.

"I hope the motorcycle cop I see driving up in back doesn't have his light blinking for us," Dixie Jean said.

It was too late for me to duck down, so I just put my right hand against my face, leaned against the window, like I was thinking.

His siren came to life as he sped up behind us, then passed by, hard left, pulled into the parking lot of a convenience store on the corner.

The light changed, Dixie Jean turned left, drove north while I scribbled more notes in my book.

We hit three red lights in a row. "Dixie Jean, let's scoot over to Olive Avenue, there's less traffic there, it's got to be faster than this.

"Pete, I lived on Olive some years ago," she said. "It's Speed Trap City. They're out there every day."

"So be careful," I said. I felt a twitch in my jaw.

"What chance do you think we have of catching them?"

"Pretty good," I said, watched the hidden drives as we passed slowly through a school zone. "I know Alwen was up late last night, and if her brother waited up for her, they didn't get to bed until about the time was I getting up."

"Which was?"

"About four," I said. "I don't think they would head out without getting some sleep first. I'm banking they believe they're above suspicion."

Our conversation was interrupted by a news alert. I turned up the volume, heard a deep-voiced woman say, "I'm standing outside room 318, Memorial Hospital, where a patient, Mr. Anthony Mally, an employee of a well-known West Palm Beach social club, has just been assaulted by a crutch-wielding patient from room 312, who shouted obscenities as she broke his nose, and at least two fingers on his right hand.

"The attack was witnessed by this reporter, whose news team was in room 318, about to begin an interview with Mally, when the assailant charged past us, and would not be deterred by reason, as this reporter tried to intercede on the victim's behalf. Mally, who was in traction at the time of the assault, also pleaded his case, though with no success.

"The suspect, who police have identified as Nordy Nichols, is also an employee of the same establishment. Police have taken

Nichols into custody, and have returned her to her room. They do not yet know the reason for the assault. Mally has been rushed back to surgery."

"God bless Nordy," Dixie Jean said. "I didn't think she had it in her."

"Listen to News-at-Eight for an update, and analysis of this and other news stories." The music came back on. I lowered the volume.

"She's got your story, Pete," Dixie Jean said.

"She's missing the most important part of the puzzle. Still, I wonder what my managing editor is going to say about this if the boat is gone?" I said.

"We'll know in a few minutes," she said, drove a few blocks over to Flagler Drive.

Flagler snaked a dozen blocks through a residential area, then the buildings on the right fell away, and the Intracoastal came in view. We were almost there. Back once again to where it had all started.

I sat forward, looked as far ahead as the winding road would allow. We soon came out of a bend, and there she was, on the other side of the waterway, bright red in the sun, just like Nordy said. She was tied pretty as you please on the north side of the marina, close to the bridge.

"That's got to be it," I said. "I can't quite make out the name."

"Labyrinthine Lady?" Dixie Jean said.

"You can read that from here?" I asked, delighted, anxious.

"I've got great eyes," she said.

"You're telling me," I said. "Let's step on it."

As we drove toward the entrance ramp, I noticed the bridge span, which had been open, had begun to close. "Now things are falling into place," I said.

We stopped behind the last car in a line of vehicles that stretched back to Flagler.

"Let's go, let's go," I said, watched as the span move down slowly, then stopped about half way. It bounced a little, then rose slowly back up.

"Oh, no. Don't tell me," I said.

Horns began to blow, brake lights flashed.

"I wonder if this has something to do with those trucks," Dixie Jean said, pointed to two yellow trucks parked on the grass near the exit ramp.

"I hope not," I said, looked around, saw a car coming up on our left. "Dixie Jean, why don't you back up a little, so we don't get blocked in. Just in case we have to turn around."

She nodded, backed up about three car lengths, and stopped. "Don't look now," she said, "but somebody is up over there."

I looked across the water at the boat with the red hull, saw a man in white slacks and a pink shirt walking on the deck.

Ahead of us, a car with a Department of Transportation emblem on the door backed away from the yellow trucks. The driver pulled into the turn lane, then headed our way. I got out of the car and hurried to the median, waved him down.

He pulled to a stop, rolled down his window. "Afraid she's gonna be like this for some time," he said.

"Any guess as to how long?" I asked.

"Too long for me to wait around and give these folks a chance to share their opinion on how well they think I'm doing my job," he said, laughed. "I'm about to hightail it out of here."

"That long?" I asked.

"The police are on their way to help out with the traffic," he said.

I thanked him, got back in Dixie Jean's car. "The bridge is broken. We need to turn around and head south to the next overpass."

She turned to the inside lane, then jumped the median and headed back south. As we drove away, I looked across the water, saw the man still walking about on the deck. "Step on it, Dixie Jean," I said.

We drove the winding road back, past the residential area, back to the next bridge. I looked north on the Intracoastal. Try as I could, I could not see the marina. I felt my stomach tighten again.

"This isn't a good place to get caught speeding," Dixie Jean said. "I think I should slow it down a little, don't you?"

She was right, Palm Beach was a place with more cops, in and out of uniform, than almost anywhere else in the universe.

I agreed. "Hopefully there won't be any traffic this early on A1A. It should be a smooth run to the marina."

Dixie Jean drove around the curve, and ran smack into a city road crew trimming trees. Braked hard.

I figured the flagman, a City of Palm Beach employee, didn't cotton to the notion that the folks in the economy sedan had almost hit him, then honked at him. He waved the flag more like he was on an aircraft carrier than A1A, and saw to it that the southbound traffic cleared completely before letting us pass.

We drove past the road crew, began to move along briskly, before just, up the road, a tourist from Ohio pulled out of a side street, led us on a slow drive while he and his family got their fill of looking at the Palm Beach mansions that lined the road on the left.

"Want me to pass him?" Dixie Jean asked.

"Yeah, just not too quickly." I took a deep breath, tried to relax. "We're so close, let's not blow it now."

Dixie Jean accelerated, drove around the tourists, cruised at the speed limit until we got to a place where the business district began.

"Where's the best place to turn?" Dixie Jean asked.

"Worth Avenue," I said, "Just ahead on the left."

We turned left onto Worth Avenue, drove slowly past the merchandisers of the rich. It was still early for Worth Avenue, the street was quiet.

We turned right at the Everglades Club, and drove directly to the parking lot.

"Bingo." The boat was still there.

Chapter 34

"Well, there she is," I said, saw its two tall masts reach upward above the tree tops. "Time to initiate action." I reached under the seat for the gun.

Dixie Jean put her hand on my arm. "We're going out there together," she said.

"I can't let you," I said, turned my eyes away from her, watched the morning sun cut through the leaves of a palmetto, cast razored edges of light on the trunk of a royal palm.

"Pete, they're both killers," she said. "Please don't go out there alone."

I shook my head. "Truth is, Dixie Jean, I need to do this by myself."

I shifted on the seat, half-turned so I could look directly at her. "How about you wait here, and if I'm not back real soon, call the police." I noticed the green collar of her light brown rugby shirt was crooked. I reached over, straightened it, brushed her cheek with the back of my hand.

She didn't say anything, just nodded, turned away from me, sat quiet.

I got out of the car, tucked the gun, still rolled in the towel, under my arm, and walked quickly away.

I passed the small marina office, noticed there were lights on inside, and was relieved when I didn't see anyone around. I went through the gate, walked out on the wooden dock, and noticed the yacht was not actually tied at the marina dock; rather, it was tied between old construction pilings closer to the bridge.

There was a ramp, but it ran from the boat to the edge of the seawall, off the marina property. The area, I remembered, had been dredged, and the pilings driven years before when a commercial ship hit the bridge and caused enough damage that major repairs had to be made. The pilings had held a very large construction barge.

Looking across the waterway, it had seemed to be at the marina. I wondered how he got permission to tie up there.

I walked back to the park, and over to the ramp which was anchored to the seawall. She was a stately lady. Hard to believe behind the spit and polish, behind the bronze, the varnish, the select hardwoods, was a death ship.

The heavy aluminum ramp flexed as I walked across it. I didn't see anyone on the deck. I did notice that the low cabin, which I judged to be between fifty and sixty feet long, stretched almost the entire length of the boat. I took a deep breath, stepped aboard. The hard leather of my shoe hit the teak with a crack. I froze, listened for any kind of commotion inside the cabin, didn't hear anything.

Carefully, I crossed the deck, stepped into the steering area at the stern, went down the stairs to the cabin door. I tried to look through the two small portholes, one on each side of the door, but they were tinted. I couldn't see anything, no movement or light that would indicate they were waiting on the other side of the door for me.

My jaw tightened as I slipped my right hand in the towel, felt the weight of the gun. We weren't strangers, Alwen and me. She had already tried to kill me once, and I was about to give her a second chance.

I turned the door knob, felt a click. It was unlocked. I walked down, into the cabin, looked around a room that served as galley, dining room, lounge. I heard a boat pass outside, honk for the bridge. Inside it was quiet.

I walked past the galley, past the dining room, the lounge with its onyx bar and Waterford crystal. The whole thing was luxury-class, a magazine photo layout waiting to happen. It looked more like a penthouse apartment than my idea of a sailboat.

There was a door at the end of the lounge. I turned its brass knob, dug the exquisite work of hinges that moved silently, found myself alone in another room whose owners had a taste for expensive furnishings. This room doubled as a study on one side, and bedroom on the other. It was understated elegance, though, I guess there wasn't much that was understated.

On the right were book shelves, a writing table with matching chair. There also was a leather chair at the far end of the room, and a reading light next to it. All museum quality furnishings.

On the opposite side of the room, there was a bedroom set, two chests of drawers, a night stand and an end table at the head of a king-size bed. A large trunk sat at the foot of the bed. Beyond that was an assortment of gym equipment. Plenty of chrome.

I moved through the room, past the books and leather chair, past the weight stuff, to a door at the end of the room. As I walked, I tried to judge distances. If I had figured right, I was near the end of the cabin area.

As I neared the back door, I thought I heard something outside. I tensed, went quickly to one of the portholes, opened it. There was no one on the ramp. I listened for the sound of anyone on the deck, but didn't hear anything. I left the porthole and walked back to the back of the cabin.

The last door was a replica of the first two, smooth, silent. It opened into a gold-fixtured bathroom. I heard a soft noise, turned fast, thought someone was in back of me, then noticed the door had slipped shut. I opened it, made sure it hadn't had help, found I was still alone.

I searched an assortment of drawers next to the small sink. Bathroom goodies, a tube of toothpaste carefully rolled from one end, toothbrush, short-bristled hair brushes, cologne. I smelled the cologne. I was in the right place, but something, someone was missing.

I went back to the bedroom area, rummaged drawers, found men's clothing, pants, shirts. As I returned to the front cabin, I felt something was wrong, wondered why there was only one bed.

This time through the lounge, I noticed the place had a feel of not being used. There was no sign that anyone had sat in the chairs, placed anything on the tables, no page-folded magazines, book-marked books, coffee cup wet spots. An empty feeling engulfed the place.

My first impression had been correct. It was nothing more than a high gloss how-the-other-half-lives magazine spread, intended to evoke esteem, envy. Instead, it looked lonely.

The galley shelves, as you would expect on a boat, had everything locked down tight. Nothing looked out of the ordinary, nothing stood out as being the wrong thing in the wrong place.

I made a quick turn around the lounge, then went back to the bedroom-study. I shuffled through the papers in the writing table drawers. No dirt, no receipts for hardcore anything, no bills of sale for drugs, prostitution, death.

I noticed the trunk again. Like everything else in the place, it was solid, in this case, solid mahogany. A small lock, solid gold, glistened from the hasp. I pulled it, found that someone had done me a favor, hadn't clicked it shut.

I removed the lock, lifted the heavy lid, and got a glimpse of Alwen.

"Mr. Krekow, we meet again."

I looked up, froze.

"I just stepped out for a bite of breakfast," he said, "and who do you think I found waiting for me in the parking lot?"

They stood together in the doorway, Dixie Jean nearest me. Doc stood slightly behind, but close to her. His left forearm rested on her left shoulder. In his hand he held a carving knife, the blade moved in tight circles near her throat.

His right hand held a small calibre automatic pistol. It was aimed at my chest. "If you would," he said, "kindly toss your weapon on the bed, and raise your hands. Open palms toward me."

I did what he said.

"It seems, Miss Dixie Jean, we have captured an intruder," he said, leaned forward, whispered something in her ear. She shook her head, looked at me. I saw sadness mixed with fear.

I wanted to run to her, to protect her. But it was impossible to ignore the long, thick silencer screwed on the end of the automatic. It made the small gun look larger, even more dangerous.

I tried to gauge the distance that separated us, knew there was too much real estate.

Dixie Jean tried to pull away, pleaded with him to let her go.

I watched as the tip of the blade pressed into the soft part of her neck, just below her jaw, forced her head back toward his. A thin stream of blood ran down her long neck, onto the green collar of her polo shirt.

I started to move forward, stopped when the gun spit fire. I felt the hard smack tear into my left shoulder.

He pulled out the tip of the knife, took his arm from her shoulder and pushed her toward the bed. She held her throat, bloodied her hands. Tears flowed down her cheeks.

"Don't drip on the floor," he said, took a handkerchief from a top drawer of a chest nearest him, tossed it to her. "Here, press it tight."

She did.

"This is messy," he said.

I held my shoulder, surprised I didn't feel pain. The front of my jacket showed only a slight rip, a dab of blood. Inside, blood stained the shirt, spread slowly around a small hole.

He pushed Dixie Jean down on the bed. He kept the pistol aimed at me while he put the knife on the bed, grabbed up my pistol and put it in his jacket pocket, then retrieved the knife.

"I'd like to remind you that I had a nice little talk with the guy over in the marina shack on my way here," I said, lowered my head to make hard eye contact.

"I find that interesting because we just passed the day-shift guy in the parking lot, who was relieving the night person you would have talked to," he said, met my gaze, "and who, further-more, is a gal."

I shrugged. "Your neighbors saw you bring Dixie Jean aboard," I said. "When the police begin asking questions, like how two more floaters ended up across the waterway against the seawall, they'll remember her. Then they'll remember Ivy. Then, they'll come looking for you." I looked at Dixie Jean. She held the cloth tight against her neck, cried very softly.

"Dixie Jean and I came back to the boat, found you here," he said. "You killed her in a jealous rage. Then, unfortunately, I was forced to kill you."

"What about Alwen?" I asked. "The police might find her interesting."

"She won't be difficult to deal with," he said. "Stand over there." He pointed to a place at the end of the bed, near Dixie Jean.

I walked over, stood by her. She seemed not to be aware of me, or of what was going on around her. Her hands shook. I reached over, about to put my hand on her shoulder.

"No touching," he said, walked to the trunk.

Dixie Jean looked up at me, then at him. "Alwen?"

He set the knife on a corner of the trunk, put the pistol on the edge of the open lid, and reached in. "Here, you want her?" He pulled out an armload of clothing, threw it at Dixie Jean, who muffled a scream with her bloody hand. "I give her to you."

"There was a little girl," he said, placing a blonde wig on his head. He shook the curls and smiled, "with a pretty little curl."

"Oh, God," Dixie Jean pleaded, "please don't do this."

"Right in the middle," he let out a slow hiss, said something so soft-slurred that I couldn't tell what it was.

"There is no Alwen," I said.

Dixie Jean seemed still not to understand.

"Of course, there's an Alwen," he said, picked up the gun, walked to where I stood and took the photograph from the table, walked back to the trunk.

He looked at the picture, made a childish face, was quiet for a very long moment. "'How pretty is Alwen?' Mother would ask, and we would giggle together. 'So pretty' I would say. 'So very pretty.'" He wiped his eyes with the sleeve of his jacket. "So pretty."

I looked down at Dixie Jean, tried to hide my fear with a smile.

He looked at us, then at the photo. "Perhaps I have only to deal with you, Mr. Krekow," he said, put the photograph and the pistol on the top edge of the open lid. He took off his jacket, put it in the trunk, and took out a full-length, black formal evening gown.

He held it up, looked in a mirror that stood near the gym equipment. "Lovely, don't you think?" He turned to us, posed. "Miss Dixie Jean and Alwen would make a stunning pair on the Mediterranean. They would drive the little boys mad, wouldn't they, Mother?" He looked down at the photograph.

"What happens to Dixie Jean when the cruise is over?" I asked.

"Lovely, don't you think?" He looked again in the mirror, modeled. "You do like watching Alwen pick out clothing, don't you?"

"Not particularly," I said.

"It lacks only a medallion," he said. "You will help us with that, won't you?"

"I don't know what you're talking about."

He picked up the pistol, aimed it at a place directly between my eyes, said, "I was on the pistol team at prep school."

I told him it was in my pocket. He nodded, did not shift the pistol.

I reached in my pocket, removed the medallion, held it in my open palm. "I didn't know they had pistol teams at private schools," I said.

"You never know when you might have to shoot a poor person," he said, picked up the framed photograph, sunlight reflected off the glass as he held it close to his face, kissed it gently.

"Like Robbie Provot?" I asked.

"Provot put his hand between Alwen's legs," he said, "but what he discovered there was not nearly as great a surprise as the one Alwen had in her handbag."

"I hear you," I said. "What about Marbles?"

"Ugh!" He made a face, a sick mask. "That wart tried to blackmail Alwen. And, get this, darlings, he tried to force her to make a movie of all things. Well, she simply lost her head."

"His head didn't do well either," I said. I was about to ask him about Ivy when I heard Dixie Jean make a muffled sound. I looked down. She was pointing to my jacket which was stained with my blood.

There was shock in her eyes. I realized she had not known I was wounded. I tried to stop what was about to happen, tried to calm her before she began to scream, tried to set in motion a different set of events than those about to be played out.

I moved toward her, heard the metal strike her throat, saw the soft, white flesh torn, hemorrhage blood. I was next to her when the second bullet slammed into her neck.

The bullets had to be stopped. I had to do something, anything. I felt a metalic snap as my fingers broke the chain, tore it from the medallion and threw it with an explosion of madness, toward the open porthole.

Doc watched, distracted, as the medallion, spinning, hit the edge of the porthole. I was in motion, my first step a beat behind the follow-through, the arc of my arm and spring in my legs behind the small, gold disc.

Then I felt my left foot slip, my knee began to buckle. In that split second, I saw the medallion ring the edge of the porthole, balance on its edge, then fall out of sight, into the water. I heard him cry out, and saw a flash from the muzzle of his gun.

A sharp, hot pain creased the edge of my forehead. My right leg came under me, absorbed the weight of my fall forward. I pushed, and with an enormous heave I leapt at him.

The gun flew out of his hand as I grabbed his arm, brought my body under his, picked him up and slammed him into the wall. He hit with a shattering crunch, his foot smashing against the edge of the open porthole, driving it closed with a crash. Then he fell to the floor, limp, unmoving.

I picked up the gun, tucked it behind my belt. I quickly took a piece of cord from the trunk and tied his hands behind his back. He lay still while I pulled the rope tight into his wrists. I was tying the knot when I saw Dixie Jean slip forward.

I rushed to her, grabbed her before she fell to the floor. I held her, rocked her gently, told her it was over, everything would be fine. I felt her finger nails dig into my back, knew she couldn't say anything.

She tried to cough, I felt a spasm tear at her so violently that it shook us both. Then I felt her relax. I knew she was dead, but I couldn't let go. I held her, rocked slowly, felt my tears soak her hair where I rested my head. I hummed a slow melody, one that Robin liked when she was little, a lullaby with no name.

I thought of the first time I had seen Dixie Jean, of the time I pulled in front of her house, saw her dressed in her gardening outfit, that large straw hat, the first time I saw her smile.

I gently put her on the bed, closed her eyes. I slipped out of my jacket, folded it as best I could to keep the blood stains from showing, and covered her wounds. I kissed her on the forehead, then I heard a noise behind me. I turned in time to see Doc, with the cord I had used to tie him dangling from one arm. He was heading toward the trunk.

I stood, and fired a warning shot at him. He grabbed the knife which was close to him and ran for the bathroom. He went in and I heard the lock snap.

I ran after him, turned the knob hard a few times, banged my shoulder against the door. It held tight. Then I thought about what Barbara Dreggs had said about her father snapping a door like kindling. I stood back, hit with my shoulder lowered, a full force blow that snapped the lock, drove the door open, and me into the opposite wall.

I bounced back hard, my hands clawed air. I reached for Dixie Jean's murderer with a determination to tear him to pieces. Only, he wasn't there.

The light from the open hatch in the ceiling caught my eye. He was gone. The hatch was too small for me to slip through, so I turned, forgot the bathroom door had a way of closing on its own, and ran smack into its edge. I didn't feel anything as I hit the floor.

I awoke not knowing how long I had been out. The gun was lying by my side. I picked it up, stood, put it back behind my belt, and stumbled through the length of the boat and up the stairs.

On the deck I looked for any signs of him, but he was nowhere in sight. A shudder ran through me.

I ran down the ramp, saw a guy with the marina shirt getting out of a car in the parking lot. I asked him if he had seen anyone pull out.

He looked at my bloody clothes, looked frightened, said, "He headed that way, towards Peruvian."

"What kind of car?" I asked, wondered what my chances were of the keys to the car being anywhere around, knew I was in trouble.

"He's on foot," he said, moved quickly away from me, toward the marina.

I didn't take time for a sigh of relief or a prayer of thanks, though both we in order. As I hurried across the parking lot, I shouted for him to call the police, tell them the man I was after just killed a woman on the boat.

I stopped at the corner of Peruvian, looked in all directions. Doc wasn't around. Where the hell was he? Which alley, side-street, walkway had he ducked into? There were a mess of them. The place was built like a movie set.

I headed across the street, dodged a compact car that was headed my way, almost hit me. Its horn honked, brakes screeched.

"Daddy," Robin shouted.

I stopped, looked in the car, saw Lennox behind the wheel, heard the door slam as Robin jumped out of the passenger side and ran around the car, and into my arms. "Daddy, you're bleeding."

"Robin," I said, exhausted, held her tight. "What are you doing here?"

"We have an appointment, remember?"

"Cartier," I said.

"Of course, Cartier," she said, "but what's happened to you?"

"It's just a scratch, nothing to worry about," I said. "But what I'm going to ask you is very important." I described Doc, asked if she had seen him as they drove down Peruvian.

They agreed in unison.

Robin said, "Sounds like the man we saw across the street, back there." She pointed at a white building that fronted the sidewalk. "We noticed him because he was limping, and it looked like his ankle was bleeding."

"He went into that alley," Lennox said.

I was in motion before I had a chance to thank them. I ran toward the place she indicated, which was half way down the next block. It turned out to be a narrow walkway between two white, one-story buildings.

As I entered the alley, I thought I heard Robin shout something, but I was already through the archway, already running on the narrow path that led through this tiny community of small homes with flowered window boxes.

It was not long before I was at the end of the path and found that there was no place to hide. It ended abruptly. Doc leaned against one of the buildings.

He was a pasty white, his body stooped in pain. His ankle was soaked in blood.

"So you win this set," he said, whispered. "Sorry about your friend."

"How about the knife?" I said, held my hand out.

"Oh, I don't think so," he said, brought his arm around, held the knife pointed at me. "Match point. You take it from me."

I noticed it must have been garbage pickup day, shiny aluminum trash cans were near the doorways. I took one of the lids, walked toward him. He moved away, I ran into him, slamming the lid into his knife hand, and punched him hard in the gut with my other.

"Match point," I said.

He fell against the wall, tripped as he tried to get away. I dropped the lid, grabbed his arm, twisted it behind him, took the knife away. He groaned in agony.

"Daddy!"

I turned, saw Robin rush toward me. "Stay away," I said, felt pain explode in me as Doc shifted his weight, brought his right arm back into my groin. I doubled over.

He turned, moved in on me, kicked me hard in the stomach. I fell against the front of one of the buildings, smashed my head into a window box, fell forward onto my knees.

As I fell, I felt him tug at the gun in my belt. I clamped one hand on his, tried to keep his finger from finding the trigger. I pushed myself up with the other, but he leaned hard on me.

"Shelly, do something," Robin shouted.

"Get her out of here," I yelled, brought my fist down hard on his bleeding ankle, then hammered his knee with my elbow. His leg buckled, and he fell into me, we both went down.

I heard a door open near us, heard someone yell, "Miss Ina, call the police, call the police." The door slammed shut.

We struggled, I felt the gun pull free, the barrel turn away, toward the voice, toward Robin. The gun fired, I saw a large chunk from a stucco wall next to Robin blown away.

The knife had fallen near me, I grabbed for it with my left hand, and chopped hard, hacked a slice of knuckle and finger. He groaned, but managed to hold onto the gun. I pulled his hand under my arm, he fell flat on the ground, on his stomach, with me tight against him. The gun under him.

I could hear Lennox try to get Robin away, then heard her pull free, shout, "Daddy, Daddy." She sounded close.

I felt my hand slipping away, felt the gun twist, pull free.

This time I didn't hack at him, I swung. Swung hard.

The gun fired, and I heard Robin scream in pain at about the same time I drove the knife down into flesh and bone. Still, he fired again. I felt the garbage can lid next to me, lifted it and hammered down with all my strength on the knife that stuck out of his back. He wailed. I thought of Dixie Jean, felt her last breath, and brought it down again, and again. Buried it to the hilt.

Chapter 35

I sat next to Robin, held her hand. Two Palm Beach police officers stood nearby, one on each side of me. Sheldon Lennox talked to a third, described what had happened.

"It hurts, Daddy."

"I'm sorry, Robin. I know it must be awful," I said, heard the siren of the ambulance in the distance. "I wish I could do something to make it better."

"Where's Shelly?"

"He's behind us," I said. "I can see him from here."

"I love him, Daddy," she said, her face grimaced in pain.

"I know," I said. "I like him myself."

She was quiet a bit, then said, "We talked last night, decided it would be best if I finish my next year here, before moving to California."

"Whatever you decide, I'm certain it will be the right thing," I said. "I'll support you in any decision you make."

She smiled. "If it were up to me, I'd go now," she said. "It was Shelly who said we should wait."

"How do you feel about that?" I asked.

"I don't know. Scared maybe," she said. "Frightened he'll forget me."

"I don't think you have to worry about that," I said.

"I hope not," she said. She closed her eyes, lay quiet a minute, then soft smiled. "Daddy?"

"I'm here, Robin," I said.

"You said you'd support me in any decision I made?" She reached over, held my hand.

"Count on me."

"I want to live with you, Daddy," she said. "How about it?"

"The place is kind of small," I said, saw her eyes show hurt. "But, well, if Frankie can't figure how to remodel it so we'll be comfortable, we could always move you in with Willie Dee."

She smiled, closed her eyes. The ambulance doors sprang open.

Chapter 36

I sat with Joseph in a sheltered clearing that Willie Dee had engineered for us at the center of a large area of heavy foliage at one end of the Rainbow property. It was, I suspected, the place he used to call home. Anyway, the little guy, who was still dressed in his Robin Hood outfit, was thrilled about having an honest to goodness Sherwood Forest to hide in. He sat with his weapons, sword, bow and arrows on one side and a small stack of books on the other.

I watched him read a hardbound copy of Treasure Island that I had bought him earlier in the day. It was the same edition I had when I was about his age, one with illustrations by Norman Price. They were as timeless as the story. I watched him read the words, look at the pictures, leave the twentieth century behind.

And I took comfort in knowing that on the other side of the yard was the small butterfly garden I had planted under the window of apartment number two. Willie Dee had cleared a nice area for me to dig, let me feel the warmth as I gently pressed dark soil around the roots of small plants. It gave me time alone, time to think about Dixie Jean. I suppose it gave us something special to share, a garden, something I would remember about the lady who had touched my life so briefly, yet, with so much color, intensity.

While Joseph wandered the shores of Treasure Island, I touched my pocket, felt the outline of the folded pages I had torn from consecutive days in the newspaper. I carried the pages with me, but had not read them since they had run. Still, it felt good having them nearby. Both stories had played above the fold, alone across the top of page one. I was back in the reporting business.

I had filed the first-day story from the emergency room, where Robin was rushed to surgery. They removed two bullets. She almost didn't survive, and that was a story in itself.

My bullet wound paled in comparison. It was removed without complications, bandaged, and fortunately, it healed quickly.

I wrote the second-day story in the office, and on the third day Barbara Dreggs, who was now solid in my camp, announced she had awarded me an Editor's Choice award. I was back at my desk, back in the newsroom. And there wasn't a damn thing Latham could say or do about it. I was on a roll again.

But I just couldn't get that kid in the Easter dress out of my head. And I was also having a hard time knowing that not far from my desk, back in the library, in the morgue, there was a small file marked Dixie Jean Evans, and that that file would never get bigger, instead it would collect dust, turn yellow with age.

I don't know, you try to put the pieces of the puzzle together, try to make sense out of life. You wonder why so near the Mitchell and Evans files there is the file of a tortured man who had too much money, too much time on his hands. A man who, it turned out, had a mother and sister who didn't care enough about him to get him locked safely in a padded cell years ago. They gave him a boat instead. Maybe they did what they thought was right, but he died alone, with a carving knife in his back, and not a soul in the world gave a damn.

In the yard, Harry kicked a football around. I saw Joseph look up from his book, then hunker down in the brush, glad to be isolated, away from his brother. I knew Crystal and Robin were inside cooking lunch, and that Willie Dee would be placing flowers around the apartment. I had seen Sheldon Lennox off a few days earlier. He was pleased that Robin and I were going to spend the next year together. I was delighted.

At the funeral I had met Dixie Jean's sister, who was very nice, and also fond of gardening. I was glad the little house on Flamingo was going to be lived in by someone who would look after the front yard.

After the funeral, Crystal and I went off alone, had a long talk. I think Dixie Jean would be pleased. Crystal really likes me. And I think, maybe after Robin leaves, it's time I stopped sitting alone in a dark room, watching the Christmas tree lights blink.

Perhaps it's finally time -- go ahead, hit the switch.

www.ingramcontent.com/pod-product-compliance
Lightning Source LLC
Chambersburg PA
CBHW070858180626
46817CB00003B/821